women for hire

The Ultimate Guide to Getting a Job

women for hire

The Ultimate Guide to Getting a Job

Tory Johnson

Robyn Freedman Spizman

Lindsey Pollak

A Perigee Book

A Perigee Book
Published by The Berkley Publishing Group
A division of Penguin Putnam Inc.
375 Hudson Street
New York, New York 10014

First edition: September 2002

Visit our website at www.penguinputnam.com

Library of Congress Cataloging-in-Publication Data

Johnson, Tory.
    Women for hire : the ultimate guide to getting a job / by Tory Johnson, Robyn
Freedman Spizman, Lindsey Pollak.
        p. cm.
    Includes index.
    ISBN 0-399-52810-5
    1. Job hunting. 2. Women—Employment. I. Spizman, Robyn Freedman. II. Pollak,
Lindsey. III. Title.

HF5382.7 .J638 2002
650.14'082—dc21
                                                                        2002025122

Printed in the United States of America

10   9   8   7   6   5   4   3   2   1

To smart, savvy, and hardworking women past, present, and future.
We salute you!

CONTENTS

Contents

ACKNOWLEDGMENTS

We extend our greatest thanks to the women and men who went to work for us by sharing their knowledge and insights and whose advice appears throughout the book. To our dedicated literary agent, Meredith Bernstein, who supported our vision of a book just for women and helped make it happen. To Jennifer Repo, our editor extraordinaire, and the team at Penguin Putnam including Christel Winkler, copy editor Collette Stockton, and especially Perigee publisher John Duff for enthusiastically embracing us. To the hundreds of Women For Hire clients and the thousands of women who attend our events, thank you for making our network so successful.

From Tory Johnson: To my husband, Peter, and our children, Emma, Jake, and Nick, whose endless affection, cheerleading, and love of life and all things wonderful keep me going—even at three in the morning. I'm grateful to Cici Prendamano for giving me the gift of peace of mind knowing that my family is always taken care of. I have enormous appreciation for my talented brother David Beilinson, who helps me dream big; my inspirational grandma Evelyn Goldstein; my devoted in-laws, Stella and Jim Johnson; and my generous parents, Sherry and Les Beilinson, especially my mom, who works tire-lessly fussing over every detail to always make me look good, which I know is no small task. To Tess Johnson whose love and endless chal-lenges keep me on my toes. To Stephanie Biasi, Dora Dvir, and Melissa Corrigan-McCarthy and Ryan O'Keefe for believing in our mission, wearing many colorful hats, and working so diligently—between breaks for Tasti and fountain DPs—to spread the word. Love to the ladies of An's who keep us pretty in pink. Thank you to Mordecai Budner, Rachel Tarlow Gul, Carter McDonough, Jennifer Richards, Beverly Walters, Lindsay Weitz, and Katie, Nick and Zach Werner for staying interested and always looking after us. To Erez Barnavon, Jodi Goldman, Kristine and Jim Goldstein, Jason Hirschhorn, Kate Johnson, Margaret Johnson, Nicole Johnson and Barbara Lundblad, Rob Kaplan, Scott Seviour, Natasha Gregson Wagner, and Genevieve Wood—thanks for your unconditional friendship and unwavering support. To Maurie Perl, Lynn Sherr, Stone Phillips, and Bob Brown for taking a chance by giving me my first real job. To Donna Weitz, whose friendship and work ethic are an essential part of the glue that keeps this all together through the general chaos of life. To a bunch of great women and a few good men—Reba Amdur, Nola Firestone, Phyllis Goldfarb, Randy Green, Marvin Michael, Frank Redican, Lisa Revesz, Gaylen Robbins, Samantha Steinberg, Sandy Steinberg, and Ken Weitz—I'm a lucky girl to have each of you on my side.

From Robyn Freedman Spizman: To my wonderful husband, Willy, and our children, Justin and Ali, who support me in all of my liter-ary endeavors and continue to make my work worthwhile. To my devoted parents, Phyllis and Jack Freedman. What a lucky girl I am to have you as role models. My lifelong thanks to my amazing brother Doug and his real life Genie. And to Dr. Sam Spizman, Gus

Spizman, Lois and Jerry Blonder and Ramona Freedman who have cheered me on to success. To Meredith Bernstein, who has stood by me for twenty years of my literary ideas with her unwavering friendship and ongoing support. To the highly competent and creative Paige Janco of The Spizman Agency, my endless thanks, and to Suzi Brozman and Hilary Munson for being talented women with whom I'm fortunate to have worked. And my endless thanks to Bettye Storne, who is my right arm and incredible assistant. Plus, a world of thanks to my incredible circle of close friends, extended family and co-workers who honor me with their presence in my life. You encourage me at every turn and I count my lucky stars because of each and every one of you.

From Lindsey Pollak: Special thanks and love to my parents, Jane and Bud Pollak, who support and encourage me every single day. To Rob (Guns n' Roses) and Laura (nmi) Pollak, for being both siblings and friends. To the rest of my family, especially my grandmother Anita Goodman, for your endless generosity, and Aunt Meri for your advice and special friendship in the city. To my close friends Danielle Calnon, Derek Billings, Jill Fromson, Gillian Epstein, Laura Santaniello, Cassandra Krause, Jason Criss, Meryl Weinsaft, Cheryl Gulden, Natasha Hoehn, and especially Paul Wasserman for all the love, laughter, fun, and encouragement I could ever ask for. Many thanks to the great staff of Women For Hire for welcoming me to your group and helping so much with this project. And lastly to Miss Corcoran, who always said I should be a writer.

PREFACE

My career began with communications positions at ABC News, NBC News, and Nickelodeon, where I helped promote the work of network superstars like Barbara Walters, Jane Pauley, and Maria Shriver.

While that was wonderfully rewarding, after several years I decided to turn my attention to a group of people who I thought could benefit from my work a whole lot more: ordinary women in the early stages of their careers. I discovered that many women had stellar academic backgrounds and solid professional achievements but did not know how to conduct a successful job search. In July 1999 I founded Women For Hire, a company that produces career fairs specifically for them.

I wanted to give bright women an exclusive place to feel comfortable while meeting face-to-face with top recruiters. One thing that is critical when looking for a job is maintaining and exuding self-confidence. Really being your best. Most women appreciate an environment that is supportive of them and conducive to making them feel their best while learning about career opportunities and interviewing for jobs.

I also wanted to offer leading employers a place to tap a diverse group of terrific talent. We know one of the greatest challenges in corporate America is finding qualified candidates in a time-efficient and cost-effective manner. Diversity is not a cyclical issue or a meaningless buzzword. It is a bottom-line necessity that makes good business sense—regardless of how high or low the Dow or NASDAQ are—and most companies wrestle with it. Women For Hire is very successful on this front. Just ask recruiters at Microsoft, Merrill Lynch, Lockheed Martin, Abbott Laboratories, Guardian, Crate & Barrel, Zales, the FBI, Teach For America, and many others.

How'd I get the idea? In early 1999, I was hanging out with a bunch of my brother's girlfriends just before their senior year at New York University. These were smart, sophisticated gals—no lack of egos among this group—so I expected tremendous excitement and enthusiasm about finishing up and getting out on their own. Instead, I learned they were so anxious about how they would land jobs. They were genuinely concerned about their ability to get in front of employers, to beat the competition, and to begin their careers.

While the Internet clearly plays an important role in recruiting, the value and importance of real-world interaction—shaking hands, not clicking a mouse—must not be underestimated. Even as technology grows more impressive every day, job seekers must not rely exclusively on online services for their job hunt. That is just one piece of the overall program.

My intention in creating Women For Hire was and is to help women with all the elements that go into job hunting. In addition to connecting job seekers and recruiters, Women For Hire events often feature a special guest—a prominent woman who has achieved great success and serves as a role model. That is how I met Robyn Freedman Spizman.

An accomplished consumer reporter, co-owner of an Atlanta-based public relations powerhouse, and author of over sixty how-to books for women, Robyn graciously agreed to spend hours talking to job seekers and offering them constructive career advice. She was impressed by their enthusiasm and focus. But she was more concerned about the women who seemed less confident, did not make eye contact, fumbled for their resumes and failed to introduce themselves by name. That is when she approached me about writing this book. An enthusiastic mentor and promoter, Robyn spotted the immediate need for a guide jam-packed with smart advice and savvy insight. She envisioned offering women an insider's view on the pulse of the job market from people who live it everyday.

To round out our effort, we enlisted Lindsey Pollak who has worked tirelessly to promote Women For Hire events to a broad base of professional women. As a Yale graduate, an accomplished speaker on women's issues, and a well-connected networker across several industries and dozens of prominent associations, she understands the frustrations faced by job seekers who have sensational education and experience, but just do not know how to plan and conduct an exhaustive job search. Lindsey leads dynamic Women For Hire seminars for thousands of job seekers and she uses her enthusiasm and expertise to coach hundreds of women through one-on-one sessions.

With extensive research and over seven decades of navigating the job search process between the three of us, we collaborated on this book to fill a need. *Your need to get a job.* Forget boring career theory. Never mind "feel-good" spirit builders. Nobody has time for long, dull manuals. We know women today want expert ways to make it happen now. Finding meaningful work takes hard work, but does not have to sabotage your spirit or totally wear you out. We will take you step-by-step through every aspect of the job search process—from getting started and getting noticed, through the crucial first days of a new position, to the challenges of changing jobs and career direction—and we will address all the bumps and detours along the way.

Nothing is more rewarding than getting an e-mail from one of more than 30,000 women who attend Women For Hire events each year thanking us for impacting her career. We also receive tremendous feedback from those who do not land jobs immediately, but who say it was well worth the experience because these events improved their networking skills, which is invaluable for all future success.

Robyn, Lindsey, and I hope our suggestions and guidance inspire you to take the necessary steps to land the right job and launch or leverage a truly successful career.

Good luck!

Tory Johnson
Founder/CEO
Women For Hire

Introduction

Let's not kid ourselves: Finding a job is hard work. Whether you are a new grad, a pink-slip party girl, or a semi-seasoned pro primed for a change, it takes time and commitment to forge a career path. We know you have worked hard to plan and prepare for where you want to go in life. But finding that dream job can be a nightmare. Pounding the pavement is about as much fun as changing a flat tire and the competition is as fierce as a half-off designer sample sale. It is no secret that women often face unique obstacles in their job search—from a total lack of confidence to an aversion to networking. But these are not brick walls—we promise.

Among the challenges we will address throughout this book:

- **Contacts/Mentors.** Since most women do not have an "old boys network" to lean on for career issues, we will offer you extensive tips and information on the value of identifying potential mentors and building a network of personal and professional contacts to aid your job search process.

- **Networking Skills.** As many as 80 percent of job openings are filled by networking, which means solid networking skills are essential, especially in an increasingly competitive economy. We'll address ways for you to develop these skills and put them to work.

- **Self-Esteem/Confidence.** When it comes to job searching and interviewing, women sometimes lack the same level of self-esteem and confidence as men. We are generally not as competitive either. Through specific advice, exercises, and inspiring examples, we will help boost these key elements to the search process.

- **Negotiation Skills.** If single women earned as much as single men, their incomes would rise by 13 percent. Collectively, women lose over $100 billion annually in wages due to pay inequity. This is due in part to an unwillingness and insecurity in women to negotiate effectively. Our real-world strategies will aim to empower you to do better for yourself in this crucial area.

- **Glass Ceiling.** Even with millions of dollars devoted to recruiting women, we continue to face a glass ceiling in the corporate workplace. We truly believe that providing women with early and mid-stage career advice helps all of us to prepare for greater success down the road.

- **Appearance.** Women face unique issues of appearance that are different from men's issues of appearance. This may seem petty, but how you look is critical to first impressions in networking and interviewing. Cosmetics, fragrance, accessories, clothing, grooming, and handbag really do matter and must not be overlooked in the process.

- **Resources.** There are a wide variety of career-related resources available to women (government agencies, websites, grants, free counseling, etc.), but most women do not know they exist and therefore cannot take advantage of them. We identify some of the best resources and we will help you navigate them.

Women For Hire: The Ultimate Guide to Getting a Job will help you put your drive to succeed into gear. This is a step-by-step guide to figuring out what you want and then making it happen. Securing a job is a full-time job, and a smart job seeker learns to turn every interaction into an opportunity. We will show you how to build your job-seeking muscle with everything from an upbeat attitude and effective networking plan to an unbelievable resume and flawless interview style. Then we will help you tone that muscle, flex it, and work it until you get that offer. You will find practical tips, interactive exercises, resource lists, and real-life anecdotes—all designed to help you get hired. Take advantage of the space provided and the suggested activities to assess your skills, map out a plan, take notes, and keep track of your daily progress.

All work and no play is awfully boring—not to mention unhealthy too. Work/life balance is a huge issue for all of us. Women place a much greater priority than men on balance, ranging from flextime to child care to our own personal health. Remember that job seeking is work too—it's hard work—so you'll need balance as you look for a new position. Our "Wait a Minute!" sections throughout the text are designed to encourage you to take a breath to smell the roses or in some cases eat a little chocolate. We will address issues that we hope you will consider in your daily grind.

The other sidebars offer the "Inside Scoop," which is excellent advice and anecdotes from professionals whose experiences enhance the key messages throughout, as well as "One-Minute Mess-Ups," which are career blunders and major and minor mistakes to avoid along the way. And last, at the end of this book is a checklist to help keep you organized with the job-searching process.

Our first tip: Get started today.

CHAPTER ONE

Attitude: You Are Now a Job Seeker

KEEP YOUR COOL

You're at a party, a barbecue, a concert, the mall. You're having a great time until someone, suddenly, asks that dreaded question feared by job seekers everywhere: "So, found a job yet?" We know—it makes your stomach turn. This doesn't feel like your life. You've done well in school, you have lots of friends, your ambitions are high, but at this very moment you don't have a job and you feel like an exile from the Land of Employment.

Here's the truth: It happens to all of us at one time or another. Even the smartest, savviest, hippest women have to job hunt once in a while. We know that looking for a job is hard—most of all on your self-esteem. But don't let yourself get depressed: There is light at the end of the tunnel. If it makes you feel better, think of all the unpleasant situations much worse than job hunting. Would you rather be job hunting or carry six screaming kids across the Oregon Trail? Interviewing at a corporation or facing the Spanish Inquisition? Writing a resume or taking the SATs again? See, it's not so bad.

But seriously, depression can indeed creep up and it's crucial to stay positive and focused. Remember Eleanor Roosevelt's famous line: "No one can make you feel inferior without your consent." Easier said than done? Here's how to keep your spirits up if the job hunt starts to get you down:

- **Don't panic.** Freaking out over your inability to find a job only causes more stress and headaches—two things you really don't need. It's important to stay calm and in control of your emotions, because a levelheaded job seeker is more successful than a frantic one.

- **Rise and shine, baby.** Don't fall into the trap of sleeping late and lounging around in your pj's. Wake up early and start your day as if you were reporting in for a full-time job—because job hunting *is* your job now. Waking up on a regular schedule—even if it is an hour or so later than normal—will keep you motivated and feeling like your time is valuable.

- **Don't become a hermit.** Socializing, also known as networking, which you will read about in every corner of this book, is a critical piece to your success. Tell everyone you meet that you are in a career transition right now and ask if they have a good connection for you. Remember the old cliché, it's *who* you know, not just what you know. Your friends and acquaintances can be the best source of job leads. There will be plenty more on this throughout the book.

- **Find a partner in crime.** The best way to feel like you're not alone in your job search is not to go it alone. Go out of your way to find other motivated women who are in the same boat and commit to doing this together. Impromptu brainstorming sessions with this support person or group can lead to new ideas and new opportunities. If you don't know anyone who's looking, try attending job search seminars and lectures at local colleges, libraries, and community organizations to find simpaticos. Just like having a gym buddy, a job-seeking pal helps keep you going.

- **Do it daily.** It's important to schedule job-hunting time into your calendar, especially if you are working full-time or part-time or you tend to procrastinate. We recommend at least three hours a day—whether it's working on your resume, making networking calls, scanning online job boards, or meeting potential connections. By giving your job search the same, if not more, importance as any other activity in your routine, you are more likely to accomplish your goals.

- **Let's get physical.** Pounding the pavement shouldn't be the only exercise you get. This is definitely a great time to start or step up your regimen. Lifting weights can lift your spirits too. Exercise is a great deterrent to depression. From an hour at the gym to an extra walk for the dog, the message is keep moving, because an adrenaline boost can do wonders for the psyche.

- **Avoid strangling your parents, husband, partner, or children.** Concerned family members—to put it mildly—want to know why their angel isn't having much luck. Parents have spent a pretty penny on your education or they know you're the greatest thing since sliced bread—maybe even both. Perhaps an unfeeling significant other grouses about the piling bills. Their anxiety and pestering can drive you nuts. Instead of screaming at your loved ones, enlist their help. First have a calm conversation in which you explain how difficult this transition is on you, and while you appreciate their concern, it's also distracting to deal with. Then ask them for contacts and suggestions. You may be surprised at who they and their friends know.

- **Keep your eyes on the prize.** There's an old dieting trick of taping a picture of a svelte lady to the fridge, and many swear by it. Why not hang a photo of a savvy businesswoman above your desk—right near the phone you use to set up interviews? Or write out your dream job and tape it to your mirror. These constant reminders will help keep you motivated when your energy starts to wane.

- **Don't be ashamed of part-time work.** It's completely acceptable to take a part-time job while you're looking for your next big move. Even in an interview part-time work deserves a positive spin. If someone asks what you're doing, try this response: "Actually I'm waitressing right now, which is great because I can't afford to be without any income and the schedule is quite flexible, which allows me to focus a lot of time on my job search. And you never know who I might meet!" Part-time work in a job environment that you are interested in might also lead to a full-time position. Don't be shy about considering any position that will get you back to work, even if it's not quite at the level or in the industry you want. Not only would that provide some income, it is also good experience to list on a resume. Plus it can be easier to find a job when you have one.

- **Don't focus only on one particular position.** Just like that hot guy you obsessed about in high school, it's a natural tendency to aim all of your energy in one direction. But in a job search it is a huge mistake to set your heart on one job or even one company. You cannot count on any single opportunity working out, no matter how perfect it seems. If you see a listing screaming your name, it may be filled internally before you even apply. You may have wanted to work for IBM your whole life, but this may be the season they have a hiring freeze. Cast a wide net, and do not let one position consume too much of your search time.

• **Don't let one rotten apple spoil the bunch.** A smart, highly educated pharmaceuticals industry executive was looking for a new position with a bigger company. She got in touch with the alumni association of her M.B.A. program and asked for a contact name from each of the companies she was interested in. So far, so good (in fact, we recommend this exact strategy and extensions of it a few chapters from now). But when the job seeker made her first phone call, introducing herself and mentioning their connection, the M.B.A. colleague rudely rejected her and said, "Just because we went to school together doesn't mean I have time for you." The woman was horrified (and rightly so, there's no need to be so rude!) and vowed never to make another cold call, deciding only to look for jobs on the Internet and through close friends. This fear of cold calling probably cost her many good opportunities. Rejection is going to happen. It's an inevitable part of job searching. Rejection from others, particularly other women, can be very upsetting, but you have to get over it and move on. The next phone call could be the winner.

• **Reward yourself.** Looking for a job can be a long and arduous process, so it's important to enjoy small achievements along the way. Set goals (our exercises will help you) and assign an affordable reward for getting things done. How about a manicure for every ten resumes sent? Or a night at the movies for each informational interview? No cheating!

Wait a Minute!

Get Out the Popcorn You've job searched all day and now it's night. You're exhausted and you want to spend time alone, or maybe cuddling on the couch with your significant other. Video Night is calling. We understand the impulse to rent a corny Farrelly Brothers comedy, or even a Marx Brothers romp. But why not use the opportunity to inspire your job search? Here are some films to make you feel like a Career Queen, even in the dark:

9 to 5: Indulge in the classic kill-your-boss fantasy film with great songs from Dolly Parton.

Working Girl: Applaud as Melanie Griffith takes over the boardroom.

Sliding Doors: Watch Gwyneth Paltrow apply for a loan, start her own PR firm, and plan the launch of a new restaurant.

Baby Boom: Marvel as Diane Keaton proves a woman can have it all—a successful business, a beautiful daughter, and Sam Shepard too!

My Brilliant Career: Sink into the life of a brilliant young Australian woman pursuing a writing career at the turn of the century. Best of all it's based on a true story.

Mr. Mom: Cheer Teri Garr as she advances her career while dad—a lovable Michael Keaton—stays home with the kids.

Crouching Tiger, Hidden Dragon: Because girls can be swordfighters too.

Thelma and Louise: Okay, they aren't career women, but watch it anyway.

ATTITUDE 101

Appearing desperate and glum might earn sympathy from your mom or your best friend, but it's not going to get you a job. Your attitude affects everything you do—from preparing your resume and interviewing to performing on the job. "You must view a job not as a job, but as a launching pad to utilize your infinite potential," says Mark Victor Hansen, best-selling coauthor of the phenomenally successful *Chicken Soup for the Soul* series. "Everyone has unlimited potential, but not everyone believes it." Although a full hour of yoga or meditation would be ideal, just five minutes of mental preparation each morning of your job search will help you prepare and set the tone for your day:

- Picture yourself as a phenomenal success. If you believe it, you will achieve it.

- Think about three things that you are really great at and practice saying them without feeling embarrassed. If you don't believe yourself, no one else will.

- Promise to smile when you talk to people about your job search. Your positive energy will influence their thinking about how they can help.

- Recite some of our favorite positive mantras from women we love:

> *I'm tough, ambitious, and I know exactly what I want.*
> —MADONNA

> *All serious daring starts from within.*
> —EUDORA WELTY

The future belongs to those who believe in the beauty of their dreams.
—ELEANOR ROOSEVELT

You have got to discover you, what you do, and trust it.
—BARBRA STREISAND

Allowing anxiety, anger, and depression over a job loss or an inability to find a new job quickly will prevent you from succeeding. Those powerful emotions will take their toll and will prove to be serious barriers to your productivity.

Work It, Girl!

Goals and Rewards Remember those gold stars in kindergarten? Think of some little treats that will make you smile as you slog through your job search. Then think of the tasks you are most dreading and assign a reward to each one. Make sure that your goals are specific and achievable.

Example:
Cold call to HR department at XYZ Company = One frozen yogurt with rainbow sprinkles or a bouquet of daisies to brighten your day

_____

_____

_____

_____

_____

Special Situations

Every job search is different and some of us face particular challenges. Here are some tips for how to best use this book if you fall into one of the following categories:

- **Job searching while still employed.** Throughout the book we address job hunting as a full-time job, but many people look for a new position while still employed. The two most important mantras for employed job seekers are time management and honesty. You'll need to make time for your job search after work hours and during lunch breaks—be sure to schedule networking and resume writing to fit into your busy day. You will also need to inform potential new employers of your work status. Let them know where and when to contact you so you won't compromise your current position. Recruiters will understand, as long as you are clear about your situation. There are, of course, certain advantages to job seeking while employed, such as a steady paycheck!

- **Long-distance job searching.** Looking to relocate? Pay special attention to the sections of the book dealing with online research and networking. In our Internet age, you can access information about virtually any town or city. Be sure to learn as much as you can about the environment you are moving into—from salary ranges and work culture to industries and the current economic climate. Prospective employers will be impressed with your knowledge of their city and more likely to consider you from afar if you show them you are serious about moving and eager to learn the lay of the land. If it is your partner's relocation that is forcing you to look in another

Downtime between jobs can be stressful. Now is a good time to pull out the old to-do list. Remember all the things you always wished you had more time for? Well, now you do. Of course, the catch-22 is that now you haven't the funds, so scratch off that massive shopping spree and the trip to Europe. Instead, invest in yourself. Take a language course. Read a great book. Clean out a closet. Perfect your culinary skills. Get into great shape. Visit a museum or a matinee. Be a tourist in your own town. Write a letter to an old friend. Fine-tune a computer skill that's always been challenging for you. Take some time to fulfill your soul. When you start your new job you'll regret it if you don't.

city, ask if the new employer has HR support to help your search.

- **Career changers.** We will not kid you; it is often hard to find a job when you are starting over in a new industry. But it's certainly not impossible, and a major career overhaul may just change your life. Career changers will want to pay particular attention to self-assessment tests and activities to be sure of making the right change. Then focus on developing a stellar sales pitch, explaining why you're switching into a new career and what general skills and passion you possess to ensure that lack of experience won't hold you back. Network extensively to become known in your new field and become an expert on that field's hot-button issues, titles, salaries, buzzwords, and major employers. No one will criticize your lack of experience if you come across as focused and determined.

Understanding the Hiring Process

Even with the most positive attitude on earth, it's pretty darn hard to navigate any job search without some basic understanding of how the whole thing works from the perspective of the big decision makers. Just as success in tennis is based on the players' ability to follow the rules of the game, succeeding on this court means knowing how the career game is played. There are three main ways in which jobs are filled.

- **Empty Desk.** For whatever reason, an employee leaves a position and it must be refilled. Recruiters publish the job description and begin interviewing for the slot.

- **Dream Weaver.** A resourceful job seeker like you identifies a need for a specific position, usually based on her expertise and interests, and convinces an employer of its great benefits and worth to the organization.

- **Smart Cookie.** A decision maker identifies a specific individual who would be an asset to the employer and then commits to finding or developing a spot to place this person.

To make your job search most effective you must attack all of these scenarios with a well-thought plan. Just focusing on one of them won't do the trick.

Establishing a Realistic Time Frame

We can almost guarantee that finding a job will take longer than you think or you would like. Knowing that you're not alone often helps make the process a little more tolerable. When times are tough, expect

Those Annoying Questions All of Us Hate

One of the unspoken downers of job searching is the lack of something to say when faced with chitchat conversations about work. "So, what do you do?" seems like an innocuous question, but it can provoke sweaty palms and nervous twitching in an already stressed job seeker. Our advice: Get over it and turn an awkward moment into an opportunity.

Q: So, what do you do?
A: Actually, I'm in transition right now and looking into some new opportunities. I'd love to hear about what you do. Perhaps I could tell you about what I'm looking for and you might be able to connect me with someone you know.

Q: Are you still *unemployed?*
A: Yeah, but job searching is really a full-time job. This time off has given me the chance to explore some interesting opportunities. I've decided that I'm most committed to securing a magazine advertising sales position. Do you happen to know anyone in the industry?

a long, arduous job search effort to carry on for three to six months, sometimes longer. According to the U.S. Department of Labor, an average job hunt lasts sixteen and a half weeks. It's best to set goals and deadlines for yourself—you know your budget, your career goals, and your tolerance for uncertainty better than anyone else. Yet it is essential to remember that recruiters do not work according to your schedule. You may send in a resume that no one views for weeks, not because you aren't the most fabulous candidate out there, but because a big deadline came up or the decision maker is off on a vacation. Sometimes it's because they just don't feel like reviewing your resume. One friend of ours cried for days because she didn't hear a word from her prime contact—the vice president of Human Resources at a major retail bank—for the job of her dreams. Then that Sunday she saw the VP's wedding announcement in the *New York Times*. The executive wasn't blowing her off; she was getting last-minute dress fittings!

Although you can't control much, you can establish a time frame and specific goals for your search that you are comfortable with. They must be realistically based on the economic conditions, your skills and abilities, and your dedication to this job search. You should also set dated benchmarks to monitor your progress. It's best to work with weekly goals. Depending on your industry, each week we suggest you plan to have:

- One to three conversations with recruiters or decision makers;

- Between ten and twenty-five search-related conversations, via e-mail, phone, or in person, with networking contacts;

- One to five follow-up calls on previous communications.

KEEP A HANDY-DANDY NOTEBOOK AND CONTACT GRID

The best way to keep close track of your contacts is with a notebook dedicated to your job search. Buy one that has a bright color cover to energize you! Be sure to make note of the anticipated follow-up steps. Try making a grid or spreadsheet, like the graph produced on the next page, to monitor your progress and ensure that nothing, and more importantly, no one, falls through the cracks. Make a habit of carrying the notebook with you at all times. Whip it out any time something in your surroundings triggers a great idea to help fuel your progress. Refer to the notebook several times each day to stay on top of your tasks and goals.

READ OUR LIPS: IT'S ALL ABOUT SALES

No matter what your industry, level of experience, or special situation, if you learn nothing else from this book, remember one key theme: Job searching is about sales and the product you are selling is you. During your search you will be asked to sell yourself over and over again. The very mention of the "s" word makes many women's

Contact Grid

Contact Name	Company	Contact Phone	Contact E-mail	Referred by	Notes	Initial Contact Date	Appointment Date/Time	Outcome	Thank You Sent	Next Steps

skin crawl—we cannot help but picture used car salesmen and over-zealous commission-crazed department store clerks harassing you in the dressing room. Erase these stereotypes and revise your image of what it means to sell, because during your job search you will be selling yourself until you are blue in the face. You may as well learn to embrace it.

Why is the concept of sales particularly unappealing to women? Perhaps it is because we have been socialized to act reserved and polite in public. We do not want to appear to be too pushy, overly aggressive, or money hungry. Many women shy away from careers in sales for these reasons, but remember that sales is the driver of all for-profit businesses. You cannot have a company if you can't sell your product, and you can't get a job unless you sell yourself.

Selling oneself is both the hardest and the easiest form of sales. It is hard because it feels immodest and self-promoting. But think about the positives—you know the product better than anyone else, you can answer any questions about it, you can adapt it to various situations, and you are in control of its future performance. Also remember that you have sold yourself many times before: from selling maturity and trustworthiness when negotiating curfew with your parents and ambition and aspirations when applying to college, to selling charm and affection when accepting a first date and skill and passion when going after previous jobs.

How can you get over the negative issues you may associate with selling yourself? Our best advice is to practice on friends and family. We all know that the cold call—selling to someone you have never met before—is the most challenging form of sales, so start with an easier audience. Next time you meet your best girlfriend for coffee, tell her about your achievements, your ambitions, and your experience. Tell her why you are the best person for the job you want. Sell yourself with words, enthusiasm, and specific facts. Then ask her to critique your sales pitch. Would she hire you on the spot? What aspects of your "product" are most convincing? Least convincing? Professional salespeople make hundreds of sales calls a day—they know their pitches backward and forward and this constant repetition makes selling less scary. The more you practice, the better your pitch and the easier selling becomes.

Remember the Rule of Seven

Sales and marketing executives know that it is rare—nearly impossible—to close a deal on the first try. The rule of thumb is that the average prospect needs to be exposed to your sales message at least seven times before becoming a motivated buyer. Does this mean that you'll get a job if you call a recruiter seven times? Not exactly. But it does mean that persistence pays. So remember to follow up with all job opportunities because it is likely you will not be offered a position on your first try. Or your second . . . or your third. But ultimately persistence enables you to stay top-of-mind.

LISTEN UP!

Former Miss Kentucky Diane Sawyer didn't get to the top rungs of ABC News just because she is pretty. It took perseverance, hard work, and a little bit of luck. But another element to her success was—and remains—the ability to listen. Sawyer has said there is no substitute for paying attention. But it's not a subject most of us think about. Listening is part of our subconscious and we are either good at it or we're not. Now is the time to be a *great* listener.

Television superstars Barbara Walters and Oprah Winfrey are known as top interviewers, which we tend to associate with being able to ask the right questions. Yet those questions aren't merely drummed up by behind-the-scenes producers trying to make their bosses look good. Much of Walters' and Winfrey's success comes from an ability to pay careful attention to their guests and to take cues from their responses to ask some of the most probing questions. "The point of listening is not just to be polite; it's to get information," says ABC News correspondent Chris Wallace. "When your mission is to get a job, you're trying to get information from and about the person you're talking to: What they say, what they don't say, how they react to your questions. It's almost like a submarine sending out sonar and gauging the way the beams bounce off the target."

DON'T PROCRASTINATE!

So many bright women postpone their dreams and give up too soon because they are afraid of rejection. You will only delay your success if you let the frustrations of job searching stall your progress. We won't kid you—there will be frus-

Inside Scoop

Wisdom from CNN's Larry King

"As an interviewer, listening is as valuable a tool as asking the right questions," says legendary broadcaster Larry King, who's been asking questions for forty-five years. "As the saying goes, 'I never learned anything when I was talking.' The simple rule is to pay attention and here's why:

"It's 1992, Dan Quayle is the guest, and he's running for reelection as vice president. I asked him a question about family values and to paraphrase he says, 'Isn't it funny that if my daughter wants her ears pierced, the school has to call home for permission. But if she wants an abortion, that's nobody's business but her own.' My immediate follow-up was: 'How would you as a father react if your daughter did tell you she was going to have an abortion?' The lesson here is obvious. By not thinking ahead to the next question, but totally focusing on his answer, I elicited a response (he would support her) that made headlines the next day.

"There is no secret to listening. People love to know that they are being heard, so look the person right in the eye and don't think ahead to the next question. If your prospective employer is explaining the job requirements for a position you want, listen to every word and ask questions about anything you don't understand. This will also save a lot of headaches later on."

21

trations and rejections along the way. But remember, half of success is just having the guts and tenacity to show up. We will show you how to embrace rejection and learn from every experience. So leave those procrastinators in your wake and get started on your quest. Step one: Figure out where you are going.

CHAPTER TWO

• • •

Find Yourself:
Personality/Skills Assessment

If you are just starting your job search, there is a lot of soul-searching to do. If you have been looking for several months and nothing's clicking, this is a good time to rethink your approach, which requires the same kind of self-assessment. Ultimately, knowing what your skills are and determining exactly what you want to do will make all the difference in your job search because you won't be wasting precious time going after jobs that just aren't for you.

When we ask recruiters at our events to share the biggest mistake they see in job seekers, their answer is clear: lack of focus. While being flexible is fantastic, it's easy to blur that line with indecision. Jodi Goldman, human resources manager at a *Fortune* 500 company, tells us, "I'm never impressed by someone who says they'll take anything, that they just want a job. It's a sign of desperation. I'm most impressed by a potential candidate who comes in with a clear objective and focus. They may secretly have eighteen other career possibilities they're pursuing, but when they're interviewing at my company I want to feel like the job that I am talking with them about is really and truly their dream job."

Many women really aren't sure exactly what type of job they are looking for. College students often graduate without a clue and experienced pros can find themselves lost and uninterested in their previous line of work. You may very well be open to just about anything. "I have so many interests, I could pursue several of them" is a common refrain. While being flexible is definitely a good thing, learning how to position that flexibility and knowing when to use it is the key to career success.

How do multitalented women find focus in their search? There are countless books devoted exclusively to finding the perfect career to complement you (see our reference guide at the end of the book), but on the next several pages you will find practical, easy, and fun ways to narrow your interests and skills into specific jobs and companies to target. Remember, you spend a ton of time at work so it's best to spend it on something that appeals to you. And you're bound to be best at something you love. Nationally certified career counselor Jennifer B. Kahnweiler, Ph.D., president of About You, an Atlanta company that specializes in career development, says, "While there are many types of assessment tools, it's highly beneficial to go through self-exploration first. I firmly believe that we need to use assessments to gain insight into patterns and establish the 'must have' criterion that drives what occupations you'll be looking at. What excites you and what do you desire in your work to use your gifts to the fullest? We're trying to surface what drives you. With this knowledge at hand, you will have that awareness and know the steps to take for life."

Determine What You Love to Do

Take a deep breath and get ready for some serious soul-searching, sister. We all act as amateur therapists for our girlfriends. Now it's time to turn the mirror on ourselves. Finding the perfect job consists of a balance between working in the right industry and performing the right job function. The following activities will help narrow your focus to the industries and functions for which you possess a natural affinity.

The best way to determine what your interests are is to write them down. Spell out your wishes on paper. The very process of writing your dreams and goals is the first step toward figuring out what you really want and achieving it. You'll refer back to this often, so write neatly! See, good penmanship does count for something. Here are some questions to ask yourself to get the juices flowing:

1. What is your dream job at this moment? (It's okay to have a few possibilities.)

position that allows me to be indulged w/in co. Upper level position - with my own office

If your dream job is a pie in the sky, think about other, more attainable, positions that might be closely related to it. For instance, if your fantasy is to be the women's singles champion at Wimbledon, think about what other options (marketing, sales, promotions, public relations) exist in such organizations as the United States Tennis Association, Nike, or a small racquet maker. If you envision yourself an international rock star, but lack the talent of Madonna or Whitney Houston, try exploring a host of exciting behind-the-scenes opportunities in the music and entertainment industries.

2. Based on my dream job(s), I would also be happy working in the following environments:

_____

_____

_____

3. Sit down with a highlighter and the Sunday Help Wanted section of your local paper and mark all of the jobs, companies, and position descriptions that hold any interest for you, even if you are not qualified. Go with your gut—mark even the smallest word or phrase that speaks to you. Then make a list of everything you've highlighted and search for patterns and repetitions, answering these questions:

What position titles attract you?

_____

_____

What industries attract you?

_____

_____

What size company are you naturally drawn to?

_____

_____

4. Do some serious soul searching to assess your genuine strengths and weaknesses. Consider areas for growth.

What do you consider to be your biggest strengths?

_____

_____

What are your biggest weaknesses?

_____

_____

What developmental opportunities might help you overcome those weaknesses?

_____

_____

What skills are you most proud of?

_____

_____

What skills would you most like to develop in your next position?

_____

_____

How can you add value to an organization?

_____

_____

5. Ask at least five people who know you well—especially friends and family—what specific jobs, industries, or companies they envision when they think of you. Jot down the responses and suggestions below and then look for overall themes. You may be surprised at what you learn about yourself. If your mom always says you could sell ice to the Eskimos, then maybe you should consider a career in sales. If pals constantly call you for advice when they are shopping for the perfect gift, you might think about being a buyer or merchandiser for a retail store.

PERSON   SUGGESTIONS

_____

_____

_____

_____

_____

6. Figuring out what you *don't* want is just as important as knowing what you do want. Answer these questions to assess what tasks, job functions, and companies you want to avoid:

What were your least favorite aspects of the jobs you've had?

_____

_____

What were your least favorite subjects in school?

_____

_____

7. Are you a multitasked individual enjoying the eye of a tornado or do you prefer a calmer environment doing one thing at a time in a predictable manner? In what environments (large, small, rural, urban, loud, quiet) do you produce your best work and feel the happiest?

_____

_____

8. Make a list of things you've loved to do in past jobs—projects you've loved working on, events you organized, clients you worked with:

_____

_____

_____

_____

9. Now that you've developed a better sense of what you like and don't like, make a list of the specific careers you'd like to explore. Include the dream job you listed at the beginning of this exercise, then add new ones you've discovered through the process. Try to put the jobs in order of your interest level, given what you know about them already. Then use this list, and all of the above activities, as a guideline for later chapters on resume writing, research, networking, and interviewing:

_____

_____

_____

_____

_____

UP, DOWN, OR SIDEWAYS?

Among the issues to consider in your job search: What kind of move are you willing to make—a lateral move, a vertical move, a step back? Many companies are committed to promoting from within. Starting in an entry-level role, which for some people means taking a step back, allows you to learn a business from the ground up and enables you to interact with customers, gain invaluable product knowledge, and adapt to the company culture. If you're entering the job market full-time for the first time, expect to take an entry-level position. Even though this is a temporary stepping-stone to greater things, it's smart to treat this job seriously. A chief complaint among managers of first timers is a poor work ethic. These candidates refuse to stay late, they ask for too many days off, and they rarely go out of their way to help. Knowing up front what's expected and mentally committing to give it your all makes the experience of entry-level jobs all the more successful. You'll stand out in an interview for an entry-level position by making a point of saying you look for ways to make the office a better place than how you found it. For example, you're a stickler for detail and organization who likes to make sure the printers have paper and the staplers are filled.

Getting into the company of your choice may require a step back. Even though there may be a temporary decrease in your salary, title, or responsibilities, think about this as a time to learn the business of a new employer while proving yourself each day. Companies that make a policy of promoting from within usually move talented players up the ladder quickly. For example, within the retail industry many Estée Lauder executives launched their careers at the cosmetics giant with positions behind the counter. Selling at the store level enabled them to immerse themselves in the company and its product line while gaining valuable insight to the brand's powerful connection with customers. Estée Lauder trains its retail staff on the art of the sale, reading customer reactions, and running a business—all of which are desirable and transferable skills across many industries. After a successful stint at the counter, there are many avenues to pursue in the field and in the corporate offices, all of which include raises in compensation and responsibilities. There is little doubt about the value of a corporate marketing executive's strong perspective on the consumers' use of cosmetics after having attained firsthand knowledge in the retail field.

Other industry recruiters agree. "Store associates have a better understanding of their customers, the merchandise, and the company's mission, environment, its objective for the bottom line and how to obtain it," says Sharon Sam of Talbots, the classic clothing chain. Having worked at the retail level "allows the individual to have a better understanding of the bigger picture when they are promoted into a corporate position." When a retailer hires or

Inside Scoop

Fear Not, Liberal Arts Majors!

We know you. You followed your heart. Changed majors six times. Now you have graduated, and still cannot seem to find the category for East Asian Philosophy majors in the help wanteds. Don't despair! The liberal arts led to inspired careers for these accomplished women:

- Andrea Jung, chairman and CEO, Avon, English literature major
- Carly Fiorina, CEO, Hewlett-Packard, medieval history and philosophy major
- Sally Ride, astronaut, English major
- Dianne Feinstein, senator, history major
- Maxine Waters, U.S. congresswoman, sociology major
- Jodie Foster, actress/director/producer, comparative literature major
- Carole Black, president/CEO, Lifetime Entertainment Services, English major
- Claudia Kennedy, Lieutenant general, U.S. Army, philosophy major

Opportunities abound to put your top traits to work. Great oral and written communication skills, analytical problem-solving skills, good organizational skills, flexible thinking, and the ability to see the big picture and relate effectively to many different people are some of the talents that translate well to many different careers regardless of your major.

Careers for liberal arts majors include:

- Advertising and Public Relations
- Buyer/Merchandising
- Commercial banking

continued

- Consulting
- Counseling
- Film and TV Production
- Financial Planner
- Fund-raising
- Government
- Human Resources
- Insurance
- International Relations
- Journalism
- Law Enforcement
- Library and Information Sciences
- Management
- Marketing and Sales
- Museums
- Public Policy
- Publishing
- Research: Technical/Scientific/ Health Care
- Social Services Administration
- Social Work
- Sports Management and Recreation
- Teaching
- Technical Writing
- Writing/Editing

promotes a planning specialist, it looks for individuals who are familiar with the product line and practices. A bachelor's degree in business or merchandising can be helpful, but that in-store or actual experience is invaluable. Visual merchandising professionals contribute to the development and execution of seasonal plans and they usually have backgrounds in graphic or fine arts.

Large retail chains like Federated Department Stores, which owns Macy's, Bloomingdale's, and Burdines, have formal management training programs for entry-level candidates, which combine hands-on experience with behind-the-scenes learning. Those part-time positions—behind the register, on the floor, or in the stockroom—that many of us took just to earn a few bucks can easily lead to more solid careers. Take an interest in a store's seasonal sales strategies and their type of clientele. Talk to district managers about opportunities that grow in responsibility at the store level and lend themselves to corporate promotions. And don't forget the added bonus of employee discounts!

Formal Assessment Testing

There are wide ranges of tests called assessment tools that are available to assist you in defining your career interests. They can be utilized for personal insight, yet are not always considered a definitive evaluation of your ideal career match for life. Your choices include career assessment tools, career tests, career interest inventories—the list of assessment possibilities is truly staggering. While these tools are designed to help you gain insight into your best attributes and how they relate to your work life, all assessment tools aren't created equally. Check out the resource guide at the end of this book for a list of some recommended assessment books and websites.

Unfortunately no assessment tool, no matter how fabulous, can provide a quick fix or instant answer. They may provide recommendations but not prescriptions for your success. The best ones give you a mirrorlike image of your strengths and point out some of the weaknesses you might have swept under the carpet. In other words, just like the informal exercises above, formal tests should make you think and take a closer look at your likes and dislikes, patterns of work, strengths, and specific interests.

The best assessment tests will spark you to consider a few new possibilities, but trust yourself to know what you want to do with your life. The hard truth is that experience and trial and error are often the greatest indicators for successful career matches and determining what we really love to do. Yet few of us have the time, money, and energy to survive job surfing. Think of assessment exercises as a road map, hopefully with a minimal number of detours.

Then give yourself some leeway to try things out by applying for positions in fields you've always wanted to explore. Be willing to take risks and follow your bliss. Keep in mind that by age thirty-two, it is common for most people to have had up to nine jobs—often in different fields. As long as you are constantly learning and developing skills, no job will be a mistake.

When You Don't Have Experience

Wait! We know what you're thinking. We haven't yet answered the crucial question, asked primarily by recent grads and job changers, but feared by everyone entering a new position: "How do you get experience without a job and how do you get a job without experience?"

It's no secret: At some point in your career, particularly if you want to break into a competitive field such as finance or media, you will have to pay your dues—start at the most basic, low- or nonpaying position available. But how do you even land those jobs? It's all in the spin. That's right, sales again.

Instead of worrying that you have no *professional* experience performing a particular job function, think about the *amateur* experience you do have. Sarah Hughes, Michelle Kwan, and Kristi Yamaguchi didn't start out as Olympians, did they? No. They were doing somersaults and back bends on the sofa just like you were. Everyone has to begin somewhere. So, when thinking about your professional aspirations and what level of jobs you can consider, do not discount your nonprofessional experiences.

Women are often shy about promoting their natural talents and life experiences. A job hunt is not the time to be modest. Think hard about *all* of your abilities and take credit for your distinctive achievements and talents. And, most importantly, get comfortable telling people what you do best. Employers want confident employees who are not afraid to share their ideas and apply their talents.

When you look at the requirements outlined in formal job listings during your research, you'll notice that many of the skills and abilities are not only developed in the professional world—communication skills, tough skin, energy, hard work, and an analytical mind—but also are used in everyday life. Just because you learned the basics of balancing a budget while managing your weekly grocery expenditures does not mean it is any less of a skill. Think about what else you have mastered in your life—finding bargains, negotiating on the telephone, getting organized, putting people at ease—and value that as much as a potential employer will.

What do you have to offer an employer? What qualifies you to perform a job effectively? It is important to realistically assess your education, experience, and skill set and learn how to promote your talents. Remember, the best companies want a whole person, not just a one-dimensional type. There are skills you learn outside the workplace that can become an asset to your performance on the job. For example, coaching Little League games or mentoring kids on weekends demonstrates your ability to relate to people at all levels, which is an invaluable skill. Do not forget to include volunteer work or personal accomplishments in your skills assessment. And when you are matching your skills and interests to jobs, do not ignore positions that ask for a bit more "experience" than you have in the workforce. If you really do possess the skills and ability to excel, you will not be overlooked.

CULTURE CLUB

We've talked a lot about likes and dislikes, dreams and skills, but there are some hard-core realities that are also important to determine before you venture out into the jungle of job searching. Keep in mind that where you work is as important as what you do. An organization's location, size, and atmosphere all make up the culture of which you'll become a part. Consider the following issues, and write down your comments in that handy notebook:

- **Getting to and from your job.** How long are you willing to commute? Do you need a job that is accessible by public transportation? Are you willing to relocate?

- **Workin' 9 to 5.** Do you want regular hours? How do you feel about overtime or weekends? Does your family situation require that your employer allow flextime? Remember, there's an awfully big difference in the time commitment between, for example, retail and tech consulting.

- **Closet space.** What do you want to wear to work every day? Do you want to shop for work clothes at Ann Taylor or Levi Strauss?

- **Naming rights.** How important is your title?

- **Brand equity.** Is it important to you to work for a name brand, well-known, prestigious company?

- **Size matters.** Are you looking for a big, corporate environment or the intimacy of a small family business? Will you feel comfortable in a cubicle or do you need open space to get your work done?

- **Good works.** Is it important that your employer be socially responsible or environmentally aware? Are your ethics in line with those of your company? Do you mind if your employer manufactures guns or tobacco?

- **Gender issues.** How do you feel about a firm heavily dominated by one sex or the other? Fashion magazines are predominantly female, while construction companies or defense contractors tend to be filled with men. You'll be spending as much time with your colleagues as you do with your family, so be sure you're comfortable with the group dynamics.

Keep these answers in mind as you think about the many different types of organizations where potential jobs exist, a topic we'll explore in detail in the next chapter.

Brainstorming Your Career

As you search for the job that you want and is best for you, we truly believe that anything is possible, but realism is pretty darn important. As determined as you are, you're unlikely to find a job as a film publicist in Peoria. Or an aeronautical engineering post at a small mom-and-pop shop. You won't make six figures as an entry-level nurse, and you'll never make partner without passing the bar.

Start by thinking broadly. You already have a handful of industries and companies in your mind from the earlier activities. Now it's time to widen the net. Start by thinking of your top choice company (make up your dream company if no real place comes to mind). Now think about all the clients served by that company. Who are its customers? Who are its vendors? Who are its competitors? Who does it outsource work to? In what publications or television shows does it advertise? Where do its employees work when they leave? What charities does it support? What events does it sponsor? The answers to each of these questions will lead you to other businesses where you may find a job. This is a great strategy for anyone working in an industry that is currently in a downturn.

Here's an example:

I want to work in marketing for a national women's fashion magazine, *Fashionista*. *Fashionista* outsources work to magazine-insert companies, advertising agencies, graphic design firms, freelance writers, and direct-mail houses. *Fashionista* customers include fashion design houses, cosmetics companies, interior decorators, fashion public relations agencies, and fashion students. *Fashionista* competitors include *Vogue, Elle, Harper's Bazaar* and *W. Fashionista* supports Breast Cancer Awareness Month, Mothers Against Drunk Drivers, and The Girl Scouts of America. *Fashionista* sponsors the MTV Video Music Awards, the American Women in Fashion Annual Awards Dinner, and the Miss Teen USA pageant.

For the candidate interested in working at *Fashionista,* every single one of the affiliated companies, events, and nonprofits are potential sources of a job if *Fashionista* doesn't have any available positions. She can join American Women in Fashion, find a mentor at *Fashionista* to learn about future opportunities, and build a career in the industry of her choice.

THINK SMALL

Sometimes smaller companies—even start-ups—are doing well when the big corporations are experiencing layoffs. America's twenty-five million small businesses employ more than 50 percent of the private workforce and are the principal source of new jobs in the United States. The trend of corporate outsourcing has created tons of jobs in small- to midsized businesses. The trick is finding the opportunities; small businesses often don't advertise their openings, but prefer to hire through referrals and personal connections. Network and call the local chamber of commerce and local Small Business Administration (SBA) office for information about small businesses in your community. Look to local association websites where many small business members will list their job opportunities. You might even look to large companies that interest you and find out who their vendors, consultants, and advisers are—all of these smaller companies are great prospects. Find this information on the company's website or through an informational interview with someone in their purchasing or supplier diversity departments.

THINK POSITIVE

The nonprofit sector offers opportunities for job candidates with endless interests. There are organizations serving almost every "good works" cause from children to AIDS to music to sports to economic development to education to mental illness to the elderly, the environment, and the arts. There are a variety of national nonprofits, such as the American Red Cross or the United Way, that are as large and bureaucratic as corporations. Then there are thousands of smaller, community-based organizations that offer a more intimate work environment. If you are passionate about a certain issue, there are research organizations small and large that serve your cause.

No matter what the size, nonprofits need marketers, accountants, fund-raisers, publicists, secretaries, researchers, event planners, and human resource specialists just like any other industry. Of course the challenge of nonprofits is that they raise their operating budgets through donations, foundations, membership charges, and program or service fees. While you can help society at a nonprofit, it's no secret that you will often sacrifice a higher salary.

Many industry and trade associations, a huge component of our networking chapter, are also nonprofits. If you're having trouble breaking into a particular industry, why not apply for a job at that industry's trade association? For example, many associations employ administrative assistants, event planners, accountants, marketing managers, and grant writers. On that note, don't overlook the organizations that fund nonprofits. Private foundations are another industry sector off of most people's radar screen.

UNCLE SAM REALLY DOES NEED YOU

A whopping twenty million people work for the local, state, or national government in the United States. Full-time and part-time jobs exist at all levels. Just like nonprofits, the government employs specialists in all job functions at every stage of experience. Think national parks, the CIA, the IRS, tourism offices, embassies, public schools, post offices, offices of elected officials and judges. Though some of these jobs change with each political cycle, many government positions are incredibly secure and offer the best benefits imaginable.

Government job listings can be found on several websites including www.govtjobs.com and www.usajobs.opm.gov. Government agencies are regularly represented at career fairs. You can also network for government positions at the government's own events. If you are thinking of a career in the public sector, start attending meetings of your local town or city council and make yourself known. And when you are not out schmoozing, keep your TV tuned in to C-SPAN or cable news so you're up to date on changes in legislation that might create more openings.

In the federal government, your application and resume play a far more significant role than when applying for private sector positions. Because government agencies are accountable to the public, job descriptions for these positions are very specific in terms of requiring a certain amount of experience or specific skills, leaving little room for leeway. Be sure to match your resume precisely to these requirements. Applications are also standardized so be prepared to list all of your previous positions, contact information, and skills. There is no cutting corners when applying for a public sector position.

Federal job postings are typically called vacancy announcements, which describe all of the required information to complete an application. This includes the minimum required qualifications; knowledge, skills, and abilities (you'll hear about the importance of KSAs in chapter eleven) that are used to rank applicants; a specific description of the job; where to send your application; and the closing date. Some positions require interested candidates to apply through automated procedures. Follow all the instructions because an incomplete application or resume often knocks you out of the running. The majority of federal jobs are filled under a merit system. You're competing with similarly qualified applicants and must be found among the best qualified in order to be referred for further consideration. Depending on the position, testing may be required as well. It's a time-consuming process, but usually worth the wait for the right spot.

AT-TEN-TION!

In recent years, and especially since September 11, 2001, the military's appeal has grown in popularity among women who are eager to serve their country. Opportunities are listed in local recruitment offices, on military websites, and at career fairs. Requirements vary based on the division and area of interest.

Entry Level Is Not So Bad

Monica Bernstein, Channels editor of www.clubmom.com, recalls her first job and sings the praises and promises of entry-level positions.

"My first publishing job was at *McCall's* magazine, where I worked full-time, four days a week as an intern during college. I got paid ten dollars a day—just enough to cover lunch and my subway fare—and attended classes on Fridays. It was by far the best way to break into the magazine business. I realized quickly that the magazine business, like any industry, had its own unique, 'insider' culture. If I was going to be part of it, I needed to be able to identify which players were already successful and why, and then learn by their example. I also needed to show the right people that I had what it took to be successful, so that they'd think of me when job opportunities opened up. Most important, I realized that what goes around comes around: If I expected people to help me out, I needed to do the same for others—and be genuine about it. Better to surround myself with a team of people I thought were equally talented than to always compete against them. If you're trying to break into a new industry, expect to start at the bottom and be pleasantly surprised if you can start higher up. I'm a better editor today because I observed how to write cover lines while serving coffee at cover line meetings, and direct photo shoots while taking lunch orders and dressing sweaty fashion models!

"There's always some part of a job

First Sergeant Pauline Keehn retired after a long career in the U.S. military, where her last assignment was in Saudi Arabia with the 101st Airborne Division during the Persian Gulf War. She offers firsthand advice on the awesome advantages of making the military your mission: "If you're looking to make money, don't join the military. If you are looking to find out more about yourself and to become a leader, there is no better place than the military. College gives you book smarts, but the military offers the best people education. It teaches self-confidence and self-discipline. You are taught how to meet a problem head-on and overcome it—not always by using the obvious solution because the materials are not there for that resolution. It teaches you that no one is irreplaceable and that the most successful functioning units work as a team. It teaches you that as a team, everyone has something to contribute and how to work each individual to their best advantage. It teaches you that as a leader, not all decisions or work fall directly on you. The military teaches you how to be personal without stepping over the line. There are so many intangibles that you get from the military. The best thing about being in the military is the opportunity to expand your horizons and take a hard look at yourself. It draws the very best out of you whether you want it to or not.

that isn't appealing to the person applying for it. I'm impressed when someone is honest about what they're not looking forward to in a job description, but is able to tell me why that part of the job still has redeeming qualities. For instance, transcribing other reporters' interviews is tedious, but doing it helps you learn the tricks of the trade."

"The biggest reward in the military is not the chestful of medals or the promotions that you receive, but the admiration and trust that your soldiers have in you. It's going home at the end of the day knowing that you have contributed to something bigger than yourself. It is the pride of putting on the uniform of the nation you love."

PUTTING THESE ASSESSMENTS TO WORK

Once you've started narrowing down your interests, skills, preferred work environment, and personality type, you can start applying your new self-knowledge to focus your job search. You can say, "My greatest strength lies in dealing with people. I have strong communication skills coupled with an ability to organize details and achieve results. Therefore, I'd like to work in a position where I can manage other people." Or, "I love music but I also have a keen mind for financial analysis. Therefore I'd like to work for an accounting firm with clients in the entertainment industry." Or, "In exploring career options, I have learned that I am most happy in healing, nurturing environments. Therefore, I'd like to work in a health care facility or nursing home."

Your focus may change over the course of your job search, but having some focus—any focus—is a crucial starting point. Now, before passing "Go" and collecting $200, it's time to determine if your wishes are realistic.

Wait a Minute!

You are not all about your job. What are some of the other things you do well? Think of hidden talents and hobbies that you love and create an inventory of self-worth. Write it down on pretty stationery and stash it away for those inevitable moments of despair.

CHAPTER THREE

The Truth:
Job Functions and Industries

Industries A–Z

Lots of professions *sound* interesting or glamorous (hey, any job sounds good at this point, right?) but do you know what certain positions require on a day-to-day basis? We've taken some of the most popular fields and broken them down to their essential elements, with a bit of brashness, of course!

Accounting: It's not just math. Accountants are number crunchers who spend a whole lot of time focusing on details ranging from budget forecasts to pricing analysis. Whether you work for a large firm or a small business, accounting requires a willingness to keep up on ever-changing tax regulations while never ignoring the bottom line, and always being a trustworthy resource for your clients.

Advertising: Do you thrive on stress, creativity, and working with others? Can you spend long hours each and every day discussing the merits of a single product? Cleverness is key, but groovy advertisers

Q & A with a Financial Planner

Dee Harrington is a well-respected financial professional with The MONY Group, a leading financial services firm. She also manages many of the company's initiatives to attract, develop, and retain women to the position of financial planner. It's not an easy job—less than 15 percent of MONY's planners are female. Harrington helps explain why and offers encouragement for you to consider.

Q. Describe the typical responsibilities of a financial professional.

"At MONY and most similar companies, the planner offers people in the community financial services and products that can help them build their assets and fulfill their dreams. This includes saving for college and planning for retirement. To achieve success a planner is trained extensively to evaluate an individual's financial needs and to recommend products to maximize their savings potential. It's up to the agent to build a network of possible clients to meet with for consultations with the ultimate goal of selling the company's financial products."

Q. Why aren't women traditionally attracted to the positions as career agents and financial planners?

"I believe fear of math, fear of sales, and fear of an industry so long dominated by men are the main reasons women keep away."

Q. What are some of the downsides in the early stages?

"The early years are hard much like a doc-

spend a lot of time analyzing market research and Nielsen ratings. Remember that advertising agencies are split into two very different disciplines—media and creative. Do you want to brainstorm and design campaigns or do you want to deal one-on-one with demanding clients? Pleasing clients requires being totally attentive and quick thinking, and working long hours to make sure you stay ahead of the curve. You can't let stress get the best of you in this fast-paced, highly charged, competitive atmosphere. Rejection is high in this industry. You are only as good as your last big idea, ad slogan, or brainstorm, and it's an industry notorious for its obsession with youth.

Architecture: Even though Mike Brady made it seem so cool in his den on *The Brady Bunch*, architecture isn't as glamorous as it looks. Architects are mathematicians and artists at once. You will spend hours at the drafting board and rarely building neat models. The field is very selective, so it's highly recommended to intern with a well-established architect. Don't expect to design the next great landmark overnight; this is a profession that demands you serve your time and prove your talent on the small stuff before you're handed larger projects.

Banking and Financial Services: Do you *really* like money? It sounds like an obvious question, but people who work in banks are there to make money and nothing else. Job functions vary tremendously based on the type of bank you're in, and advancement is all about performance—making money for the bank and your clients. Can you deal with frantic phone calls when the market goes down? It's a male-dominated field, but the major firms have committed big bucks to the

tor who stands on his feet for eighteen hours a day and deals with blood and other unmentionables. The early days in this line of work are less challenging than all of that and we make more than most doctors at the end of the 'internship,' but it takes time to learn the business, build your market, and to focus on success. When it's done, most of us would never want to do anything else."

Q. Is cold-calling the only key to success?
"It's essential to market yourself in person and employ a variety of sales techniques. This includes mailings with follow-up calls, utilizing referrals, and conducting seminars at schools and small or large organizations. There are a lot ways to achieve success besides cold-calling, but that's still my favorite. I seldom get to do it anymore because referrals are still flowing from when I did just one year of calling in 1997.

"To be a successful financial planner you need the heart of a social worker (to really want to help others) and the head of the business person (to be able to keep doing this great business). Women are naturals!"

recruitment and retention of women. There's no substitute here for an outstanding knowledge of the financial world—the *Wall Street Journal* is essential reading for any aspiring banker. As an analyst in the commercial banking field you'll be running numbers day in and day out, reviewing spreadsheets and financial statements. As a financial planner or money manager you'll be dealing directly with your clients. Are you comfortable advising someone where to invest their life's savings? There's a ton of responsibility and no room for error because people will count on you to make intense decisions daily.

Seasoned Broadcaster

Shirley Washington, a successful anchor for Fox in Dallas, broke into television by pounding the pavement and networking and more networking.

"Most news directors don't like to be bothered with phone calls from out-of-work journalists or those trying to break into the business. However, I believe calling shows initiative and aggressiveness—valuable tools of the trade. So pick up the phone, call, and schedule appointments. Face-to-face contact is very important. When you get the opportunity—and you will—don't sell yourself short. Sell yourself as the greatest journalist since Barbara Walters or Katie Couric! Don't exaggerate your skills, but implement a powerful sales presentation. Be determined and dedicated to the craft—live, eat, and breathe news. Keep abreast of what's going on internationally, nationally, and locally. Check television trade magazines. Go to journalism conferences and workshops. Join professional organizations and let them know you're available. In fact, make it headline news that you're looking for a job."

Biotechnology: Do you have the mind of an inventor and the heart of a physician? Are you prepared to commit years to a vision and twenty-four hours a day to fulfilling it? In biotechnology, you'll be applying scientific research to the creation of new products. Continuous education is the name of the game. You'll never stop learning, especially in today's ever-changing biotech world. Be ready to be a pioneer, but be prepared to spend long hours in a lab. As a woman and as a scientist, you'll be breaking new ground in your work. It's essential to associate yourself with success because only proven laboratories are awarded grants, which are crucial to biotech research.

Broadcasting: Are you a public-speaking, news-loving, up-to-the-minute workaholic who doesn't mind braving an overnight shift or chasing breaking stories at 5 A.M.? Are you gutsy as hell? It's hard to break in and you often have to work in small markets in low-level positions before landing a highly visible job in a major city is even a possibility. When ratings are down, you might be too. You need to be thick-skinned and very persistent to make it in this competitive and often cutthroat world.

Consulting: Are you a thorough problem solver? A people person? Do you enjoy conducting qualitative research, brainstorming ways to improve efficiency, and then guiding others to put those big ideas into action? To consult in any arena, meticulous organization, vast experience, and credibility are key. You will be forced to constantly build credentials, a track record, and proof that you know your industry inside and out. Be prepared to envision multiple scenarios and present a range of solutions for your clients. Developing an instant rapport and bonding with clients is essential.

Inside Scoop

Consulting 101

Dr. Ava S. Wilensky, human resource consultant and co-owner of CORE InSites Inc., offers suggestions for aspiring consultants.

"You have to be flexible and want to go into multiple organizations and work with a myriad of people and be comfortable dropping into other people's cultures. Consultants are project oriented and most comfortable with clear beginnings and the goal of closure. Consultants are results-oriented and solution-driven people. Consultants do what they do best since they are experts from the outside. The strength of being a consultant is you have to want to help people and see your success tied to the success of others."

Customer Service: Are you an organized, outgoing, do-what-it-takes personality with a desire to please even the most difficult people? Do you enjoy solving problems, helping strangers, and putting others' satisfaction before your own? Get ready to be slammed on an ongoing basis and serve as a calming force to help sort out problems. Be willing to accept blame, even when you have nothing to do with the problem. "I'm so sorry" will be your mantra, which is a difficult thing for even the most innocent people to say. The upside of customer service is the satisfaction of calming a complaint and turning around someone's attitude about your company.

Gutsy Literary Agent Tells All!

"Most people who hustle are successful because they work their butts off," says literary agent Meredith Bernstein. "They don't wait for someone to hand them the silver platter. In fact, when that platter passes by they grab the choicest canapé." Bernstein should know. She's our ace literary agent in an industry that is built on hustle, which is how she worked herself up through the ranks to achieve prominence in her field. Bernstein, who began as an assistant, shares the story behind her success. "I was at the job for three months when a friend suggested I meet her at a writers' conference. I approached my boss and asked him if I should go. He said, 'These things are usually a waste of time, but try it.'

"Not only did I go—I told everyone there I was a literary agent and I convinced the woman running the conference to let me give a little talk about what literary agents did. I was never short on moxie. Naturally, not everyone is as adventurous as I was on this occasion. But if they are they should see the opportunity and grab it. It also happened that at this particular conference was a young writer who I felt was a kindred spirit. I approached her and asked if I could read her book; she agreed and I read it on the train ride home. I loved it. That Monday when I got to work I told my boss I wanted to call the one publisher I knew. The publisher asked me to messenger the book over, he read it overnight, and called me the next day. 'Meredith, I want to buy the book.' That is how I became a literary agent.

"For women who want to break into

Editorial and Journalism: Do errors in the daily newspaper make you cringe? Do you like to interview people and dig for facts, even when those people and facts don't necessarily want to be found? Can you work long hours and write under deadline pressure? Can you stand to see someone hack apart your masterpiece? If you'd like to work at a major publication, you will pay your dues for years. You may also consider making money independently as a writer, from writing newsletters to editing brochures and authoring a book. Ultimately a writer's job is to communicate information in a reliable, clear, enticing style. As a journalist you need to get it right the first time, not just spelling and grammar, but the facts. No fabrications, no half-truths, no insinuations. The best journalist is the one who lets the story tell itself, accurately.

Engineering: Whether it's chemical, electrical, structural, or computer, are you a math and science whiz who thrives on developing logical solutions for complicated problems? You'll have to train yourself to accuracy. No mistakes allowed when you're responsible for a structure's safety and integrity—both online and in person. In this still male-dominated profession, you'll need to ally yourself with a mentor who has a strong standing in the industry. Be ready to prove yourself over and over again.

the publishing business, I suggest majoring in English and loving to read. There are a few courses—like the Radcliffe Publishing Program—that provide a taste of the industry, but by and large it is often just a matter of canvassing publishing houses or literary agencies with a letter and resume. One can also find employment agencies that specialize in the field."

Event Planning: Are you a detail-oriented multitasker? Can you deal with multiple vendors from caterers to musicians to florists to sound engineers while keeping everything organized perfectly? Can you manage the delicate balance between asserting your opinions and pleasing your client? Can you accommodate styles and tastes that are different from your own? Something always goes wrong, so you'll have to stay cool under pressure and handle emergencies with grace.

Fashion Design: Do you have impeccable, forward-thinking taste? Do people always compliment your outfits? Consider learning a basic understanding of sewing to enter this profession. If you don't understand how a garment is constructed, how can you ask anyone else to make it right? You'll need to know how to draw, or at least sketch, as well. Don't count on being Vera Wang or Betsey Johnson tomorrow. Try an apprenticeship with someone whose vision you respect and keep working for the day when the final bow on the runway will belong to you!

Film: The film business is a fast-paced industry where you can be yesterday's coffee girl, today's star, and then tomorrow's forgotten

The Wedding Planner

Bridal consultant Sue Winner, coauthor of The Complete Idiot's Guide to Budgeting for Your Wedding, *shares her tips on succeeding as an event planner.*

"I learned almost everything by the seat of my pants, coordinating weddings based on what I'd read, which included everything on the subject, and then reviewing each wedding I did to see how I would do it differently to avoid whatever glitch I felt could be improved upon. When I hire someone, I look for candidates who are calm by nature (or who can appear to be calm) and who think well on their feet. I plan for some emergencies at weddings, but have to be able to shift gears and make things work when the unexpected happens. Outwardly emotional people don't do well in this situation, you have to look like you have everything under control and know exactly how to fix it when the unexpected happens. The client needs to believe you can do this. I hire people who are not afraid of hard physical work, runs in their panty hose, or broken fingernails, and who can think about options quickly and implement smoothly."

news. You can pay your dues for years, and then be discovered or discarded in a heartbeat. Grow a tough hide that will let you take rejection and start fresh over and over again. Geography plays an important role since Los Angeles and New York get the most action. Who you know is often more important than what you know or even what you've done before. The industry is full of freelancers, many of whom hold other jobs while pursuing their big breaks. Hone your communication skills so you can promote your talent to a variety of business and technical people. Writing proposals, sketching characters, creating scripts and story lines are all part of selling yourself. Remember that lots of jobs exist in the industry that support the film-making process—production companies are full of accountants, lawyers, marketers, publicists, and support staff.

Fitness Training: Are you blessed with endless energy, athletic talent, stamina, and drive? You can't jump in as an Olympic gymnast at twenty-eight, but you can become involved in the sports world at any age. If competitive sports are beyond you, consider applying your talents to high school coaching, personal training, or physical therapy. Gyms are booming all over the country, hiring personal trainers, aerobics and spinning instructors, nutritionists, massage therapists, and customer service staff. Clients tend to require endless motivation to keep them moving, and many will rely on your expert knowledge of nutrition and sports medicine as well. For scientific-minded exercise enthusiasts, check into certification and courses in anatomy and physiology.

Graphic Design: Are you equally at home with words and pictures? Can you take somebody else's ideas and make them blossom into a stunning presentation, and then change everything based on their nonexpert opinion? You have to be ready to sublimate your sense of style to your client's wishes. If they want the photo upside down, or a glaring purple header, in the end it's their money. Strong up-to-date computer skills and ability to communicate are key in this field. You'll definitely need a portfolio, so keep track of everything you have done and display it to your best advantage to attract clients.

Hospitality: From caterer to concierge, do you enjoy taking care of everyone's constantly changing needs? Do you love the challenge of finding tickets to a sold-out Super Bowl, chasing down a rare book,

> ## Inside Scoop
>
> ### Swell Fashion Tips
>
> "First of all," explains designer Cynthia Rowley, "everybody thinks fashion is so glamorous. But most of it is really hard work that's not glamorous at all. It's important to be prepared for that. The way we hire—and I think the way a lot of people hire—is from our internships. That's the best way because interns really get to see the whole thing. You see what you like, and we see how you are too. At least half our staff comes from interns."
>
> Rowley, also the coauthor of *Swell: A Girl's Guide to the Good Life,* believes that creativity in this industry goes a long way. "If you're in design, send a sketch along with your resume. It's always an advantage to have something really visual to go along with that piece of paper. It's important to be willing to start at the bottom and work your way up. That's how fashion works."

or providing just the right setting for a romantic marriage proposal? Diplomacy and perfectionism must be part of your personality. Your clients are always right, and they want your help yesterday. Get to know everybody and everything about your city—where to go and what's in vogue. Shrug off anxiety as you juggle a thousand details, a hundred contractors, and a dozen problems all at once without going crazy.

Human Resources: Are you a natural go-between and a good judge of character? Do you thrive on promoting healthy relationships and motivating large groups of people at work? Are you willing to stay up-to-date on the ins and outs of health insurance, equal employment law, and worker's compensation? Could you fire someone if you had to? Hiring and firing require very different emotions, both of which deserve an always steady hand and an objective eye. Whether you're a generalist or a specialist, maintaining confidences and coaching people to reach their potential is your daily routine, as is networking to recruit the very best talent. There's lots of paper pushing and upkeep on employment legislation and company policy, which means attention to detail is key.

Information Technology: Do you know what HTML, C++, and Java stand for, but more important, can you explain the terms to laypeople? Is building a website or troubleshooting computer glitches a piece of cake for you? Can you work alone or as part of a functional team? The high-tech, wired, networked world demands lots of logic. When things go wrong, you have to stay calm and be able to see through a computer. There's no substitute for a strong skill set here.

Insurance: A big chunk of business in this field is in sales. Beyond that, other opportunities allow you to apply strong quantitative skills. Do you like to investigate mysteries? Do computing numbers and making settlements keep you interested? Could you call on friends and network round the clock to make sales for a product that many people don't want to talk about? You'll never skip the fine print because someone's benefits could be at risk, and you'll talk endlessly to convince people to protect their assets, which includes bouncing back quickly from rejection and moving nonstop to find and retain clients.

Interior Design: Do you have a sense of style, love matching fabric samples, rearranging rooms, beautifying interiors, and enjoy interpreting other people's ideas and influencing them with your own? Do you understand enough about architecture to read and interpret a floor plan? Successful decorators know how to not be overbearing or overwhelming. Regardless of how much you have to spend, you'll need to be resourceful, creative, and upbeat. Client satisfaction is the most important aspect here.

Investment Banking: As with other areas of finance, you must be extremely money conscious, an accounting expert, and have a detail-oriented mind with a full understanding of the financial world. Self-confidence will have to be your middle name since you will be entrusted with enormous amounts of money and proprietary information. Personal integrity and an understanding of investments will be your strongest selling points. This is one field where image is all-important. Look the part with your wardrobe; act it with your confident posture, your impeccable manners, and polished speaking style. And be prepared for some long hours and sleepless nights.

Law: Are you a quick-thinking tough negotiator? Could you slog though a contract, analyzing every single word? Do you want to work in an industry known for some very difficult personalities? If you're not sure about the law, find work at a law firm as an intern, paralegal, or clerk first; three years is a long time and a lot of money to invest in schooling if you don't absolutely love the profession. Investigate the many different forms of law practice, and find one to suit your personality type and strengths. Are you fast on your feet with a rapier mind? Try litigation. Great with numbers and you love research? Perhaps real estate law or contracts would be your choice. Have a soft spot for kids? Consider child advocacy or family law.

Manufacturing and Production: Are you technically skilled, level-headed, attentive to detail, and able to creatively improve processes? Nuts and bolts and attention to the bottom line are the prime movers in this field. You'll have to understand the process before you can improve on it. Competition is keen, and the pennies you shave off of costs make you the heroine. "It's a man's world" is still the image in both the factories and executive suites of manufacturing companies, so be ready to defend your opinions with fact and to show the men a female brain is not just as good, it's often better!

Marketing: Do you ever wonder why you're loyal to Coke? Or why you'll only wear Levi's? Do you enjoy knowing a single product or brand inside out, backward, and forward? Do you possess strong quantitative and analytical skills to measure the effectiveness (read: hard-core financial reports and ratings numbers) of marketing campaigns? Marketing is a head game—lots of brainstorming and thinking outside the box to get your message through. Make it your own by studying psychology, journalism, advertising, and media. Learn to put aside your own prejudices and listen to others talk. There are many faces to marketing; pick the one that most interests you, from market research to planning campaigns to figuring out what the market wants and developing a product to fill the niche. As a marketer you'll likely start out as a marketing coordinator, carrying out the ideas of more senior staff. Be prepared to learn from assembling PowerPoint presentations, organizing spreadsheets, and editing copy.

Medicine and Health: Extensive professional training is of course the first requirement for this field. Are you a strong-stomached, highly attentive, dedicated, calm person who deals well with illness and emergencies? Can you handle the chaos of a busy hospital or clinic? Expect long hours and big demands on your time if you're pursuing this industry, which is made up of various levels from home attendants and nurses to dentists and surgeons. You need to be an expert at handling stressed personalities at all levels. Nothing is easy about this profession; however, the rewards can be very meaningful. With the aging population this will be a growing field for many years to come.

Nursing: Are you a compassionate, patient, dedicated, quick thinker with an incredible bedside manner? Is the mix of science, people's problems, and the world of health appealing? Nurses need to be highly compassionate, instruction-following individuals who don't mind being the front line for a doctor. Long hours are a big part of nursing, and you must be able to deal with stressful situations with poise and grace. It helps to have a calming personality and the ability to relax even when everything around you is chaotic. This is a growth field as the nursing shortage is expected to continue for years.

Performing Arts: Are you a highly expressive, outgoing, passionate person with a thick skin and impressive vocal or acting abilities? Does the sound of applause motivate you and make your spirit soar? Can you handle rejection? To break into this field, you need to be willing to try a variety of related disciplines from scenery to stagehand. Few people land the leading role and it's a business with a high rejection rate regardless of how talented you are. There's no substitute for training and preparation. You never know when the lead of a play will be out sick!

Politics: Are you able to multitask and change direction at a moment's notice? Can you work well under pressure and focus all of your attention on a single politician's success? Do you have strong feelings about public policy issues? This is a field where you can take on as much responsibility as you can handle, and it often spills into your nights and weekends. Political staffers and elected officials are very intense people so be prepared for superstrong personalities. And know that if your candidate loses, you'll have to look for another job.

Psychology and Counseling: Are you interested in how the human mind works and its influence on our behavior? More important, can you keep your spirits up after listening to people's problems all day long? You have to be on call around the clock, and keeping up with voice mails and dozens of telephone calls can be mind-boggling. Being empathetic is also on the front burner. A compassionate heart is absolutely necessary, as is the ability to separate work and home life, since the demands on your time can be totally consuming.

Public Relations: Are you a creative thinker with an outgoing, fearless, cold-calling, rejection-proof personality with excellent communication and writing skills? Do you like planning and executing events? Can you handle a sudden crisis? Internships and working in the field or at a media outlet are very important. Contacts are crucial because you are your Rolodex. Persistence is also a necessary quality. You have to think on your feet and deal with an endless variety of personalities and win them over hourly. This career is very demanding on your time and often suits workaholics.

Residential Real Estate: Do you have an ambitious and entrepreneurial spirit and thrive on working long hours independently, especially on weekends? Does the rush of sales, closing deals, and working on commission energize you? This business is ideal for a strong personality who will go after what she wants. You can't be timid in this arena. Connections are also important here and you must be very personable. You need to know what you are selling inside and out and you must have a strong understanding of how to assess a situation so you can qualify the buyer and the seller.

Research: Do you have a curious mind, a passion for data, and a nose for knowledge? Can you spend long hours in a library or in front of your computer screen? It's necessary to have a strong foundation of computer and research skills to be able to find hard to locate information. A good researcher knows that the really good information is not the easiest to find. An analytical mind is a positive trait since quantitative and qualitative research demands that you compare and contrast volumes of information. Communication skills are also essential so you can share and apply the facts you uncover.

Retail: Do you like the idea of totaling numbers, counting inventory, increasing sales, and helping a product reach the consumer? Retail demands that you do everything from cleaning up a stockroom to answering the phones. Multitasking with enormous energy and a positive attitude is a must. You'll pay your dues before landing that glamorous buyer's job with its attendant travel and perks and even then, much of the job is nitty-gritty number crunching. While it seems exciting, most retailers will tell you it's plain old hard work that gets the job done and the sale rung up.

Sales: Above all else, sales is about building relationships. People are your audience, your focus, and your target. You'll need a persuasive personality and a fearless attitude. Are people naturally willing to take your opinion and lead? Are you motivated by the bottom line and willing to work long, hard hours? In sales, self-motivation is key. If you don't go after the appointment, nobody's going to do it for you. Customers will rarely beat down your door begging for your time. In addition to being a self-starter, you'll need excellent record-keeping and follow-up skills. Getting one order is relatively easy, but it's customer service that will get you the reorder. Make yourself known as the salesperson who's willing to go the extra mile for your customers and you'll keep them coming back for more.

Science: Do you dream of being the first woman to discover a new galaxy? Or creating a new energy source to replace gasoline? Or finding a cure for the common cold? Maybe the research lab is the place for you. Start early. You'll need vast knowledge of what's already been done before you can go forward where no man or woman has gone before. Be prepared for the tedium of repetition, dead ends, and disappointments, sparked with the overwhelming joy of accomplishment when an idea leads to positive results. Learn to look for productive work environments, groups of researchers who push one another to achieve even more, and who attract funding for their achievements.

Secretarial: Are you a highly organized, detail-oriented, skillful grammar expert and letter writer with an upbeat personality who takes direction well? Whether you think of secretarial work as a stepping-stone to higher responsibility or as a career in itself, make it count. If you don't shine, your boss won't either. A warm personality and an ability to work with others are pluses here; you'll have to run interference, handle communications, and even occasionally take the blame for your superiors' mistakes. Grasp of language, computer and phone skills, discretion, and perfectionism will all work to your advantage in the secretarial world.

Social Work: Are you unselfish, a great listener, highly motivated, caring, and anything but a pushover who can deal with tough times and tough people? Your heart of gold will have to be encased in steel if you're going to help those in need. You have to be able to smell a con game from a mile away, and to put aside your personal convictions to give aid to people you might want to despise. You'll need a solid grounding in psychology, law, human services, and available social services to be effective in your work. Dealing with people can be very discouraging sometimes no matter how hard you try to reach them. Teach yourself that a failure is not your failure.

> ## Inside Scoop
>
> ### *Consider a Career in Sales*
>
> If you're more of a generalist without a specific skill or some strong technical area of expertise, you ought to consider sales—at least as a starting point. We know sales typically conjures up unsightly images of some boiler-room braggart who'd sell the shirt off his grandmother's back. Don't be alarmed: The industry as a whole isn't sleazy at all.
>
> Quite the contrary.
>
> Sales jobs can be big moneymakers, especially if you're good. Such opportunities are ideal for women with great personalities, endless energy, and solid people skills. Not only does sales strengthen these traits, the profession also builds confidence and teaches us how to think quickly on our feet. The perks are fabulous and it's often the fast track to some of the biggest and best corporate jobs. It's a great first step to marketing, business development, senior management, and other areas. Everyone loves someone with a solid record of generating revenue. Your best bet is to find a job selling something you already like—a product or service you use or believe in. But keep in mind: Thin skin won't cut it. There's lots of rejection in sales, so strong confidence is essential.

Teaching: Teaching is all about preparation and communication. A command of knowledge is imperative as well as the ability to be able to share your topic. And above all, you must really like kids! The upside is that you will have the amazing opportunity to influence others, impart knowledge, shape lives, build character, and be a role model. You'll need to be content doing important work at modest pay. Are you comfortable disciplining children? Teachers primarily work with students but you'll need to handle parents and school administrators too.

Visual Arts: Are you a creative personality with training in art and design? Do you want to express your ideas in a form other than words? Be honest with yourself. Are you an artist? Does your work have a creative spark? Are you willing to struggle for the years it might take to get recognition for your talent? The best strategy is to find your niche. Work in your field, even if it means painting backdrops for plays or illustrating magazines. Being a snob about your work will get you nowhere. Follow your heart, but listen to people you respect. Learn to live with rejection. It's a cliché, but remember that most famous artists were ridiculed and many never achieved recognition during their lives.

Web Design: Do you possess the cool combo of creativity and a strong understanding of Internet use? Whether you want to work for yourself or in a corporate setting, if you can show your creativity, technical skills, and command of technology, you can be a cyber-star. Refine your skills, learn to talk to people and sell yourself if you want to run your own web design business. Be the innovator and focus on pleasing your clients. Approach the large names in the computer field and find mentors to sponsor your work. You have to be able to communicate in cyberspace in a way that attracts people and signs them up for your services.

Work It, Girl!

Survey Says . . . If you have followed our exercises, you should know what your skills are and what jobs exist. It's time to sum up the results. Come up with a one- or two-sentence description of the job, industry, and culture you are looking for. It's okay to have two or three possibilities, but make them each as specific as possible.

Write your "perfect" situation—job function, industry, and culture—in the space below.

Example: My ideal opportunity is as a junior publicist in a music-related cable television company in Los Angeles. The office will be hip, fast-paced, and located near public transportation.

_____

_____

_____

_____

_____

_____

Researching Companies

As you begin to hone in on your ideal industry, job function, and culture, it's also important to start sniffing out specific companies that appear to be a good match. Begin to develop a target list of companies—twenty to twenty-five is a good start—and begin to research them for clues on whether or not they'll be hiring in the near future. Have they experienced recent layoffs? How's their stock price? Did they recently expand to larger office space? All of this information will come in handy later when you begin the interview process, but for now it's important for realism's sake. If a company is experiencing massive layoffs or its stock just plunged 20 percent, it won't be impossible to get a job there, but it won't be easy.

BECOME AN EXPERT ON YOUR INDUSTRY

Aside from assessing your own skills and interests, it is essential to get a grip on the industry and specific field you are interested in. You may be thinking about a marketing job in the world of health care. Not only will marketing trends be important to you, but also you have got to get in tune with the latest on the health care industry as a whole, including nonmarketing related issues. This process will open your eyes to a myriad of possibilities and will provide you with valuable content for upcoming conversations with contacts and interviewers in the field.

WHY FOCUS MATTERS

Over the course of your job search you're going to be asking a lot of people for help. At various stages you'll be requesting networking contacts, resume advice, negotiating tips and, most important, you'll be asking for a job. Remember that most people—especially your friends and family—want to help with your job search. But no one can help unless you're clear about what you need. The more focused your request, the more likely people are to respond. So the next time someone says, "I wish there was some way I could help with your job

Work It, Girl!

Becoming an Expert Conduct an online search, read industry publications, and talk to peers in the field(s) and identify the top three current trends affecting each of the industries of interest to you. For the moment, do not worry about the job function you would like to pursue. Focus instead on the field, keeping in mind the health care marketing example above.

Field of interest:

Major trends:

_____

_____

_____

_____

Field of interest:

Major trends:

_____

_____

_____

_____

Field of interest:

Major trends:

_____

_____

_____

_____

search," your response should be, "As a matter of fact, you can!" But rather than saying, "Please let me know if you hear of anyone who's hiring," be specific: "I'm really interested in finding a copywriting position at a large advertising agency with a focus on consumer products. Do you know anyone at one of the major ad firms?"

Even if your contact can't give you a specific name at BBDO, Saatchi & Saatchi, or TBWA\Chiat\Day, she is certain to keep you in mind if someone from those companies crosses her path. The more focused you are, the more memorable you will be.

Volunteering and Internships

There are many ways to gain experience, even while you are job hunting. We strongly believe that it is better to be working than not working. Any job, paid or unpaid, full-time or part-time, may lead to a permanent opportunity and always leads to more contacts. Consider offering your services as an outside contractor, temp, or volunteer. You can check out the environment, wow them with your skills, and be on hand when full-time opportunities arise. Here are some ideas for maximizing temporary opportunities.

VOLUNTEERING

Besides giving back to your community, volunteering offers yet another great way to connect with potential employers or networking contacts and to build your resume. And there's nothing like a dose of reality to keep your own work woes in perspective. Volunteer opportunities are endless and exist everywhere. From spending one Saturday a month cleaning up a public park to volunteering your accounting skills to balance the books of a day care center, nonprofit organizations offer numerous ways to contribute your time. When choosing a volunteer organization, remember the following tips:

- **Be up front about your commitment level.** Many nonprofit organizations "rely on the kindness of strangers" as Blanche DuBois might say, so they understand that you have other commitments and they are usually willing to take as much time as you can comfortably give. Be clear about the time you have and that you may cut back your commitment when you find a full-time job. This will help the organization give you tasks that can fit into your schedule.

- **Share your goals.** It's okay to tell a volunteer organization that you are there to help your career and job search. As long as you are genuine in your desire to help, they will more than likely be happy to give you tasks that will advance your skills or allow you to meet more people in your industry. For instance, you can volunteer to work on a fund-raiser attended by executives in your field if you want an inside route to a media company, or you can volunteer at an animal shelter if you aspire to be a vet. Often your industry association can match you with a volunteer organization looking for help.

- **Volunteer at a company.** There's no rule saying that only nonprofits can accept volunteers. Why not donate a few hours a week to the company you would most like as an employer? If you can spare a few unpaid hours, this could be a great way to get a foot in the door, particularly if you are just starting out in your career or changing careers. This is a great tip for working your way into a small or midsized company.

From Volunteer to Employee

Jamie never got to use her B.A. in anthropology. A winding career path veered from bartending to managing a marina to becoming a Montessori teacher. During a breather to contemplate a career change, but not knowing in which direction to go, she began volunteering to lead tours at a local historical museum—a job usually reserved for retirees. Learning the local lore was right up her alley, and she found her head bursting with ideas to excite public interest. After only a few months of volunteering, Jamie had shown she was reliable, responsible, and capable of adding immense creative energy to the museum. Serendipity! A new career—with a paid position—was born.

- **Volunteer in politics.** Republican, Democrat, Independent, or Green, political candidates are always looking for enthusiastic volunteers. Working on a political campaign is exciting, interesting, and often exhausting! Campaign staff will often give you as much responsibility as you can handle, so be prepared to work hard, especially as a campaign nears its conclusion. But the long hours put in by many volunteers can have a nice payoff: When candidates are elected, they often hire campaign workers to serve as fully paid members of their staff.

INTERNSHIPS

You want to go to work, but you don't know where or how or why or for whom? Maybe you've narrowed the choices, or maybe you've invested some time in career testing and counseling. But the road map to that perfect career path still eludes you. Sounds like you ought to be looking at an internship.

Internships are one of the most outstanding ways to increase your skills and circle of influence. An internship is typically a short-term work experience, usually for students with some academic background, but not always. Some pay, some don't. And many, while done for academic credit, can lead to full-time work later.

Internships can be local, across the country, or halfway around the world. They can be during the school year, structured during your semesters or quarters, or in the summer, days or evenings. Many colleges have internship programs where you can even earn course credits. Internships are an important resume builder and way to establish connections and insights into what you are good at and enjoy doing most.

Employers love interns (no Monica Lewinsky jokes, please). For starters, it's cost-effective labor for a company without expensive benefits. Employers love to hire job candidates who have similar work experiences that illustrate they've been there and done that. Internships also show that you've already sampled the industry you're exploring; they teach you skills and help you begin building a network of contacts and experiences that can be of major assistance in the future.

Almost every industry offers internships to promising candidates. You can check out websites like www.wetfeet.com and www.internweb.com for hundreds of listings. You can also call a company directly to inquire about internship programs. Corporate websites offer this information online. Smaller businesses are likely to be more flexible and open to your suggestions about what a mutually beneficial internship situation would be. Just remember, never say you'll work "for free." Use the term "unpaid internship."

TOP TIPS FOR PICKING AN INTERNSHIP

- Remember that the early intern bird catches the job. Each company differs, but traditionally you should apply up to three to six months ahead of when you are interested in interning and begin correspondence to determine if an opportunity exists. Some companies—particularly in the media, finance, and consulting

Take a Page for Success

The NBC Page Program, which is based in New York and Burbank, California, has a long history of success as a training ground for developing industry talent on-air and off, dating back to its origin in 1933.

Alexa Levin, a 2000 cum laude graduate of the University of Pennsylvania, was accepted to the program in 2001, after completing the highly competitive application process. "There's a series of two interviews. The first is one-on-one with the head of the program, and the second is a panel with other potential pages and about four people from NBC asking everyone a series of questions," says Levin. NBC guarantees one year of work, but "encourages each page to look for full-time jobs throughout the program as the page can leave at any time."

Levin started her stint by giving guided tours of the NBC studios, then moved on to a variety of ten-week assignments throughout the network. "I was chosen to assist the president of NBC, which gave me an insider's look into the business. After that I moved to the *Today* show, which meant being at work at 5:30 A.M. I was responsible for getting all of the live guests to hair and makeup and then to the studio on time for their segments. I met extraordinary people, from Matt Lauer, Katie Couric, Ann Curry, and Al Roker and the producers and crew to amazing guests—celebrities, authors, chefs, athletes, politicians, and more. By working on the set, I learned that I wanted to try my hand on-air. I had the opportunity to make a resume tape and was coached

industries—accept applications a year in advance and the competition can be steep, so do not procrastinate and be sure to get the facts. Many smaller companies welcome a call and might not work as far in advance, while others prefer you apply online. It is important to determine the company's internship application policies and guidelines to jump-start the process.

• Ask other people you know for contacts and referrals who might be searching for interns. Most companies love having interns help them and even if they don't have an internship program, you just might initiate one and be the first.

• Check with your career counselor at your college to determine what internship programs are available through your university, even if you graduated several years ago. Many colleges have internship programs available to help assist their students in securing internships. Take advantage of these services.

- Check with someone who has interned at a specific company and see how she liked it. What did she learn? Was she a coffee go-getter or did she really learn specific skills?

- Don't be afraid to interview a company if they are offering an internship. Find out what they will expect and all details

while reading the news, and now I have something to send out for potential jobs. I've also met many people who may be able to help me kick off my career. If not, I certainly have mentors to look to for advice. The Page Program is a great feeder into many diverse and great jobs at NBC."

Visit www.nbcjobs.com for information on applying to the Page Program, as well as details on other news, entertainment, and sales training programs offered by NBC for college graduates.

possible. Observe the environment you will be working in and see if you can meet the people with whom you will be working. Be enthusiastic as you check them out and make a fabulous first impression.

- Pick an industry that appeals to you—high tech, entertainment, media, medicine, law, nonprofit, and read all about it. Don't go in without some idea of what you are getting yourself into and check out alternatives.

- Set realistic goals—do you want to learn about an industry or dabble in several? Are you using the experience to get a foot in the door at a specific company? Is the job most important, or the opportunity to travel or meet people?

- Pick the kind of learning experience that appeals to you—service, where you work under a professional; apprenticeship, where you learn a skilled trade; externship, which allows you to experience a career for a short time as you shadow a professional; co-op, which may last longer and alternate with classroom work; or practicum, another one-time experience.

- Understand the options: paid versus unpaid, full-time versus part-time, school year or summer, for credit or not.

HOW TO SUCCEED BY REALLY, REALLY TRYING

If you land the internship, remember to have a positive attitude—do whatever you're asked to do, even if it's menial. You're not the boss—yet! But this may be the first step to a great full-time job in the company. It's important to communicate with your boss about your schedule so that she knows when to expect you and any holidays you need to take off. Treat it as you would a full-time job and a commitment. Create a Rolodex card for the boss's desk with your contact information to make it easy to reach you at all times.

An intern position is the time to be willing to learn all you can about the company. So take direction and constructive criticism with a smile. You'll learn more if you're tough-skinned, so when someone suggests a different way of doing something or shows you an error you've made, appreciate the time they took to teach you. An internship is a safe haven for learning. You'll never learn anything if you think you know everything!

Don't forget to say thank you. Thank your boss or coworker for helping you, teaching you, and offering you assistance when the copy machine jams. Every day is a new opportunity for your success. Do more than you are asked to do and make a difference. And leave the office better than you found it. From replacing paper clips to replacing paper in everyone's printer, it's the little things that count. Consider ways that you'll be valued. From helping organize the office supply closet to alphabetizing a file cabinet, volunteer to make things better and you'll definitely be appreciated and noticed. You can always ask for assignments that fall outside of your duties. Once you fulfill their requests, offer to do more and be specific.

MAKE THE INTERNSHIP EXPERIENCE A BUILDING BLOCK
FOR FUTURE SUCCESS

- Find a mentor. Making yourself useful and doing it cheerfully will get you noticed. Remember, you're building a network of contacts as carefully as you're building a resume and a file of job skills.

- Learn everything you can about the business or industry. This is a golden opportunity, so do not waste a second of it.

- Utilize your internship to learn how to polish basic skills like writing a correct business letter, using basic equipment like a fax or copy machine, and mastering the learning curve.

- When the internship is over, stay in touch, first with a thank-you letter to everyone who's helped you, and then with thoughtful e-mails, calls, or notes that express how those people mattered in your life and helped you learn, grow, and gain confidence to move up the ladder. Make your last day a memorable one for everyone involved by expressing your gratitude.

Inside Scoop

Job-Hopping

Temping, freelancing, and interning are great, but can these temporary arrangements ever backfire? Can "job-hopping" eventually cost you a job that you really want? Like Nike, we say just do it. Take any job that teaches you something, then hop up to a better opportunity. In today's job market, due to corporate downsizing, global competition, advances in technology and a rising cost of living, it is not unusual for a person to have several jobs throughout their career. In many cases, it depends on your field. For example, in certain technology specialties, moving around a lot is considered routine; however, in the educational market, job-hopping would likely be frowned upon. If you have moved around a lot, it is important to have different reasons for each. "It just wasn't the right job for me" will only work once. No matter what the circumstances, pay careful attention not to burn bridges when you opt to jump ship.

- Before you leave your internship, ask your employer to read your resume and make suggestions before you go. Also, request a letter that can be attached as a reference to your resume. You've dedicated yourself for weeks or months to the company, and it's totally appropriate to ask for some "me" time. It's also a great idea to ask for any contacts they might have that can help you with your job search. If you don't ask, you'll never know. A job could be right under your nose or around the corner.

CHAPTER FOUR

The (Gulp) Resume

You have worked hard to decide what you want and you have worked hard to get the experience you need to land a great job. But no one will ever know how wonderful you are unless you have a phenomenal resume. It is often the first point of contact with a potential employer. Will Rogers summed it up best when he said, "You never get a second chance to make a good first impression." A resume can make yours a lasting one.

Before you decide what to wear to the big interview or what to say to the recruiter, before you even step out the door, make sure you get your foot *in* the door with a top-notch resume. You won't land a job based solely on your resume, but if it's smart and well written it can lead to a world of opportunities. A sloppy, poorly written document will end up in the circular file, along with your career prospects. Think of your resume as your new best friend and concentrate on making it perfect. Your resume is an advertisement: The product for sale is you. It's the marketing tool you use to pique the interest of recruiters. You've got to make them want to take a closer look.

First things first: Never lie no matter what. Everything on that resume is verifiable by a potential employer. They can confirm your education, previous employment, association memberships, and more.

Honesty is not just the best policy; it's the *only* policy when it comes to resumes. Stretching the truth on your resume will almost always haunt you. Unless you want to spend the rest of your career looking over your shoulder, we warn you not to do it. Not only do some companies conduct background checks on many prospective employees, but also in some industries you never know who knows who. Meaning the person you are about to present with a phony resume may very well be friends with your former employer. Since you never know whom you may encounter, it is safest not to lie. Background checks may include verification of your previous job titles, dates of employment, day-to-day responsibilities, and education history. If you are two credits shy of a bachelor's degree, do not check the B.A. box on an application. In some cases, even that small stretch will prevent you from ever being employed by that company.

You don't have to shy away from boasting about significant

responsibilities and successful contributions. For example, if you are confident that your individual efforts on a team project helped save your previous employer money or generated profits, you may say that you "spearheaded" or "led" this particular effort. Just be prepared to justify the credit you are taking should an interviewer choose to focus on it.

By the way, there is no rule that says someone else can't prepare your resume. If you are really unsure of your writing skills, go ahead and talk to an expert for one-on-one advice. But remember, just because you shell out a hundred bucks for a resume professional doesn't mean you have a better chance at getting the job. We believe that nobody's better at creating a solid representation of your background than you are.

CHRONOLOGICAL VERSUS FUNCTIONAL

For most job seekers, we recommend a standard, chronological resume that lists your professional experience beginning with your most recent position. Chronological resumes are essential for job seekers applying to large, traditional companies as well as for job seekers with solid work histories.

If, on the other hand, your recent work history is spotty or not really relevant to the job you're looking for, perhaps a functional resume is more suitable because it highlights specific skills rather than your chronological work experience. This also works for those with limited job history, but good technical knowledge in a chosen field. If you've acquired skills through academics, unpaid work, hobbies, or other avenues, group them into categories. For instance, a would-be photographer would list under skills: types of cameras, darkroom equipment, and computer programs she's proficient in, even if her last job was in sales. Use phrases like "proficient in, familiar with, knowledge of, managed, coordinated" to introduce those skills. Abilities that will translate to any field such as "successfully handling customers" should be noted. Choose your words carefully to convey what you can do. Be accurate, but creative, and always show your resume to several people you admire professionally to make sure the functional format best reflects your skills and experience.

Top-to-Bottom Resume Guide
for Chronological Resumes

CONTENT

There are countless resume styles and designs, but our experience shows that a simple, straightforward resume works every time. Perfection is the name of the game, so be sure to follow these step-by-step guidelines:

Personal Contact Information

All contact information should appear at the very top of your document. Be sure to provide an e-mail address that you check frequently. If your regular e-mail address is funkymama@whatever.com or vodkaqueen@funmail.com, it is definitely time to set up a separate e-mail account using your first and last name specifically for your job search. (Hotmail and Yahoo! offer them free and both enable you to check your account from any Internet connection worldwide.)

Make sure your phone number is correct with a professional voice mail or answering machine message on the other end. Skip the punk music, pet greetings, and goofy jokes. Definitely list a cell phone number, with an equally professional greeting, if you have one.

Objective

One of the problems with some resumes is the absence of a clear objective. Way too many otherwise smart people plug in the old standby: "Seeking a position with a multifaceted company that will put my talents to good use while enhancing my skills." Huh? That's a bunch of nonsense that does not impress recruiters. If anything, it's a huge red flag letting them know that you're completely unsure of your career goals.

Look back to the section where you created a one- to two-sentence description of the job function, industry, and culture you most want. This is the first step to creating a great objective. If you're applying for an entry- or mid-level position, a short and meaningful objective will get your resume off to a winning start. Here's the lowdown on the best objectives sure to make your phone ring:

- **Narrow it down.** The recruiter wants an idea of what you want to do; be specific and indicate what you're seeking. Don't be scared of being pigeonholed into a dead-end job. You can target the industry, the specific job title, or both.

  Bad Example: "A position in a corporation solving complex tasks."

  Good Example: "A position in accounting."

  Great Example: "A position in accounting focusing on internal audit."

  A Very Specific Example: "A position in accounting focusing on internal audit in the entertainment industry."

  Bad Example: "A position in a nonprofit that helps children."

  Good Example: "A marketing role in a child-focused nonprofit organization."

Great Example: "A strategic marketing role in a child welfare agency."

A Very Specific Example: "A strategic marketing role in a government-funded child welfare agency."

- **Short and sweet.** Ya got it? No clichés. No long drawn out explanations about your experience or education that go on for line after line after line.

Before: "A full-time permanent position in the field of marketing utilizing my exceptional education and skills to make a contribution to a growing company."

After: "A marketing position utilizing skills in event planning."

- **Don't be obvious.** If you're applying for an advertised position, don't make it obvious that you changed your resume's objective just for that job. Don't include company names or the exact job title if it is obviously for that position.

Wrong Objective: "A position as master of creativity at CompuMedia Design."

Right Objective: "A position as website designer in a media design firm."

- **Why bother at all?** The main point to an objective is to show a potential employer that you know where your career is headed (at least for now!). Recruiters will rarely help a wishy-washy candidate make career decisions in an interview. Further, if your experience or education doesn't match those of the position, an objective can help reassure the recruiter you did indeed mean to apply for that job.

- **Changing objectives.** It is okay—in fact, encouraged—to have different objectives and even different resumes depending on the job for which you are applying. It's very common—even expected—to promote different skills to different companies depending on the position for which you're applying. That's how smart people operate. Remember, this is a sales pitch and you want to offer the right product to each potential buyer.

- **Don't get lazy.** We've seen a lot of otherwise decent resumes get chucked because of offensive or irrelevant objectives. No potential employer wants to read that your goal is to find an "easy" job or something "laid back." Nothing on that resume—especially the objective—should even remotely imply laziness.

An alternative to specifying an objective is to provide a summary of your professional accomplishments. This is especially effective if you have depth of knowledge in one or two key skills within an industry. It's also a good format to provide when networking and a too narrowly focused objective statement might limit your opportunities.

Education

- Leave off your G.P.A. if it's any lower than a 3.5. You are by no means required to provide your G.P.A. on your resume.

- List honors, exceptional course work, majors, minors—anything that enables you to demonstrate your acquired knowledge.

- If you're in college or have earned a degree, eliminate references to high school.

- List the dates and relevant course work if you have attended college but have not graduated.

Experience

- You don't have to list every single job you've ever had. Emphasize the most recent and most relevant. Describe your responsibilities with action verbs. For instance, rather than saying you were "responsible for in-store promotions," tell employers that you "planned, executed, and managed in-store promotions." Always keep it to the point. Pare down by asking yourself, "Will this statement help me get the job?" If the answer is no, ditch it.

- Use present tense for your current job, past tense for all previous employment.

- Be direct and concise. "Supervised staff of five" is better than "was responsible for supervision of five staff members."

- Turn responsibilities into accomplishments. "Pitched media stories generating 100 news articles per month" is much better than "Wrote and promoted press releases."

- Demonstrate how you have found solutions to organizational challenges. Think of your accomplishments in terms of the problem faced, the action you took, and the results you achieved. Recruiters like to see the progression from Problem to Action to Results.

- Quantify whenever possible. "Increased sales by 12 percent," "Generated $1 million of new business," or "Repeatedly exceeded monthly quotas." Numbers are impressive, but be sure your references will confirm the figures if asked.

- Use a better term than "temping" for temporary positions you've held. Avoid the term consulting (it has a very particular meaning), but words like "freelancer" or "independent contractor" sound more impressive. In temp situations, list the name of the company where you worked, not the temp agency, although be sure to specify that your position was in fact a temporary assignment. One note of caution: When completing employment applications, include the name of the temp agency as well. Do not imply that you were on staff directly at the company.

● Research job listings to see what skills are asked for. Match your vocabulary to the employers'. Use buzzwords specific to an industry. This is especially important when resumes are submitted online as many recruiters search resumes by keyword. If your resume mentions "Internship at ABC, freelance production work for HBO, and various commercials for key cable clients," but never mentions simple words like "television" or "broadcasting," your resume may never appear in an online search performed by a busy TV station's HR manager.

● Keywords include industries, companies, products,

Inside Scoop

Slingin' Your Experience

A common concern among entry-level job seekers is how to translate retail sales and waitressing positions into meaningful experiences that potential employers won't just overlook or dismiss. It's all in how you spin it!

You've been out there working your butt off instead of sitting it on the couch whining about lack of opportunities—that right there shows drive and a great work ethic. Let them know exactly what you've learned from your experiences. Sales and waitressing positions are full of interactions with other people. Both put you in positions to deal with difficult and demanding people, frustrating situations, and stress. Those are skills that you can apply in any corporate position. Employers today are extremely customer-oriented, and any employee that comes in with successful experience in handling customers has a head start.

The words you select to describe what you took away from such experiences are key to making a deeper impact. A waitress undoubtedly used interpersonal skills, exemplified patience, and paid attention to customer satisfaction. As a salesperson, you researched your target market, used various techniques to sell to your clients, and engaged in practices to build and retain your customers. Don't ever hide from the good, honest work in your past. Be proud of the responsibility you have shown.

and software programs that prove how qualified you are for a particular position. Your college English professor may have told you to avoid jargon in formal writing, but resumes absolutely require it. You must let employers know you possess the right stuff, which often includes very specific, name-brand knowledge or qualifications such as SQL, Java, or Series 7.

List any related activities that illustrate your experience or connections in a specific industry. Connections and a mastery of a related target base could separate you as a quick study for that career field.

- The best keywords are brand names. Use them wherever possible. Perhaps you worked for a small, relatively unknown public relations agency, but worked on major accounts. List the big clients or products you were involved with.

- Give a one-sentence description of any company or organization where you have worked, unless they were major corporations. Do not assume that anyone knows what Purple People, Inc., actually is.

THE ONLY ACTION WORD LIST YOU'LL EVER NEED

It is imperative to start every sentence in your resume with an action word. Action words convey focus and drive. Guess where we found the words on this list? In the resumes of people we've hired, as well as the resumes of our clients' favorite candidates.

Keep in mind that it's important to vary your word choices— no recruiter wants to see eight sentences beginning with the word *managed*, which is among the most overused in resume history.

accelerate	coach	distinguish	head
accomplish	collaborate	diversify	identify
achieve	collect	double	illustrate
adapt	compile	draft	implement
address	complete	edit	improve
administer	compose	educate	increase
advance	compute	eliminate	indoctrinate
advise	conceptualize	enable	influence
align	conduct	encourage	inform
allocate	consolidate	engineer	initiate
analyze	contain	enhance	innovate
appraise	contract	enlist	inspect
approve	contribute	establish	install
arrange	control	evaluate	instigate
assemble	coordinate	examine	institute
assign	correspond	execute	instruct
assist	counsel	expand	integrate
attain	create	expedite	interpret
audit	critique	explain	interview
author	cultivate	extract	introduce
automate	cut	facilitate	invent
balance	decrease	familiarize	launch
budget	delegate	fashion	lead
built	demonstrate	focus	lecture
calculate	design	forecast	leverage
catalogue	develop	formulate	maintain
chair	devise	foster	manage
champion	diagnose	found	market
clarify	direct	generate	mediate
classify	dispatch	handle	mentor

Work It, Girl

Using Action Words Form sentences beginning with ten of the above words, based on your own experience:

_____

_____

_____

_____

_____

_____

_____

_____

_____

_____

_____

_____

moderate	orient	process	reconcile
monitor	originate	produce	record
motivate	overhaul	program	recruit
navigate	oversee	project	reduce
negotiate	partner	promote	refer
nurture	perform	provide	refine
observe	persuade	publicize	regulate
obtain	plan	publish	rehabilitate
operate	prepare	purchase	remodel
orchestrate	present	quadruple	reorganize
organize	prioritize	recommend	repair

represent	shape	supervise	trim
research	solidify	survey	triple
restore	solve	tabulate	update
restructure	specify	tailor	upgrade
retrieve	stimulate	target	validate
revise	strategize	teach	work
save	streamline	train	write
schedule	strengthen	translate	
screen	summarize	travel	

Skills and Interests

- Activities and skills that demonstrate leadership roles, honors, or special talents and abilities should be listed at the bottom of your resume. This includes languages in which you're fluent or conversant and specific computer programming skills. List personal information, such as hobbies and interests, only if it relates to the job. Unless you are applying for a position as a rock and roll publicist, no one needs to know that you are president of the Britney Spears fan club.

- Professional affiliations, such as associations and volunteer organizations, are definitely worth noting. Employers want employees who are involved in their industry or community. It is always impressive to list any offices or special roles you have held in these organizations. This is especially crucial for career changers or recent grads—if you have limited experience in an industry, you can prove your commitment by listing organizations you have joined to get involved in your new field (so be sure to join!).

- Extra activities and associations are especially key to the resumes of career changers. If you are switching into IT sales after ten years in pharmaceutical sales, you'll need to demonstrate your seriousness about the IT industry. Listing an IT industry association affiliation or adult education certification in that field proves you are serious about the change.

- Avoid the obvious! We'll scream if we see one more resume that proclaims, "I'm a real people person." Your skills need to be specific, unique, and measurable. If you do consider yourself to be a good people person, explain in what way—like excellent negotiating skills, strong leadership experience, or persuasive sales style.

- Don't overdo it on the most basic word processing stuff. These days everyone knows Microsoft Word—or at least they should—so there is certainly no need to list every version of this popular program. Unless you are applying for technical positions, be selective about the computer programs you list.

What to Leave Out

- Do not write "Reference available upon request." It is assumed that you have good references. If the employer wants to contact them, he or she will ask you for names and numbers. Use the space for more valuable information.

- An employer cannot legally ask for your age, marital status, or family situation, so you do not need to provide this information on your resume.

- Salary history does not belong on your resume.

- Pictures, symbols, graphics, or other gimmicks should be excluded. If you're in a creative field, this supporting material can be used in a portfolio, not a resume.

PRESENTATION AND STYLE

Once you've mastered the content, keep the presentation simple. Resumes today must be compatible with technology. It's safe to assume the recruiters at big companies will scan all resumes into their database. If your resume isn't scannable, it may never be seen at all.

- Avoid long sentences: Use bullet points and be concise.

- Skip the marble-textured paper. White is best.

- Forget fancy fonts. Arial, Helvetica, and Times New Roman are the most commonly used. Book Antiqua, Courier, Futura Optima, Palatino, and New Century Schoolbook are also acceptable.

- Eliminate underlines and italics unless they are essential.

- White space is perfectly acceptable—don't feel pressured to fill every corner of the page, especially if you have minimal work experience.

- No typos, no excuses. Proofread, proofread, and have a friend proofread.

- Limit it to one page. Professionals with ten or more years of experience may expand to two pages, but any more than two is an invitation to be overlooked.

HOW TO HAVE YOUR RESUME ASSESSED

Ask friends and professionals to review and critique your resume. Beyond checking for mistakes, this enables you to test its overall effect. Find out if your objective is clear, if your experience seems to lead to the position you say you are looking for. (An added bonus:

Having friends, family and career counselors review your resume may just spark a great contact in their minds.)

Here are some questions to ask resume assessors to make sure you are presenting an accurate and positive picture of yourself, and to anticipate questions from recruiters:

- After reading my resume, what do you think my ideal job is?

- Which of my experiences are most impressive?

- Is anything unclear, inconsistent, or confusing?

- Is there anything positive you know about me that does not appear on my resume?

In addition to your friends and professional contacts, find a stranger and ask her the same questions. The best idea is to find another job seeker and swap resumes. Someone you've just met will likely have a different—and more neutral—perspective. Listen carefully and take notes on your resume reviewers' responses and address any concerns they raise. Comments of friends, family, and new acquaintances are bound to be very helpful and much nicer than feedback from a confused recruiter.

IT'S FINALLY DONE. NOW WHAT?

- Have a hard copy and electronic copy ready at all times—they're equally important and you never know which version a contact or potential employer will request. You should have your resume available in both a Microsoft Word document and a text-only file.

- Stock your drawer with full-size manila envelopes, stamps, and computer disks. Be prepared to send your resume at any time in any format. Smart job seekers carry a computer disk and hard copies of their resume at all times—what if you're far away from your home computer and you meet a potential contact on the bus who asks you to e-mail your resume that afternoon? Never be caught off guard. Disks are small—don't leave home without them! There will always be a Kinko's or quick copy shop nearby.

VIRUS PROTECT

In this era of annoying viruses that can lead to serious damage, many large companies block attachments from being received by internal e-mail if they are not virus protected. Don't fall victim to the pitfalls of technology. When attaching a Word or text document in an e-mail, be sure to give it a clean bill of health with a virus protect. Free downloads can be found at websites such as www. mcafee.com.

Inside Scoop

Tips from Anne McKinney, Editor of the Real-Resumes Series

"Remember that a resume is designed to reveal or hint at what you can do for the company or organization. Most people are very good judges of their own resumes. So be honest, look at your resume, and decide for yourself: Is it a limp, boring 'laundry list' that would make good bedtime reading for an insomniac, or does it communicate aggressively in such a fashion that the only obvious next step after reading it is to want to dial your number in order to at least talk with you and perhaps meet you? Remember that's the goal of your resume: to motivate the reader to want to meet you. But first the reader has to be aroused to dial your number, e-mail you, or write you. We've heard a lot about how 'every vote counts.' Well, on a one-page resume, every word counts. Present the duties, achievements, licenses, affiliations, and other facts about you that will motivate the reader to want to meet you. (Forget the unimportant or 'old' stuff; for example, no one really cares if we won the third-grade spelling bee.) Although you certainly don't want to misrepresent anything on your resume, you don't need to reveal everything about yourself either. For example, if you resigned from a former job because of a personality clash with the boss, don't volunteer this information on your resume. Never put anything on the resume that will encourage the employer to screen you out."

Resume Template

Fabulous Job Seeker's Name

Street Address, City, State ZIP

Telephone, Fax, Cell Phone, E-mail Address

SUMMARY or OBJECTIVE

Your summary is your sales pitch. Use two to four sentences to explain your key experience and qualifications and what type of position and industry you are seeking. This introduces you to potential employers and allows them to place you in context, while the rest of your resume provides supporting information. It's a sales pitch, so be positive and persuasive!

EXPERIENCE

**Most Recent Impressive Job Title, Company, City, State
(Month Year–Month Year)**

Here you can present a brief overview of the position's responsibilities. Also include an explanation of the company's business if it is not a well-known organization.

- Outline the most impressive accomplishments of your position with bullet points. Always focus on the results of your actions, not just your responsibilities. Include industry buzz words and tangible numbers to support your experience. The eye is drawn to figures, especially on a sales resume!

- Demonstrate how you have found solutions to organizational challenges.

- Start every bullet with an action word, and vary words throughout your resume. No action word should be repeated more than once.

Previous Job Title, Another Great Company, City, State
(Month Year–Month Year)

Keep your summaries short and relevant. Remember that a potential employer is scanning your resume to see if you merit an interview—the briefer and clearer, the better.

- Don't try to include too much. Outline your most important and impressive accomplishments, not a complete menu of every task you've ever performed. Remember to leave some white space.

- As a general rule for chronological resumes, the amount of information—both summaries and bullets—beneath each job should decrease. Your most recent positions should contain the most information to show that you've advanced in your responsibilities and achievements.

Earlier Job Title, Yet Another Company, City, State
(Month Year–Month Year)

Your earliest jobs require minimal information, though they are important to demonstrate career advancement.

EDUCATION

M.B.A., Women For Hire School of Success (Place most recent degree on top)

B.A., Women For Hire University, 2002 (Date is optional, but usually included)

G.P.A. if it is above 3.5, Honors Received (e.g., cum laude or Dean's List)

SKILLS/QUALIFICATIONS

- An optional section that can highlight specific qualifications that are either required for a particular job or are unique about you. This is particularly useful for job seekers in technological fields.

- A great strategy for online resumes that need to be chock-full of key words.
- Two to four bullet points maximum in this section, and no fancy or tiny fonts.

MEMBERSHIPS/AFFILIATIONS

Association memberships and volunteer work show your commitment to your industry and community. This is especially crucial for recent grads and career changers to demonstrate that you're making an effort to establish yourself in a new field. Always mention leadership positions and briefly note relevant achievements.

REFERENCES

References belong on a separate piece of paper that you take to job interviews to give to the interviewer or include with a job application. There is absolutely no need to write "References available upon request" on your resume.

Sample Resumes
Sample #1

Emma Consuelos

10374 North Shore Drive • Miami Beach, FL 33141 • 305.555.5555

emmaconseulos@email.com

SUMMARY

Dedicated and team-oriented business professional with a unique blend of asset and knowledge management experience with Fortune 500 communication companies. Outstanding leadership skills in developing, implementing, and tracking company projects simultaneously with detailed orientation and proficiency.

PROFESSIONAL EXPERIENCE

ACCENTURE CONSULTING, Miami, FL
Technology Analyst
October 2000 to May 2002
Client ABC: Assisted the implementation of a customer interaction configuration to increase efficiency and manage a large increase in customers.

- Conducted client interviews for implementation of Management Training Tool.
- Developed training materials for Outsource Vendor.
- Comanaged the proposed Customer Access Solution Strategy.
- Commended by senior management for gaining cooperation and trust among clients.

Client DEF: Oversaw support for the Customer Relationship Management strategy team in implementing a plan to apply best practices within the Computer and Web Telephony Integration industries.

- Influenced determinations of Interactive Voice Response Systems best practices.
- Acquired and evaluated trending and competitive information on Web Telephony.

Client GHI: Managed the completion of the Conceptual Design activities for PeopleSoft projects and Asset Management modules.

- Maintained version control to avoid duplication of efforts.
- Verified that PeopleSoft applications could effectively interface with legacy systems.

EDUCATION

North Carolina Agricultural & Technical State University
Bachelor of Science, Electronic & Computer Technology, 2000 (summa cum laude)

PROFESSIONAL COURSES

Sequential Query Language, Microsoft Visio, Lotus Notes, Java

....

Why We Like This Resume: Candidate honors the confidentiality of consulting clients, which shows good judgment, while also providing appropriate amount of details to demonstrate strong technical expertise. There is a balance of soft and hard skills.

Sample #2

Caroline Smith
9040 Beach Lawn Terrace • Norwalk, CT 06851 • 203.555.5555
carolinesmith@email.com

PROFILE
- Experience negotiating and drafting multimillion-dollar commercial transactions
- Expertise in managing complex commercial litigation
- Familiar with international business practices and protocols in Europe and Asia
- Skilled in team development and project management

PROFESSIONAL EXPERIENCE

Steinberg and Revesz, LLP, Wilton, CT
October 1999 to February 2002
Responsible for assisting with acquisions, direct investments, financings, litigation defense, and general governance issues on behalf of clients of a large international law firm.
- Counseled clients and assisted with:
  - Internet company's $5MM acquisition of European financial publication to expand its website content.
  - U.S. automotive company's $14MM acquisition of Canadian manufacturer to increase its market share.
  - Renegotiation of $200MM credit facility to facilitate two major acquisitions and provide for operating expenses.
- Led support services for deal team advising a European-based shipping company on a $300MM acquisition of a competitor with assets worldwide.
- Conducted depositions of municipal portfolio managers in major U.S. securities litigation against international investment bank alleging fraud totaling over $2B in damages.

PRO BONO EXPERIENCE

Harlem Homeless Services, Harlem, NY
1999–2000
Advised community group on tax and zoning matters.

EDUCATION

NEW YORK LAW SCHOOL, New York, NY
1999 J.D., cum laude, top 6 percent of class
Honors: Dean's Scholarship; Moot Court Honor Society

UNIVERSITY OF MIAMI, Miami, FL
1996 B.A., cum laude, English Literature

INTERESTS: Travel in Australia, Europe, and Southeast Asia, cooking, biking, and karate

....

Why We Like This Resume: All responsibilities are quantified. There is a strong distinction between domestic and international experience. Pro bono experience demonstrates a community mindedness. Overall experience showcases individual and team accomplishments, which is important to most employers.

Sample #3

DANIELLA SWAEBE
4010 Market Street
Old Bridge, NJ 08857
(732) 555-5555 dswaebe@email.com

OBJECTIVE

To obtain an entry-level position to apply my analytical, communication, and quantitative skills obtained from my engineering background.

EDUCATION

Northwestern University, College of Engineering, Evanston, IL
B.S. Agricultural and Biological Engineering, Biomedical Engineering Minor, May 2001

RELEVANT EXPERIENCE

Engineering Intern, Town of Evanston, Evanston, IL, June 1999–May 2001

- Obtained information on distances and elevations from surveying various sites using level loops, traverse, and topographical survey for a variety of projects.
- Designed and managed a database on water and sewer easements.
- Assisted in computer-aided design and drafting for proposed construction.
- Received an exceptional performance evaluation and excellent feedback from management on account of independently implementing many projects.

Leadership Fellow, The Leadership Institute, Brooklyn, NY, May 1999

- Developed leadership skills through reflection, planning, one-on-one interactions, small-group feedback, and large-group training.
- Worked on a month-long project on practicing ethical decision-making.

OTHER

Electronic Highway Instructor, Northwestern University, Evanston, IL, August 1999

- Taught a workshop in network computing to over 500 freshmen.

Library Assistant, Northwestern University, Evanston, IL, August 1999

- Discharged books to 100 patrons per shift.
- Organized and shelved library materials.

RELEVANT COURSEWORK & SKILLS

Biotechnology—Solid Waste Engineering—Fluid Mechanics—Physiological Engineering—Computer Science—Microeconomics—

Macroeconomics—Engineering Economic Analysis—Statistics—Microstation SE—Eaglepoint—ArcView GIS—Matlab—FIDAP—GAMBIT—Java, C++

ACTIVITIES

Society of Women Engineers (Fund-raising co-chair); Women's Resource Center (Founding Member); Chi Omega Sorority (Assistant Secretary); Biological Engineering Society (Active Member)

....

Why We Like This Resume: This candidate shows her major and relevant course work, which is appropriate for a recent college graduate. She details strong internship experience and activities that are consistent with her academic background. Leadership and team-building skills are demonstrated through work experience and active membership in extracurricular programs and organizations.

Sample #4

Angela Matthews
100 Oak Lane • Los Angeles, CA 90049
310.555.5555 • angelamatthews@email.com

OBJECTIVE

Seeking a full-time position in merchandising.

EDUCATION

Pace University, Manhattan, New York   May 2002
Bachelor of Business Administration, Major: Marketing

WORK EXPERIENCE

Tiffany & Co., New York, NY   July 2001–May 2002
Elsa Peretti Product Sourcing
- Monitored retail pricing analysis
- Handled all local and international vendor management
- Forecasted product development

Media Dynamics Inc., New York, NY September 2000–June 2001
Research/Market Data Analysis
- Conducted data analysis of subscribers study, 60 national/local magazines
- Performed all editing of consumer, television, and magazine dimensions
- Maintained customer list management/development
Research tools included: MRI, Simmons, ABC, and J.D. Power

Elizabeth Arden, Los Angeles, CA May 1999–August 2000
Merchandising/Customer Service
- Assisted with all management relations
- Trained staff on body treatments and special services introductions
- Oversaw effective customer service program implementation

COMPUTER SKILLS

Microsoft Access, Excel, Word, Outlook, PowerPoint, MIPS

HOBBIES

Scouring flea markets worldwide for vintage clothing and merchandising props

Why We Like This Resume: This candidate uses key words that are appropriate to her background. Her resume is easy to read and concise.

THE CREATIVE RESUME

We've told you not to add any bells and whistles to your resume—no bright colors, no graphics, no glitter. So how do you show your creativity to an employer, particularly if you are a graphic artist, writer, or web designer? Remember, you're selling yourself so it's a good idea to have as many collateral materials as you can.

Create a portfolio of your achievements

This is a great idea for writers, journalists, publicists, graphic designers, event planners, and anyone whose work can be expressed in a visual medium. Put together a portfolio (a black notebook is fine, you don't need to spend a lot of money) containing press clips, writing samples, photographs of special events you've worked on, logos you've designed—anything that shows your best work. You should bring this portfolio to any job interview, informational interview, or even a large networking event where you might have some time to show your work to the people you meet. Use your judgment—just like sharing photos of your pets or your kids, you have to know when you have a willing audience.

For recent grads or career changers, a portfolio is a great way to demonstrate your commitment to a field in which you don't yet have a lot of professional experience. It's okay to include clippings from a college newspaper if you want to work at a publishing company, or photographs of you volunteering at an industry function for a field you're hoping to switch into. Even awards certificates or thank-you notes from volunteer organizations can be included if they are relevant to your job search.

You Dot Com

Design a personal website. This option certainly isn't for everyone, but if your resume says you are a high-tech wizard with great design sense or a contemporary writer with extensive Internet reporting experience, prove it! Even if you are not a high-tech genius, you can use a website design template (available on major web portals like AOL and Yahoo!). Design a simple website that shows examples of your work and your prominence in your field. You'd be amazed at the great results this can achieve. The cool thing about the web is that no one knows how big or small you are from looking at your website.

Tips on Creating a Personal Website

● Put your best work on the homepage, as well as all of your contact details.

● Just like a resume, your website should include information about your industry affiliations, honors and awards, alumni association, skills and interests, and any other information an employer might connect with. You can include a lot more on your website than on your resume, so think about everything you'd like an employer to know about you.

● Get your site linked to any associations or clubs you belong to, and link to these sites in return. You can also try to get yourself listed on search engines by including key words on your site. Some employers will check you out through an Internet search, so try to make your name appear in as many relevant places as possible.

● If you write any articles, send any correspondence, or fill out any forms (for associations, job applications, or networking event sign-up sheets), include your website address. Never miss an opportunity to promote this added sales tool.

• Include your website address on all correspondence (thank-you notes, e-mail messages, cover letters) and add it to your business cards.

• Keep your site updated at all times. A visitor might just find your website and be so impressed that they call and offer you a job!

CUSTOMIZE, CUSTOMIZE, CUSTOMIZE

Just like you do with your resume, it's essential to customize your resume extensions for every job you pursue. When you bring your portfolio to a networking meeting or formal interview, make sure the work most relevant to the person you're meeting with is displayed at the front. If you give your website address to an employer, remove any inappropriate content (photos from your best friend's bachelorette party, links to your favorite tequila lovers' website) and make sure everything is updated so your site appears relevant and dynamic.

CHAPTER FIVE
• • •

Good Cover Letters

You've written your resume and you're ready to start applying for some jobs. But, first you need a cover letter. The purpose of a cover letter is to introduce yourself with just enough juice to make the reader want to know more. Consider it a tease to lure the reader and convince him or her that the best is yet to come. Ideal cover letters are brief and direct. This is not the time to tell your life story or list every club you belonged to in college. Follow these simple tips to create a template cover letter that you can adapt to any situation.

The ABCs of Getting Noticed

The cover letter must contain three easy pieces. Consider who your reader is and customize the letter to establish a connection between the two of you. Remember, the reader can make a split-second decision whether or not to read your resume. Did you immediately engage your reader? If so, how? With lightning-strike attention spans, you must break through the barrier of their time-starved search for the right employee. Here are a few things to keep in mind when writing a cover letter that makes you stand out:

A is for Assets. A cover letter introduces your best assets, but remember to include the reader and their needs. Sum up your strengths as they apply to that company, specific job, and how you will be an *asset to them.*

B is for Best. Why are you the *best* candidate for that job? Believe in yourself—if you don't, no one else will. Your enthusiasm should shine through and your letter should be compelling.

C is for Competency. Ultimately you will be hired for your skills, so be sure to address your *competency* in terms of specific things you are great at and promote what you know how to do that would benefit their company.

Top-to-Bottom Cover Letter Guide

CONTENT

Name and Address

Be sure to follow the standard rules of professional letter writing. Type your name and address in the upper right-hand side of the page, and on the left-hand side type the date above the recipient's name, title, and address. Always double-check the correct spelling and title of the letter's recipient—a simple misspelling can turn a recruiter against you immediately. Letters that arrive at the Women For Hire offices addressed to Mr. Tory Johnson are automatically tossed out before they are opened because it's clear the sender did not do basic research about our company.

Salutation

Always personalize your cover letter. "Dear Sir or Madam" is fine if you are responding to an online job listing or newspaper ad where no name is given and where it is absolutely impossible to obtain a name, but in every other instance it is crucial to personalize your correspondence. Always err on the side of formality. Address the recipient as "Mr." or "Ms.," regardless of whether you have met the person before, spoken to them on the telephone and used his or her first name, or if you think they are married. You will never go wrong with professionalism and respect.

Introduction

- Don't begin with "Hi. My name is Sally Smith." Instead introduce yourself by stating the reason you are sending your resume. Always reference where you got the person's name if you received it from a personal contact.

- Name the exact position for which you are applying.

- Tell them who you are. Not, "Dear So-and-So, I want to pursue my aspirations in the field of communications," but basic facts that make you right for them. For example, "I'm a top-notch salesperson in search of a job at your company where I can utilize my outgoing people skills and help increase bottom-line sales," or "I'm a senior graduating with an honors degree in pharmacology and a keen sensitivity to complicated formulas and detailed directions."

- Tell them how you found them and when possible, identify a closer connection:

"I saw your ad in the Daily News.*"*

> *"Mary Jones of XYZ Corporation said you were looking for great reps."*

> *"One of my clients, Patty Brown, told me you are thinking about expanding your sales force and strongly suggested that I call you."*

- Tell them why you're writing:

> *"I've always wanted to work for the acknowledged leader in the industry."*

> *"Your approach to the workplace is exciting and I'd like to be part of it."*

> *"I know you have needs in my area of specialty due to your recent acquisition of XYZ Company."*

The Body of the Letter

Remember always to be positive about yourself and your achievements. This is not the time to apologize for any lack of experience or gaps in your resume. The cover letter's job is to sell, sell, sell:

- Give your background, briefly. Make it apply to their operation.

- State your qualifications, your accomplishments, and your job skills. Explain how your skills and experience qualify you for the position—refer to specific experience that appears on your attached resume.

- Be positive about yourself, about them, about past or current employers.

- Be honest. If you exaggerate or lie, they will find out eventually.

• If you do not have any previous employment and this is your first job, focus on your experiences, internships, study abroad, or special projects or organizations where you have exhibited qualities that illustrate your strengths.

Address How You Will Benefit Their Company

Once you have their attention, focus on them, not on you. Here's how: I want to work for *you* because . . . *You* need my skills because . . . I can bring *you* these skills. Make them want you by showing what you can do for them:

• Show them that you have done your research:

> *"I've always wanted to work for the industry leader in conservation."*

> *"My background in career counseling, coupled with my degree in engineering and extensive knowledge of and experience in the field, makes me the perfect candidate for your IT human resources department."*

• Let them know how you can help them:

> *"I can bring to your company an insider's knowledge of the media, including print, radio, and TV, with extensive contacts across the county that would offer increased visibility for your PR clients."*

Ask for Follow-up and Include an Action

• Thank them for taking time to read your letter and attached resume.

• Tell them you will be contacting them at a specific time. Include an action or next step. Then do it.

- Enclose a personal business card as one other way of making your contact information readily available.

Closing

Complete your letter with a formal closing. "Sincerely yours" or "Best regards" are foolproof choices. Then type your name several lines below the closing and sign your name under the closing in blue or black ink.

AVOID SALARY HISTORY

Many job listings ask applicants to provide salary information. It is not essential to do this, and in fact, we suggest that you leave it out. That's right, it's okay to ignore the directions—just in this one instance! If you send a fabulous cover letter along with your perfect resume, it is unlikely that you will be taken out of the running just because you've conveniently omitted your salary history. If you feel absolutely obligated to address salary in some fashion in your cover letter, you may opt to provide your desired salary. When doing so, be sure to offer a range with a high and low spread, which increases your chances of falling somewhere in between what the position pays. Any time you suggest a range, you should be willing to accept the lowest figure because it's likely to be what you are offered. There will be lots more on salary issues in the coming chapters.

PRESENTATION AND STYLE

- Keep it simple. Avoid complex sentences with lots of commas or a laundry list of details.

- Be accurate. Get the names right, and do not misspell anything.

- Limit your cover letter to two or three short paragraphs. Now is not the time to write the great American novel.

- Be confident. Show that you believe in yourself.

- Be sure to use some of the words included in the job description when responding to a job listing.

- Be consistent with grammar and style. Writing professional correspondence will come up at some point in your next position—this is your first opportunity to prove you will do a great job when you are hired.

- Use appropriate stationery. White or off-white and heavy stock is best. This is a business correspondence so avoid frilly or casual paper.

- Watch for smeared ink! If the letter does not print perfectly, redo it.

- Print your cover letter and resume on the same type of paper.

- Check with the contact or representative to see how you should submit or send it: mail, e-mail, fax, or all three.

Inside Scoop

Explaining Relocation in a Cover Letter

Resume guru and author of *Resumes and Cover Letters That Have Worked,* Anne McKinney reminds us that the cover letter can often say things that the resume may not say. For example, if you are relocating to Des Moines, Iowa, because your spouse has recently been promoted to a position in that area, then you can tell the prospective employer in the cover letter: "Although I am excelling in my current position and can provide outstanding references from my employer, I am resigning from my job in order to relocate to Des Moines with my spouse, who has recently been promoted by his company. We are looking forward to making our home in Des Moines and will be there frequently exploring housing options. I would be delighted to meet with you during one of our upcoming visits. I would like you to know that my husband's company will be covering our relocation expenses."

HAVE YOUR COVER LETTER ASSESSED

It is just as important to have friends and professionals proofread your cover letter as it is with your resume. Nobody thinks they are making spelling or grammar mistakes, but believe it or not most resumes and cover letters are littered with them. Friends, family, and professional contacts may also notice that you have left out a key selling point about yourself—sometimes we forget our own greatest achievements. Don't just ask for proofreaders; ask your cover letter assessment squad to make sure you are tooting your own horn.

THE E-MAILED COVER LETTER

If a recruiter asks you to e-mail your resume, what becomes of the cover letter? It is commonly preferred for an e-mail message to do the job of a cover letter, rather than attaching a formal cover letter to the e-mail. Two attachments are too much—the only attachment should be your resume. In this era of virus alerts and oh-so-busy execs, this gives you a better shot at having the recipient take the time to read—and respond—to you.

Chances are you will be sending dozens of resumes by e-mail. If you are responding to a specific job listing, be sure to mention the job number or title in your e-mail subject line. If you are sending your resume unsolicited or to a networking contact, use the subject line as an additional sales tool—make the recipient want to open your e-mail. Remember, having a great cover letter means nothing unless somebody reads it.

COVER LETTERS THAT SHINE

The following examples are samples of cover letters that have worked. We purposely chose letters that are not overly clever or too cutesy and do not reinvent the wheel. Instead they are clearly focused on the position and the person applying. Ask yourself after reading each one: Would you want to meet this woman?

Cover Letter Template

Your Street Address
City, ST Zip
Phone
E-mail

Cover Letter Date

Prospective Employer
Address
City, ST Zip

Dear Mr./Ms. Potential Employer (whose name and spelling have been confirmed):

First I will make a personal connection with you and explain why I am writing today. I will reference the position for which I am applying. I will briefly introduce my qualifications before outlining a few specific details. I understand that the point of the cover letter is to demonstrate my communication skills and introduce you to the highlights of my attached resume.

113

I will highlight my most relevant and impressive achievements in the body of the letter, paying attention to grammar and style. My tone will be formal and pleasant.

I will limit myself to three or four solid paragraphs and I will show my letter to a trusted professional friend for review. At the end of my final paragraph I will tell the prospective employer that I will contact him or her in the near future to follow up.

Sincerely,

Smart Job Seeker's Signature

Smart Job Seeker

Sample Cover Letters

510 Main Street

Texarkana, TX 75501

903.555.5555

Wood@email.com

March 18, 2002

Suzanne Kushner

Senior Vice President, Marketing

The Walden PR Group

3278 Oliver Street

Los Angeles, CA 90001

Dear Ms. Kushner:

I learned about your agency through Jennifer Jones and I'm so impressed by your Count On Me Ad Campaign to help kids learn about money. As a recent graduate of the University of Texas at Austin's School of Communications, I am confident that I'd add enormously to your goals of helping to communicate timely messages to youth.

Through my study of journalism, I have perfected my writing and editing skills. My professors say that my other unique strength is the ability to generate creative ideas on the turn of a dime. My proudest academic accomplishment was ranking in the top 5 percent of my graduating class, which included 10,000 students. I was also awarded highest honors for my ad campaigns for the university's newspaper.

With a keen sense of profitability, I also worked diligently to impact the financial success of the paper, and increased advertising revenue by 45 percent by designing an interactive coupon club for the campus website. I believe I would be able to apply the same innovation and bottom-line results to The Walden PR Group by combining out-of-the-box thinking with strategic planning.

As I plan to pursue a career in the Los Angeles area, I would like to discuss working as an account coordinator at your agency. I would be available to meet for an interview while I'm in town from June 15 to June 22. I look forward to talking to you about Walden's needs. I will contact you next week to determine your availability and would be grateful for your time and attention to my attached resume.

Sincerely,

Melba Wood

22 College Street
Athens, GA 30601
706.555.5555
rankin@email.com

June 17, 2002

David Lewis
Sales Manager
Black Diamond Company
11 James Place
Akron, OH 44301

Dear Mr. Lewis:

I recently saw your ad for a production analyst in the *Wall Street Journal* and I knew immediately that you were describing me. I am a dynamic, creative, committed professional with five years of experience, eager to contribute to the success of Black Diamond.

Since college graduation, I have worked in this field, gathering experience from the ground up, entry level to supervisor. I have honed my skills in communication, negotiation, sales, production services, and management, as the attached resume indicates. I am ready for a larger challenge and would welcome the chance to prove myself with you. I've read with enthusiasm about Black Diamond's forward-looking vision and innovative policies as the industry leader. I believe my grasp of the industry and my desire to succeed would be a winning blend for your organization's current needs.

I look forward to discussing your job opening and my qualifications. I will call you next week to schedule a meeting. In the meantime, thank you for taking the time to review my credentials.

Best regards,

Ellen Rankin

. . . .

7733 East Village Place
Clifton, NJ 07011
201.555.5555
tsmith@email.com

July 15, 2002

Mr. Daniel Goldstein
Recruitment Director
Melanie's Place
555 First Street
Washington D.C. 20022

Dear Mr. Goldstein:

Your advertisement for a field supervisor intrigued me. I believe I have qualifications that would be a great asset to your nonprofit agency.

For three years, I have been a full-time, stay-at-home parent, which has allowed me to pursue several volunteer opportunities and gain experience with the most prestigious organizations in Washington. I have been honing the very skills required to be an effective field supervisor for your organization. I have written newsletters and press releases, organized campaigns that raised hundreds of thousands of dollars, and chaired conventions that brought together people from around the world.

I am thoroughly at home in the world of fund-raising and political involvement, and I would love to continue in that arena with you. I would bring to your agency an invaluable maturity and depth of experience in the nonprofit world. I speak the language and I know how to apply my knowledge to the greatest advantage of whatever cause I am supporting.

Thank you for taking the time to consider my resume. I will call you in a few days to touch base.

Sincerely yours,

Taylor Smith

2332 Carrington Place
St. Louis, MO 63102
314.555.5555
sherri.langel@email.com

March 4, 2002

Ms. Margie Lyons
Sales Director
Thomas Pharmaceuticals
One Crown Place
Minneapolis, MN 55401

Dear Ms. Lyons:

Barbara Jones mentioned to me that you are currently expanding your sales force. I have worked with Barbara at XYZ for five years, and she recommended that I contact you regarding a position as Group Account Manager for your new product launch.

I am currently employed as an account executive in the pharmaceutical industry and have doubled sales in my territory in just two years. My proven track record combined with my extensive contacts would be terrific assets to help Thomas expand to new markets.

I look forward to the opportunity to discuss job possibilities with you, and I will call next week to set up an appointment. I appreciate your time and consideration.

Best regards,

Sherri Langel

Bad Cover Letters

In addition to reviewing smart cover letter options, it often helps to know what not to write when drafting your own. Below are really bad opening lines from real-world cover letters. We swear we didn't make them up! Even though each of these opening lines is made up of different words, they all convey the same message: generic, unfocused, and boring. None of them mention the name of the company to which they are applying, nor do they specify the position they're interested in pursuing. All of these candidates fail to explain what they bring to the table.

With such bland styles, we bet these writers don't wear red underwear!

"Your recent advertisement for an open position caught my eye because my qualifications are very compatible with your requirements and I'd like to interview with your firm."

It doesn't get much more vague than this.

"Please accept the enclosed resume as an expression of my interest in exploring opportunities with your organization."

Well, maybe it does!

"Seeking a new challenge, my qualifications appear on the resume attached. I am presently looking for any position where I can expand my skills and learn a new business."

Huh?

"Enclosed is a resume detailing my background and qualifications for your review for any employment opportunities at your company."

This forces the recruiter to guess what the sender wants. Recruiters don't care enough to put that much effort into the process.

"The experience that I obtained as an intern has prepared me for a long career at your company."

Most HR professionals would not read on. This would likely be tossed after the first sentence.

"I am interested in working as any type of manager at your company or organization."

This is too vague. It could mean anything—a mailroom manager, an HR manager, a sales manager, all of which are very different.

"Stop, look and listen: I'm exactly what you're looking for."

This opener misses the mark on cleverness by a long shot, and it's rude. Never order your reader to do anything.

"Hi. My name is Deborah Bingham and I am applying for all open positions within your establishment. I have a lot of years in the field to put to work for you."

For starters, leave out the "hi." Save your name for the end of the letter. Under no circumstance should you ever apply for every single opening at any company. Clearly nobody is that qualified—and if they were, their cover letter would be a whole lot better than this!

SIMPLE SENTENCE STRUCTURE

Once you know what you want to say, make sure you are saying it in the most effective way. For cover letters this means:

- Short sentences that are ideally no more than about twenty-five words each. If necessary, break one long sentence into two shorter ones.

- Paragraphs that aren't too long—five to seven lines is a good range.

- Sentences that begin with powerful action verbs from our list. If it's improper to being with an action verb, be sure the sentence contains a strong action verb.

FINAL COVER LETTER CHECKLIST

Before sending off that introductory letter, make sure it's in tip-top shape by asking yourself these essential questions. If you sense a red flag, you can bet the recipient will too.

Does your letter:

- Target a specific company and position?

- Address the skills the position requires?

- Reference the benefits you bring to the employer?

- List relevant responsibilities or previous jobs?

- Contain any typos or misspelled words?

- Convey the essential points without dragging on too long?

Once you feel confident that you have a flawless cover letter that is clear and concise, you are ready to hit the road. And, by the way, congratulations!

CHAPTER SIX

The Easy Stuff: Online Job Searching and Resume Posting

Here's where we prove how much we love you. We're going to give you a break. This chapter is all about the easy, passive stuff—the non-scary networking, the relaxed resume posting, and the lazy List-servs. Don't thank us yet—it's still work, but all of the activities in this chapter can be done from the privacy of your computer screen at any time of day, with a cappuccino in hand. This means you have no excuse not to implement these strategies. As with every single aspect of your job search, you never know which tactic will lead to the position of your dreams. We will cover other job hunting methods in chapter ten, but this is a start.

CLICK YOUR MOUSE DAILY

Even though the number of job seekers far exceeds the number of positions listed on the biggest online job boards, it's still worth your time to check new postings daily. There are tons of places to help get your resume out there for the world to see. Best of all—they're free. No gas or stamps required.

The website of just about every major corporation is designed to accept your resume. Visit the sites of the companies that appeal to you and be sure to follow the specific submission policy for each employer. Set up free accounts on the big job boards like www. monster.com, www.careerbuilder.com, and www.hotjobs.com, and check out hundreds of smaller niche sites. Often smaller companies and nonprofits don't want to receive the thousands of applications generated by a mass listing on one of the larger sites so they're more likely to post on an industry or local job board. Many small businesses will post jobs on their industry association's website as well. Depending on your interests, you can try www.nonprofitjobs. org, www.financialjobs.com, www.jobs4sales.com, www.techies.com, www.funjobs.com, www.hirediversity.com, and many others. (See the resource guide at the end of the book for a more complete list of these sites.) To make these resources work for you, it's key to follow their preferred format and instructions, which usually vary depending on the site.

Directions for submitting your resume are normally quite clear—designed for even the least tech-savvy of us to succeed. Your best bet is to cut and paste your resume into the template provided. Rarely do sites accept attached documents.

Online Resume Posting Tips

* Update your online resume regularly, even if there is no new information to add, because most recruiters search and view resumes based on the date they were posted. Just as you wouldn't apply for a job listed six months ago, recruiters want fresh prospects. Older resumes are seen last, thus lessening your chances to score an interview. To update your resume, simply view it on the site where it's posted and click "update." You won't have to

make any changes, but the website will record the fact that your resume has been recently accessed and you'll move right to the front of the line.

- Develop a laundry list of skills. An electronic resume can be longer than its paper counterpart, so this is the ideal place to list all of your skills and as many key words as are applicable. Such a list can appear toward the bottom of your resume to add more information to the skills you've outlined in your Experience section. Since recruiters search by keyword, the more matches you fulfill the better chance of yours being viewed. Use key terms from your industry, specific job titles, and skills that will help you stand out from the crowd. Association memberships and credentials are important to list as well.

- Don't limit yourself by posting your resume in a single category. If a job website asks you to categorize your resume, take the time to save it in as many categories as possible—assuming they're applicable to your background and career interests. By no means should you select "nursing" if you're looking for work in information technology.

- Double check how your formatting looks in an online version if you are cutting and pasting from a regular document. Always correct any strange indentations, capitalizations, lines, or spaces. One advantage of online resumes is that you have the freedom to be a bit longer—you don't have to worry about the content spilling over onto another page as you do with a paper resume. Don't go overboard, but you can add more to your online resume.

- Customize your resume every time you apply for a position on a job website. Add words from the company's online job description and make sure your Objective addresses the criteria listed.

On the major job websites you can change your resume as often as you like so there's no reason to send the same resume to every position. We learned this trick from a girlfriend who was job seeking and husband hunting at the same time. While using an online matchmaking service, she discovered that the best way to get the attention of the guys she thought were cute was to alter her profile to match the exact qualities the guy was looking for. We're not condoning her dishonest tactic, but we can tell you she received *a lot* of phone calls! The moral of the story is: customize, customize, customize. A generic resume sent to fifty companies won't win you interviews. Show companies that you are the best candidate for the exact position they are trying to fill.

• Stay closeted—if you'd like. If you are a passive job seeker, you do not have to let your boss find out that you are looking. All of the major job boards allow you to build and store a private resume, which is not viewable by their resume-searching clients. Use it only when you wish to apply to specific positions that are of interest to you.

Online Job Searching

In addition to posting your resume it's important to search for positions online and apply online. Start with the most popular job boards, which are also the biggest, to see what type of posted positions appeal to you. You can search by keyword, location, industry, job function, and other important criteria. Make sure your keyword search is broad—you don't want to miss any good opportunities.

Some of the sites require you to register before allowing you to access their job listings. Provide only the most basic information that you're comfortable with—typically your name or e-mail address.

Never offer specifics like your social security number, especially in connection with other personal data. The most reputable sites won't ask for this stuff.

ONLINE JOB SEARCH TIPS

- **Check out your local newspaper help wanteds online.** Visit the sites of the major newspapers in the city you're contemplating. The papers in major metro markets typically post all of their help wanted ads online, especially on Sunday. Similarly, www.career builder.com is one-stop searching for many of those papers.

- **Let some of the jobs come to you.** All of the major online job boards feature personal "agents" that will automatically e-mail job announcements to your account that match your selected criteria. Again, this is a free service that's definitely worth taking the time to register for. Check each individual site for instructions about creating an agent. By no means should you rely on personal agents as your sole means of finding a job. More often than not, the postings you receive will not be for your dream position, but they're a good way to get a daily dose of what's being advertised by employers.

- **Be discreet.** If you're currently employed, avoid signing up for job search agents using your current employer's e-mail account. Instead be sure to register for a free account with Hotmail, Yahoo!, or another leading provider.

- **Diversify your search.** Sign up for as many job search sites and agents as possible—there's nothing to lose since different employers and various divisions within large corporations use different job websites.

- **Make search engines work for you.** Search engines such as Yahoo! and Google offer the best and worst of the Internet: While they certainly deliver lots of information, it's sometimes too much. Nobody—not even the most dedicated or desperate job seeker—wants to click through hundreds of links to find what they're looking for. But search engines can be a great way to find more obscure job sites—such as those for a specific industry or locale. Try typing in your desired industry, location, and the word "jobs" and you may just get lucky. See the resource list at the end of this book for some industry-specific sites we recommend.

- **Check out specialized listings.** Industry associations, university alumni associations, clubs, and interest groups often offer a job-posting service for their members. Check the websites of any organizations you belong to and you're likely to find job listings not posted on more public websites.

- **Go directly to the source.** If you have particular companies in mind, look for a "careers" or "work for us" page on their corporate website. Check often as new opportunities may appear at any time.

SEARCH DIVA

Since there are many ways to say the same thing, you must master the art of the string keyword search to perfect the online aspect of your job hunt, especially for tech positions. Many job listings use acronyms instead of spelling out the specific skills required. For example, a total techie may look for a position as a computer administrator specializing in virtual private networks. Searching job postings by entering "virtual private network" will miss all of the listings that use its popular acronym VPN. The same is true vice versa.

The best option is to always use all possible keywords, phrases, and acronyms to cover all bases. Using the word "or" allows you to enter as many search words as you would like, thereby producing more results than a single keyword search.

Don't know the groovy terms for your field? Help is at your fingertips. A range of resources will identify the best keyword choices for your search. Sites such as www.webpoedia.com, www.whatis.com, and www.acronymfinder.com enable you to look up the meanings of hard-to-define keywords and acronyms and offer suggestions for additional terms you should include in your search. One of our absolute favorite sites is www.atomica.com, which allows you to type in any industry or occupation and it returns a slew of targeted results providing very valuable information for any job search. It's not limited to tech stuff either! For example, entering "public relations" yields a list of leading companies and professional associations to consider, along with links to their websites. It also offers keywords connected to the industry, which may aid a search. Even though it takes a few extra minutes to do the research on these sites, it is definitely time well spent because when you do hit the job boards you will turn up more thorough results for your queries.

Wait a Minute!

On days when you are feeling frustrated, rejected, and neglected, paint your fingernails a hot shade of red before doing your daily online job search. What color do you think we wore while writing this book?

CHAPTER SEVEN

Building Your Muscle:
Marketing Yourself

Courage is very important. Like a muscle,
it is strengthened by use.

—RUTH GORDON

Wonder Woman has her cape. Catwoman has her claws. Josie and the Pussycats have their guitars and drums. They never embark on an adventure without them. And we've given you your basics—the actions you can take from the comfort of your computer screen. Now it's time to get gutsy and really put your job search in gear. Eighty percent of jobs are never listed—that means they're found through personal connections and networking. So, while online job searches and newspaper want ads are important, they should only consume 20 percent of your job-seeking energy. Now comes the big stuff.

It's essential to prepare yourself with all of the tools—mental and tangible—that you'll need to conquer your obstacles and reach your goals. We believe that every smart job seeker needs to be prepared at any moment to grab the job of her dreams. Nothing should stand in your way, especially nothing that can be avoided. Think of a woman in her ninth month of pregnancy with a packed suitcase next to the door—preparation is everything!

You've already got your resume (paper and electronic) and you're ready to write a killer cover letter for every job you desire. Make sure you're set with all the office supplies you can stuff in your drawer— envelopes, stamps, paper clips, staples, computer disks, and anything else you might need to send a resume or thank-you note. Office supplies are important, but what's a smart woman's most powerful tool for success? We call it muscle. Your job-searching muscles are your arsenal of personal marketing materials—the strength you need to lift yourself to the highest career peaks. Just like the muscles in your body, all of your job-searching muscles are connected and necessary to your overall strength. We're talking about business cards, references, great clothes, phenomenal phone skills and more. The muscles you need to tone for the ultimate workout: networking. Fear not: You've got it in you and we're going to help bring it out.

Business Cards

Business cards are essential. Don't ever leave home without them. Tons of them. Even though it's acceptable in the dating scene, you don't want to resort to jotting your number on the back of a cocktail napkin at a networking event. For a reasonable amount you can create hundreds of business cards for yourself at any neighborhood Kinko's or most local photocopy shops. Cards can also be ordered online. Contrary to popular belief, you don't have to have a job to have a business card. All you need is information about how someone can get in touch with you. Trust us, it's a wise investment.

DEFINITE DOS—BUSINESS CARD COOL

- Cards must include your name, address, telephone number, and e-mail.

- Try to include an identifying detail to remind the recipient of who you are and what kind of position you are looking for. Add a title, industry, or perhaps even a photograph. This is especially important for experienced women with specific career goals.

- Like that handy-dandy Visa or American Express, don't go anywhere without your cards. You never know when you may run into a good contact.

DEFINITE DON'TS—BUSINESS CARD CASUALTIES

- Don't throw business cards in your purse or carry them in a rubber-banded wad or stuck in your wallet. Dirty business cards with dog-eared edges are turnoffs.

- Don't run out of cards. Fill a business card case with a stack of cards that's readily available at your fingertips. Refresh as often as necessary.

- Avoid having to write your information on the back of someone else's business card. If you do run out of cards, get their card, and follow up by sending your own with your resume and a cover letter.

- Don't make your printed contact information so small that someone has to strain to read it.

- Don't ever give a business card with information scratched out from your last place of employment. It's unprofessional and sloppy.

- Don't carry other people's cards mixed in with yours. You're bound to waste time fumbling for your card and could accidentally give out theirs.

Jennifer Lerner

ELECTRICAL ENGINEER

500 Waterbury
Des Moines, IA
50312

515.555.5555
jlerner@email.com

digital photography • graphic design • web content

Jamie Bondy

p: 203 • 555 • 5555
f: 203 • 777 • 7777
e: bondy@email.com

stephanie
JONES

marketing & communications

210 columbus avenue
new york, new york 10023
P212 • 555 • 5555
F212 • 777 • 7777
e-mail jones@email.com

NINA ACKERMAN

500 Grand St.
Williamsville, NY 14221

(716) 555-5555
ninaackerman@email.com

References

You will absolutely, positively be asked for references at some point in your job search, so it is crucial to be prepared. Believe it or not, some people ruin a good thing with bad references. References should help you seal the deal, not nix the offer.

CHOOSE WISELY

Who makes a good reference? Someone professional. Someone in a position of responsibility. Someone articulate and positive. Consider the position and title of your reference contact since it matters. It's okay if a reference no longer works for the company where you were employed together. It's okay if a reference lives in another city or country. Just be sure they can be contacted and willing to say how great you are and what an excellent job you did in the past. In fact, clients make fantastic references, not just bosses and colleagues.

How to maximize the effectiveness of your references:

- Ask permission of anyone you'd like to use as a reference whether it's personal or professional.

- Don't just assume you'll get a glowing report. Before giving out their name, go over a list of possible questions your prospective reference will be asked by your potential employer. Make sure their answers jive with your story. Reinforce the points you'd like them to convey about yours skills, experience, and aspirations. You are not bothering them—they will be grateful for your input.

- Have your references ready to go at all times—you never know when the opportunity may arise to use them.

- Ask your references their preferred means of contact—office phone, personal e-mail. This will ensure that recruiters aren't frustrated and references won't be bugged by countless messages.

- If your reference's name is difficult to pronounce, provide a phonetic spelling to help the employer. For instance: Jane Lukaszewski (pronounced "Luke-ah-shev-skee").

- Be prepared to explain the relevance and relationship of all references.

- When in doubt, leave them out. If you suspect that a potential reference may not say exactly what you'd like, find someone else.

Work It, Girl!

Who can you use as a reference? Make a list of five people you can ask for references. To be safe it's smart to have two or three ready to go at all times. Think about former employers, clients, college professors or deans, family friends who have observed you in a professional setting, association leaders, and others who can vouch for your experience, skills, intelligence, integrity, and positive attitude.

List your five potential references here, and then contact each one for permission. Keep track in a notebook of contact date and the person's response as well as notes from your discussion. Mark down the key points each reference agrees to highlight about you. Be sure to send thank-you notes to everyone who helps.

1. _____
2. _____
3. _____
4. _____
5. _____

PREP YOUR REFERENCES

Take the time to speak at length with your references about the image you'd like to project to potential employers. Make sure you know what your references are going to say so there are no surprises. It's important to understand what questions a potential employer will ask your references so you can discuss the answers with your references before they are contacted. Good references can make or break a job search campaign, so make sure you have great advocates prepared with great answers. Discuss the following questions with your references, as these are the most likely to be asked by an employer. Be sure you like the answers!

- What was your relationship with the job candidate?

- What responsibilities did she perform in her position with your company?

- Why did she leave that position?

- What are her strengths?

- What are her weaknesses?

- What was her approximate salary?

- Would you hire or work with this person again?

FORMAL LETTERS OF REFERENCE

In addition to references that you list on a job application or provide to a recruiter, it's also a good idea to collect letters from people who are wowed by you, your skills, capabilities, and character, and then make copies and keep the original on file. Think of former employers, clients and professors who can write letters vouching for you. If you have received letters from customers praising your work, be sure to save them for your reference file. Potential employers will want to see that type of unsolicited feedback. In sales terms, think of reference letters as your celebrity endorsements.

HOW TO GET A GREAT REFERENCE LETTER

Here are some tips for snagging a lively reference letter that makes you stand out in a crowd of applicants:

- When you choose someone carefully as your reference, it should be an individual who is pleased to help you. Don't settle for less. A referral request shouldn't be a burden or an imposition or from someone who isn't your biggest fan.

- When asking for a reference letter ask if they'd consider writing a letter of praise instead of a reference. This letter should campaign for people to vote for you rather than only recommending you for a job. Explain that you need their help with a letter that pinpoints your strong points and really sells you.

- Ask for a letter that is an endorsement of your best character traits and skills. Remind the reference of a specific capability you have that you are most proud of and ask if he or she would include it in the letter. This is not a time to be shy!

- Ask your reference if he or she would include a telephone number so that your potential employer may call without you having to ask for permission first.

- Ask for your letter to be addressed "To Whom It May Concern" so that you can use it for a while as you pursue various career choices. An incredible reference letter can go really far.

- For especially busy references, offer to draft the letter yourself. Provide your reference with the letter by e-mail or computer disk so he or she can make additions and edits and print the letter on company stationery.

HOW TO REQUEST A REFERENCE LETTER

You can request such a letter by phone, an in-person meeting, an e-mail message or a formal letter. For whatever method you feel most comfortable, the following wording can be applied:

I want to thank you for being such an instrumental person in my career and encouraging me at every turn. As one of my leading role models and mentors/most satisfied clients, I hope you will consider serving as one of my advocates. As I pursue my career aspirations, I would now like to ask you for a very important favor. Would you consider writing a reference letter that specifically addresses my strong points and why I'd be an asset to a workplace? Your letter will be instrumental in assisting my job search and your words of endorsement would help separate me from the herd of applicants.

If in fact this is in no way an intrusion on your time and you are able to help me, I would be very grateful if you would indicate in your letter how long you've known me and offer an assessment of my skills and abilities. (Now be specific. Give an example of what you want.) I'd be extremely grateful if you mention my proficiency with organizing large computer databases, any leadership abilities you witnessed while I worked with you, and how I might make a contribution to the workforce.

Please address it "To Whom It May Concern" and kindly return it to me in the enclosed self-addressed stamped envelope. I'll be certain to make you my first call when I land the job of my dreams. Please be reassured that the time you take will be well worth your effort. Thank you very much.

Sample Reference Letter

Robyn Spizman
The Spizman Agency
Atlanta, Georgia

August 16, 2001

To Whom It May Concern:

It is my pleasure to write a letter of recommendation on behalf of Hilary Jones. Hilary spent the summer semester of 2001 as an intern at The Spizman Agency, a full-service public relations firm specializing in media relations. It has been a wonderful asset having Hilary work with us. She has shown expertise and skills far beyond her years.

Hilary is a quick study and works at the speed of light. No matter what is asked of her, she rises to the occasion and figures out the smartest way to accomplish the task. Her writing skills have also been a welcome addition to our talent bank. She is such a good writer that we instantly gave her projects that will be published in well-known Atlanta newspapers and magazines. She is highly creative and attentive to detail and is also proficient in a wide range of research abilities. Able to master any task, she is a self-starter and highly motivated individual who will succeed greatly at anything she sets her mind to.

My staff and I thoroughly benefited from working with Hilary Jones and feel she will be an extremely valuable addition to any job or field she chooses. Please feel free to contact me at (801) 555-5555 if you'd like to speak with me further about Hilary's work with my company.

Sincerely yours,

Robyn Spizman
Senior Vice President
The Spizman Agency

Attire for Hire

Imagine that it is the day of the big career fair, networking event, or interview. Of course you're worried about impressing with your resume and business savvy. How you present yourself is a major factor when job hunting and meeting people. Your real first impression will likely be made somewhere between "Hello" and "My name is . . ." Yup, it only takes seconds to be looked at and judged. Sounds superficial, yet studies show that a fresh appearance definitely helps land a job, as well as a better salary.

You know that the "roll out of bed and stumble to class" look will not make the grade, but what do you pull out of the closet? Looking professional takes preparation. Here's the dish.

• Dress appropriately for the position you are seeking. For a traditional company—bank, investment, or accounting firm—lean toward the formal side. You don't necessarily need a skirt suit—pressed pants are perfectly acceptable, but a jacket or sweater top is standard. If, however, you're considering a more creative

One-Minute Mess-Up

It sounds funny, but job seekers often forget the simplest points of hygiene and etiquette. Pop a mint in your mouth before any kind of meeting. It will boost your confidence in a subtle way—plus it'll leave your breath awfully fresh.

field—design, public relations, advertising, entertainment—show a bit more individuality and flare. (We know one music industry insider who swears her tattoos made her unforgettable!)

• When in doubt, take the conservative route. You can't go wrong with neutral colors such as gray, navy, and black. Keep away from too-short skirts or too-tight pants. Any outfit that is well tailored will help you look put together, but that doesn't have to mean boring.

• Wild about animal prints but want to be an investment banker? Even though your leopard pants should be saved for a night at the club, a spotted scarf or a pair of pony-print loafers are certainly tame enough for the office.

• Do pay attention to details. Scuffed shoes with heels that double as dog chews are a no-no.

• Your fabulous sense of style will peek through when you top neat hair with a funky flowered or beaded headband.

• Manicured (no chips, please) nails are a must—even if you don't opt for polish.

• Keep your scent subtle.

• Too much makeup—like those bright red over-outlined lips and dark-lined runway eyes—is a definite don't.

• Body piercings are better left behind.

- As for cell phones and pagers, leave them off and out of sight.

- The perfect accessory with any outfit is a smile.

Developing Your Sales Pitch

Your resume is ready, printed, and waiting. You're stocked with business cards. Your clothes, hair, and accessories would make Donna Karan proud. Now you need the live version of you. Your sales pitch is the preparation you need to make the most of any networking opportunity.

You make a great contact at a function, you call a job prospect on the phone, you meet a recruiter at a job fair. You need to get them interested in you—fast. In these situations you have about thirty seconds to sell yourself. If you can't, they'll move on. This little pitch says a whole lot about you. You're giving someone a nutshell version of who you are and what you offer. The goal is to develop a style and substance that will pique their interest enough to inspire further conversation.

Similarly, a poor, pathetic pitch—one that's delivered in a boring monotone manner and lacking any clear message—will surely result in a dead end. Not too many people will go the extra mile to draw out information about you if you aren't willing or able to do your part. Think of this as a radio or television commercial all about you. You are the product. What makes you remember a great commercial? It's short, snappy, makes its point and enables you to remember the product name. So sell, sell, sell. Go for it and make it work for you!

THE THIRTY-SECOND SOLID SELL

This is an introduction to who you are and what you are looking for. Choose your words carefully—this is no time to wing it. How you represent yourself will determine if you get any further with this contact. Be short and concise, but add a specific instance to grab attention. For example, if you've got a chance to impress a recruiter at a career fair, this is an ideal thirty-second opener:

> "Hi, my name is Samantha Ward. I'm a computer science major with an art minor, and I'm really excited about combining these two interests. I've actually developed an interactive educational program to teach children how to draw. I'd love the chance to explore entry-level job opportunities with dynamic, creative software companies in the Houston area."

Once you've got an idea of what you want to say, get out a timer or use the second hand on your watch. Tape or record your pitch to make sure you like how it sounds or practice in front of the mirror or a video camera—chin up, bright smile, shoulders back. Dahling, you look marvelous!

THE THREE-MINUTE SELL

Of course the goal of the thirty-second spiel is to lead into a longer conversation. You need to be prepared with additional, specific details about your experience and goals to keep the conversation flowing. Keep in mind the principles of the thirty-second sales pitch, even in longer conversations: Be concise and sell, sell, sell. Remember, this is the live, MTV *Unplugged* version of the resume you've worked so hard to perfect.

For your longer sales pitch, be able to identify three solid accomplishments, regardless of your career stage. Some good examples: an extraordinary college project, success from an internship, saving a company money, increasing sales, balancing waitressing jobs with a full course load, or supporting yourself through college. These are awesome coups that require practice to discuss them with polish and poise.

Work It, Girl!

List of Accomplishments Make a list of twenty accomplishments—personal and professional—that promote your skills and experience. Share this list with your friends and family and ask if you are missing anything. Rank them in order of importance and prestige. Always be prepared to discuss the top three to five.

Phone Skills and Cold-Calling

Smart job seekers know that they don't know everything, or everyone. As your networking progresses, contacts will recommend that you call others who may be able to help your search. That's right, cold calls. They're not called "cold" for nothing—the thought of calling a stranger sends chills down the spine of many people, women especially.

Cold calls are essential to a successful job search (remember, it's all about sales!), so we've collected some tips on making the calling less painful. Keep in mind that your initial goal in a cold call is to keep the other person on the phone, so the first few moments are crucial. And even more crucial is your attitude about the calling itself—

good salespeople know that every call can't be a winner, so take it in stride when you speak to unhelpful, or even rude, people.

Finally, have clear goals in your mind of what you hope to accomplish from a cold call. Are you seeking advice about where to look next in your search, an informational interview, more contact names? Don't call without a very specific goal in mind. Most people are happy to answer a few questions from a genuine, polite person, but only if the questions are direct and appropriate.

PERFECTING YOUR PHONE PERSONALITY

Before you dial, do your homework. Know as much as you can before you cold-call anyone you plan to ask for an informational interview, networking contact, or general advice and information. Write down all of this information and have the paper in front of you when calling. Don't leave anything to chance.

- The name (and pronunciation) of the person you are calling and their title. Don't you hang up the phone when a telemarketer pronounces your name incorrectly?

- The correct name and acronym of the company—you'll have to refer to it in the call so don't make a mistake.

- A focused description of the job or situation you're seeking

- Any current news in your industry or at the company of the person you're calling.

BE POLISHED

- Write a script. Use one of the pitches in this chapter, but tailor it to your personality and to the company you are approaching. Keep it short: Less than thirty seconds to introduce yourself and get the interviewer hooked on hearing more about you, then just a few minutes to let him/her get to know the real you. Nobody has the time or interest to listen to your life story at this point.

- Practice, practice, practice. Use a friend to play the employer. Repeat your script until you have it perfect. Record it, listen, and improve it.

- Be ready with dates of employment, names, addresses, phone numbers of previous employers, just in case they ask.

ANATOMY OF A COLD CALL

- Refer to the person by name and err on the side of formality. Use "Mr." or "Ms." rather than a first name.

- Introduce yourself using your full name and immediately drop the name of the person who referred you. "Hello, my name is Brooke Hudson and Victoria Cane recommended that I call you."

- Always say please and thank you, especially at the end of the call thanking the interviewer for his/her time.

- Never keep a potential employer waiting. If you have call waiting on your phone, disable it before calling. Don't run to answer the door or put the phone down while conversing with an important contact.

- If you've left a phone number on an answering machine or voice mail, be prepared to talk when the call is returned. If that is impossible, be prepared to politely suggest another time for calling.

- Listen. If the person you're calling sounds busy or stressed, ask if this is a good time to talk, or whether you can schedule a better time to chat. The simple question, "Am I catching you at a good time?" will win major points.

- Tell them that you are looking for a new position or making a move in your career and you're looking for some advice or information. You don't need to directly say you're a job seeker if you don't want to. This can put people on the defensive, especially if their company is not hiring at the moment.

- Clearly state the career change or new job you're looking for, then ask a specific question: "Can you offer some advice or contacts based on your experience in the industry?" "Can you tell me a bit about your company and what opportunities might exist in the near future?" "Can you recommend some organizations I might look into to help with my job search?"

- Stop and listen. Let the person take over and offer their advice, ask you questions, or refer you to someone else. Don't do all the talking—it's important to show that you respect and appreciate the expertise of the person you're calling.

- Close the deal. Remember, good networking results in more networking. Ask for a referral to a colleague, client, or acquaintance who might also be able to help you. Ask for an informational interview. Ask if you can remain in touch and would it be convenient for you to reconnect.

BE POSITIVE

* Sit up straight when you speak. There is a clear difference in tonal quality when you're slouching from when you're upright and projecting. People will judge your telephone personality in three seconds flat. Smile when you talk.

* Let the interviewer know how excited you are about the prospect of working for his/her company or for your career in general.

* Keep the conversation short. State your purpose. Answer questions. Ask for a follow-up.

* Speak clearly and concisely. Don't eat, drink, or chew gum while you're on this call. Eating candy is a definitive don't. The phone amplifies background noise. If you have to cough or sneeze, cover the mouthpiece and excuse yourself afterward.

* No slang or profanity, ever. Sound like somebody they'll want to have representing their company.

* If you have an answering machine, make sure your outgoing message is professional. No cute jokes, music, or canned impressions will do for job seekers.

* Take notes of what you say, what they say, for future reference. But do it quietly with a pen and paper, not on your computer.

BAD COLD CALLS

Here's an introduction that is guaranteed not to work. This may sound silly, but many people get nervous and become too casual in a cold call. Avoid sounding like this at all costs:

> "Hey there. Remember me? I want to apply for the job you advertised in the paper a couple of weeks ago. I couldn't call then, but I sent my resume a few days ago. Did you see it? I've never worked in advertising, but all my friends say I'm smart and creative. Anyways . . ."

Why is this so awful? The goal of a cold call is to make it convenient and enjoyable for the person to help you. They should feel as good about the call as you do.

- Never make anyone guess who you are. No games or cutesy casual intros.

- No negatives—telling them you meant to call or couldn't call earlier puts up a red flag—why couldn't you call sooner? What was wrong?

- Don't point to lack of experience or knowledge. Rather than saying you have no direct experience, talk about your passion for your field and what you've done to become involved and informed about it.

- If you are calling to follow up a resume you sent, don't say, "I'm calling to follow up a resume I sent—did you receive it?" This adds work for the person on the phone. Make their life easy. Instead, say that you are calling "to reiterate my interest in the position" or "to ask a few additional questions." This will score points for you without annoying a recruiter with hundreds of resumes on her desk.

GETTING THROUGH TO BUSY PEOPLE

Plenty of corporate offices and human resource departments in particular are guarded like crazy from unknown callers. Many times we are told that nobody is available to take our call. Here are some tips for getting through:

- Your attitude is key and your telephone personality must be engaging, upbeat, and respectful of the busy individual's time. They know if you are listening, confident, and someone they'd like on their team in the first few moments of speaking. Many job seekers get cut off since they sound underwhelming at best and not professional on the phone. Put your best voice forward.

- Before giving your name, find out the name of the person you are trying to reach. Once you have an exact name of the right contact, call back and ask directly to speak to that person. Do not offer your name or the reason of your call unless asked. For example, "Hi, is Ms. Anderson in, please?" This will usually provoke a yes or no response. If the answer is no, you will often be asked if you would like to leave a message. Do not give your name and number because it's likely that your call will not be promptly returned.

Instead, you should let the assistant know that you will be away from your phone for a while and will try again another time. If after two or three tries you are still unsuccessful, be sure to ask when it would be good to call back. Do not leave multiple messages.

- Consider the timing. The key is to ask, "Is this a good time to speak since I am job searching and available to start immediately?" Get your key point in the first sentence. If you call an accountant during tax season it's a good chance either they'll be too busy to talk to you or thrilled you called since they might actually need an extra hand. Once you know you have someone's attention and you have stated your message, listen carefully to the answer. If the individual can't talk, ask if you could schedule a phone appointment or call back at five o'clock today. Be specific and get a commitment on the spot. When you hang up the phone you should know what to do next.

- If you can't get through to the boss, be sure to politely thank the secretary for her time. Make friends at the front line and you'll have a better chance. Immediately state your full name, "My name is Patty Brown and I am calling to speak to Mr. Jones about a job opportunity. I was referred by his friend Arthur Simon." Get to the point and instantly establish something in common. It's often who you know besides what you know. The key is to connect. Call the secretary by name and become fast friends.

- It's not easy to make contacts over the phone. Keep calling, politely but persistently, until you reach the person you need to speak to. If you have to leave a message, leave your name, the time and date of your call, your complete telephone number, and a short message. If you offer to call back at a specific time, be sure to do.

- If the boss is constantly busy, ask the secretary for her help. Say, "You are so fortunate to have such a fabulous job. Would you mind giving me some tips how to get through to Mr. Jones? I'm determined to work at the Jones Company and was told I'd be a wonderful addition to the team. I would be so grateful for any suggestions you could offer for how to reach him."

• Busy people often make promises and are often too busy to keep them. If someone says "call me back" or "contact me at a later date," be sure to include that in your communication. Say, "I was so grateful that you asked me to call you back and have looked forward to speaking to you for days. Is this a good time to talk?" Or, ask someone you know in common for a favor. Busy people are never too busy to do a favor for a friend. Consider all the options.

• Don't give up. Busy people are some of the best people to work for since they are just that—busy—and are likely to have many needs. Be sure to highlight in your conversation how you can benefit them and make their life and work easier, more productive, and successful. They are bound to listen to someone who represents progress, productivity, and benefit for their company.

INSTANT INTROS THAT REALLY WORK

Here are some great sample intros for an array of careers that are under thirty seconds in length and quick to the point. Take a look at these, but customize yours to reflect you—your personality, background, strengths, and skills. These are obviously created as a pitch. Be certain only to begin once you know you've been a good listener or you have a window to jump in and promote yourself. Employers often make quick judgments and your timing, enthusiasm, and confidence are key. The following examples are filled with quantifiable achievements, brand names, polite language, and specific requests.

Advertising

"Good morning, Mr. Nevins. My name is Ali Lauren. I am replying to your listing in Advertising Age for the entry-level copywriter position. I will be receiving my master's degree in advertising and marketing, with honors, from Emory University next week. For the past four years, I have interned at Jag Advertising in Atlanta, but I am ready to move to New York, and I think Ad Pro, Inc., offers the perfect fit for my skills and talent. My expertise is in product advertising, and your product department is simply the best in the industry. I'd love the opportunity to show you my portfolio. I'll be in New York on May 31. May I schedule an interview with you during that week?"

Accounting/Auditing

"Hello, Ms. Billings. My name is Shira Hannah. Cliff Hertz suggested I call you about a possible C.P.A. opening in your firm. I have been employed by the ABC Accounting firm for ten years. During that time I have risen from entry-level accountant to supervisor, with thirty junior and mid-level accountants reporting directly to me. I know it is time for me to transition into a larger firm, and Mr. Hertz thought we would be a perfect match, since I specialize in agricultural tax issues, which is your largest department. Would it be convenient for me to schedule an appointment for early next week?"

Aerospace Technology

"Good morning, Colonel Paul. My name is Leah Quinaz. I'm calling to inquire about openings in the air force's aerospace program. My ultimate goal is to become an astronaut. It's been a dream of mine since I watched video replays of Neil Armstrong walking on the moon. To prepare for that future, I graduated with high honors from Georgia Tech and entered the aerospace program at Cal Tech. Since receiving my Ph.D., I've been working for Northrop Grumman, developing wind tunnel experimentation devices for current space flights. It's time to take the next step toward my dream, and I'd like to fly down to Cape Canaveral and discuss possible job opportunities with you. Will you be available in the next few days? I'll be in the area from Monday through Thursday of next week."

Construction Worker

"Good afternoon, Mr. O'Malley. My name is Rene Ramon. I think you know my brothers, Justin and Doug Stuart. They work for your company, and they've told me so much about the integrity and working conditions at DBD Construction, I've decided it's the place for me too. I know there aren't many women in construction, but I've been working with my father and brothers in the building trades since I graduated from high school, through my four years in vocational school, and at Noble Construction since 1996. My expertise is in bricklaying and plastering. Can we set up a personal interview next week? I'll be available any day except Tuesday."

Chef/Cook

"Good morning, Ms. Marcus. My name is Natalie Gregson. I am a 1996 graduate of the Culinary Institute of America, and I noticed in their bulletin that you have an opening for a sous-chef in your Boston restaurant. I'm currently working as pastry chef at Les Grilles in Cambridge, but want to get back on the main line. I have cooked in several New York kitchens, including The Grill, Patsy's, and Chin Won Lee. As you can see, my skills are international, but my heart lives in French cuisine, and yours is the best in the city. May I come by and talk to you? My days off are Tuesday and Wednesday, or I am free any afternoon between three and five o'clock."

Computer Programmer

"Hello, Mr. Hirsch. My name is Tess Camille. I'm calling in reference to your job notice posted at Duke University's Computer Lab. You're looking for an entry-level computer programmer, and I'm an entry-level computer programmer looking for a job. I've been working in programming since junior high school when I began a computer consulting business, building web pages, repairing people's crashes, and writing gaming programs. I've passed that work along to my younger brother, and I'm ready to step into a full-time position. I respect the products your company creates, and I'd love to be part of your work, especially with my interest and experience in advanced multidimensional games. I hope you would be willing to schedule a meeting with me next week. I'd like to discuss the possibility of my employment with your company."

Dental Hygienist

"Hello, Dr. Garber. My name is Lisa Gomez. My friend Norma Gordon is on your hygienist staff, and she told me you have an opening for an experienced hygienist. My track record is flawless in this industry and I've been working for Dr. Smith for seven years, and he is getting ready to retire. I've done pro bono work at local retirement homes with him for some time, and I've earned extra credits in four workshops on advanced methods in the last year alone. I know most of your staff; I love the work atmosphere and I'd value being hired as part of your group. May I stop by tomorrow with my credentials at your convenience to discuss the skills I could offer your practice?"

General Office Manager

"Good morning, Ms. Jones. My name is Christine Gold. I am graduating from Syracuse University next month with my associate's degree in office management. I worked for your company each summer during high school and college as an office clerk, and your predecessor, Mr. Wills, suggested I apply for a full-time job when I graduated. I know you don't know me, but I'd like to stop in and introduce myself. My goal is office management, and with my knowledge of your systems and people, I feel we'd be a good match. May I make an appointment for some time next week?"

Lawyer

"Good afternoon, Mr. Harris. My name is Marina Cara. I graduated from NYU Law School last spring, and recently passed my bar exam. As I was contemplating my career options, I read stories in the papers and talked to various attorneys and judges about working in a small, progressive firm. Your name kept appearing as one of the most active, fair, honest, and concerned lawyers in the city. I really respect your work on behalf of the environment and fair public housing, and I'd be honored to be part of that effort. Can we make an appointment to talk in the next few days?"

Musician

"Hello, Mr. Goodman. My name is Andra Lazarus. Nicholas Freemont may have told you I'd be calling. I was the guitarist last night while you were dining at The Old Club. Mr. Freemont mentioned that you liked my style and that you might be able to use me in your blues club. As you may have noticed, I am a very versatile musician, but blues is definitely my forte. I've performed in clubs throughout the South, in Boston, New York, Chicago, and San Francisco, with some of the biggest names in the business. I've recorded with the Blues Brothers and John B. Bowles. Can we find a time next week to get together and discuss my working with you?"

Personnel Manager

"Good morning, Ms. Alexander. My name is Sybel Hoffman. I've met you several times at the Personnel Professionals' Association meetings, where I represented H. S. Bluebell Corporation. I wanted to congratulate you on your promotion to the corporate personnel vice president position, and to ask if I might be considered to move into your current job. I've been with Bluebell for eight years, and with various other companies in the same industry for ten years before that. I know it will be difficult to follow your success, but I think I'm ready to try. Our firms share the same philosophy and style, I'm sure a transition would be relatively painless, and I'd like the opportunity to work with you and learn from your triumphs. Can we get together for lunch and discuss the possibilities?"

Public Relations

Hello, Ms. Simon. My name is Mary Eve Vendreyas. I read in the *New York Times* that you are opening a Chicago office in the coming months, and I knew I had to call you. I have worked in public relations in Chicago for over ten years, and I've developed extensive connections with the media here. In the past year alone, I've booked clients on Oprah, Larry King, Regis and Kelly, as well as extensive radio and personal appearances. I know I can put my expertise and abilities to work to ensure the immediate success of your new office. I'll be flying to New York to work on a new perfume tour. Can we arrange to meet and talk about your venture?"

Secretary

"Hello, Mr. Sharp. My name is Wendy Grey. I saw your job listing for a secretary on Monster.com, and your description of your requirements sounded just like me. I am an outgoing, self-motivated, detail-oriented person. I've worked as a pool typist and secretary at IBM for five years, and I know I'm ready for more responsibility. I type eighty words a minute, I'm great at Excel, Word, and just about any other computer program you can throw at me. I can keep my schedule and yours organized, and I love a challenge. Can we set up an appointment by the end of this week to talk about job possibilities?"

Teacher

"Good morning, Ms. Attias. My name is Ellen Mittman. I heard on the TV last night that the county is looking to hire a number of teachers, and I'd like to be considered. Before my children were born, I spent twelve years teaching elementary education in the Atlanta school system. Since we moved to Columbus, I've been active as a volunteer in my children's schools, and as a substitute teacher in the county system. I've kept up my certification with annual courses, and I also completed my master's in early childhood education, with special emphasis on gifted children. Since your school has the highest reading and math scores in the state, I know you work to encourage every child to reach his or her highest potential. I share that view, and I'd love the opportunity to serve on your staff. Can we plan a time to get together this week to go over my credentials and your staff openings?"

Remember, be prepared, be polite, and be persistent. Chances are you'll be calling a lot of strangers as you advance in your career, so mastering your phone style now can only help you in the future.

CHAPTER EIGHT

Net-Work It, Girl!

Networking fills 80 percent of jobs. *Eighty percent!* Yet most people still spend the majority of their job search energy looking through websites and newspaper want ads. Think of the enormous competition when only 20 percent of jobs are found through these traditional methods! Your odds of finding a job through networking are significantly greater. But many women fear the very thought of handing out their business cards or asking friends for personal referrals. We know it can be hard to meet strangers, but networking is beyond essential. You will not get off the hook on this one. Our goal is not only to help you learn to network like a pro, but also to make you love it. Because starting now, you are going to do it every day—just like flossing.

If 80 percent of jobs are found through networking then you should be spending 80 percent of your time doing it: attending events, chatting with former colleagues, reading and responding to industry e-newsletters and websites. Throughout this chapter we'll provide our own expert tips, plus networking advice from some of the most successful networkers we know. Read on.

Networking 101:
Networking Tips of the Goddesses

The aim of networking is to develop and maintain relationships—something women are naturally good at in their personal lives, but not so great at when it comes to our careers. Don't think of this as scary—think of networking as sharing: time, information, resources, and opportunities. It can be as simple as just talking to everyone you know.

Networking is crucial throughout your career, but at this moment in time, never forget that you are a twenty-four-hour-a-day job seeker. You are networking with a purpose: to find job opportunities. Your goal is to spin a huge web of contacts who will lead you to someone who needs to hire a person just like you. The larger your web, the more prospects you'll have. The following tips and ideas will help you network like a pro, but it's up to you to take action.

NETWORKING BASICS

- **Leave no stone unturned**. Go down every path and follow every lead. A tip or contact may not sound like exactly what you want, but follow up anyway. You never know which tidbit might lead to a job.

- **Keep a Rolodex**. It's crucial to keep track of everyone you contact. We love the old-fashioned fun of flipping through a Rolodex, but you may prefer the convenience of a Palm Pilot. An inexpensive notebook, address book, or box of index cards is just as effective. Save all the business cards you receive during your networking activities, and make up cards for prospective contacts. Mark down the date of each interaction with each person—

meetings, phone calls, and resume mailings. Record who refers you to whom and how you followed up. Regularly flip through these contact cards or notebook pages to make sure no contact falls through the cracks.

● **Be resume ready.** As we mentioned before, make sure your resume is ready at all times in case you make a great contact who asks you to send your resume right away. Always ask permission before sending a copy and ask the recipient what format he or she prefers. Thanks to e-mail, your mentor can easily forward your resume and recommend you in a few minutes flat. Make it easy for anyone and everyone to help you get a job!

START NETWORKING CLOSE TO HOME

The question is: Who do you know? And the answer: More people than you think. And those people know countless others. So get the word out—seize every opportunity to publicize your job search. Shout it from the rooftops! You are in business to get a job. Tell your religious affiliation members, clergy, clubs, professional organization members, volunteer contacts, merchants, civic leaders, neighbors, and let anyone and everyone know as well. Don't leave out your classmates, former classmates, school alumni, teachers, professors, coaches, and anyone who was ever on your team or in your class. Coworkers, former coworkers, bosses, friends' bosses count too.

Remember, as you did when completing your personal assessment, be specific when you talk to your personal contacts. What kind of job are you seeking? What are your skills? Ask for specific help ("Do you know anyone who works in marketing at a big energy corporation?") rather than vague ("Do you know anyone who's hiring?").

• **Make a list of people you know**. Start with networking contacts close to home. Former college professors, for starters, are often well connected to people in their fields. Ask them for help and keep after them to prove you're serious. Whether you are at the hairdresser or your doctor's office, keep in mind that employers looking for talented people ask other talented people. Don't overlook anyone i n your circle of family, friends, or acquaintances. People you've known for years may surprise you with the network of contacts they have.

• **Be a big mouth**. Mention what you're interested in to everyone—your personal trainer, the mailman, the babysitter, the butcher, the baker—you get the idea. You never know who might know someone who knows someone who knows someone. Be the first to say hello and introduce yourself every chance you get. This is not the time to be shy or reluctant. So never, ever leave home without that stack of business cards and a determined goal to share them.

• **Be a good listener.** Even if you're not great at small talk, it's easy to be a good listener. Everyone loves to talk about himself or herself, and other people's experiences are a great way to learn about a career or a company, as well as potential job openings. Just ask a few key questions: "What do you do?" "Where are you working?" "How'd you get started?" Then sit back and soak up the information. A random encounter may spark a new job or industry idea in your head.

- **Find a reason to call.** We know it's uncomfortable to call someone out of the blue to say hello—especially when what you really want to do is scream, "Can't you find me a friggin' job?" Find articles or news programs that you might recommend to your key contacts. "I saw this article and thought of you . . ." shows you are up on your current events and that your professional life is top of mind. This tactic is sure to impress! If you can't come up with something quite as clever, invite your contact for afternoon tea or an evening cocktail at the newest spot in town. It's less expensive than a whole meal, and that drink could lead to great connections.

- **Use your alumni association.** Aside from maintaining a vast network of contacts, many of whom are ready to help fellow graduates, career service offices also offer a range of services. These include resume critiques, career assessment instruments, seminars, career days, employer information sessions, alumni networking clubs, and access to online job listings. Dr. Richard White, director of Career Services at Rutgers University, says, "Most schools around the country provide reciprocity for their alumni at other schools. I write about seventy letters a year on behalf of alumni seeking services at other career centers around the country." This is particularly valuable if you want in-person help but don't live near your alma mater. The added bonus of exploring this option is being able to connect with alumni from your school as well as another.

Work It, Girl!

Who Do You Know? Make a list of ten relatives you can call to let them know you are looking for a job and ask for any contacts or ideas they may have. Remember, don't ignore that dorky uncle you always see at family functions—he may know someone at the company of your dreams!

1. _____
2. _____
3. _____
4. _____
5. _____
6. _____
7. _____
8. _____
9. _____
10. _____

Make a list of ten nonrelatives you can call to let them know you are looking for a job and ask for any contacts or ideas they may have (friends, former professors, former coworkers, other ideas):

1. _____
2. _____
3. _____
4. _____
5. _____
6. _____
7. _____
8. _____

 9. _____

10. _____

Don't procrastinate. Commit to calling each of these people in the next five days. Always be specific in your conversations. No one can help you get a job if they don't know exactly what you want to do and what you are good at doing. Remember to use your sales pitch, even with friends and family, and always have your resume on hand to send out.

Make a list of five places you will visit this week in your ordinary routine. Commit to mentioning your job search to people around you.Some ideas: Pay attention to the person on the treadmill next to you at the gym. Look at who is sitting around you at church or synagogue, the hairdresser, supermarket, school, a weekend party.

1. _____
2. _____
3. _____
4. _____
5. _____

MAKE EMPLOYEE REFERRALS WORK FOR YOU

One great way not to feel guilty about bugging your friends and family to help you find work is to check into their company's employee referral program. "Find someone inside your ideal company to e-mail the HR department on your behalf with a strong referral," advises Nicole Nadeau of Merrill Lynch. "If a current employee writes to me saying, 'Here's someone my neighbor went to college with. I've talked to her and she sounds very intelligent. I'd like to forward her resume,' I'm much more likely to take a look at it than an anonymous resume."

Why do internal referrals work? Companies want to maintain good relations with current employees. "Even if the resume doesn't look so hot, the HR department may touch base with the candidate simply out of courtesy," says Nadeau. "Sometimes in the course of the conversation the candidate will say something to make me take a second look." Nadeau says it helps if the recommendation comes from a senior-level employee; but even an assistant's referral will get attention.

An astounding 60 percent of Merrill Lynch employees come from referrals, according to Nadeau. Perhaps that's because like most companies, this Wall Street giant offers financial incentive for referrals that lead to successful hires. But even if the employee doesn't end up with money through their firm's employee referral program, the real motivation is to get other great coworkers in the door!

Formal Networking Events

- **Mark your calendar.** Seek out professional organizations that relate to your interests, perhaps joining as a junior member. Check out seminars sponsored by places like the local Y. Listen in on a book reading at a Barnes & Noble, Borders, or a small bookseller in your area. Pay attention to campus happenings such as guest-speaking engagements. Nearly every school plays host to this kind of stuff. They're usually cheap or free—even if you don't attend that school.

* **Check event listings daily.** Every local newspaper, many magazines, and lots of websites provide event listings. Make a point to check these lists often so you don't miss out on any networking opportunities. Look for events featuring speakers in your field, general business functions, new business launch parties or anything else that interests you. Remember, you can make professional contacts anywhere—not just at business events.

> **Inside Scoop**
>
> ### *Shake It, Baby!*
>
> The Fish. That's what that clammy, weak handshake is called in the world of business. For years, men have used the handshake—firm or fish—as an instant barometer. Fishes are losers; all others hold promise. Which brings us to us. Too many women, knowingly or unknowingly, have fish shakes. Why this is we're not sure, but as Martha (firm shake) Stewart might say: It's a Bad Thing. By the way, we're not alone; plenty of men have sissy shakes too.
>
> When it comes to the workplace, other than having a large piece of spinach wedged in your front tooth, nothing is more unappealing than giving someone the fish. It makes a lousy first impression when networking or looking for a job. The same goes for anytime a woman offers it, whether at a cocktail party or at a professional meeting: You give the fish and chances are they'll judge you a wimp. Unless, of course, you're the queen of England or so arrogant that you don't care about the little things. So take it from us: Be firm. Grab that hand and shake it, baby. And while you're at it, look that person in the eye and smile.

* **Make notes.** As you collect business cards at various events, jot notes on the back of each card to remind you of the person you've met and where you met them. When you arrive home from each event, review the cards and decide what your follow-up strategy will be—who seemed to have good ideas for your

search? Who offered to help you further? Who did you speak with at length? Having notes on the back of each card will help you make a personal connection when you follow up with each person who may help with your job search.

WHAT'S IN A NAME?

There's no better way to convey that someone is important to you than remembering his or her name. Yet, particularly in a job search, when you're making lots of contacts, your brain may need to work overtime to remember everyone you meet. A few time-tested tricks can help.

● **Always repeat the name as you're introduced.** When someone introduces herself to you, your appropriate response should be: "Hi, Jane Johnson. I'm Sally Smith and it's nice to meet you." Try to say the first name a few more times in a conversation, and definitely repeat it as you're wrapping up. If it's a difficult name, don't be shy about asking how to spell it or even the origin.

● **Association is a key tool in memorization.** Do you know someone else with the same name? Is there a characteristic of the person you can identify with the name? Some examples include short Sally, long-haired Harriet, or freckled Jane. Try to form a picture in your mind of the person, a defining trait (gorgeous gray hair, dazzling green eyes, long, lovely nails) and envision their name over the image.

Informational Interviews

Once you've gathered a new list of contacts—most of whom will surely be strangers—it's time to get those people to know who you are. How do you call a stranger and ask for help? One tried-and-true method is to request an informational interview.

Although the term sounds formal, an informational interview can range from a cup of cappuccino with your personal trainer's sister to a meeting with the CEO of a major cosmetics company—especially if that person just happens to be your Aunt Evelyn's college roommate. No matter what the format, the purpose is the same: to access information and advice from a willing and helpful source. As long as you are polite and direct in your request, most people will be happy to give up fifteen to thirty minutes of their time to help a motivated person.

One-Minute Mess-Up

Easy on the Alcohol

Some nervous networkers rely on alcohol or cigarettes to become loose or comfortable at an event where they don't know anyone. We love a party just as much as you do, but now is not the time to let down your guard. Drinking too much at a networking function puts you at the risk of becoming too casual with important contacts. Or worse, you could truly embarrass yourself by saying something inappropriate or even slurring your words. Smoking is a huge turnoff as well, and often forces you to leave the building, and the networking action, for your cigarette.

Think twice about carrying around a plate of hors d'oeuvres as well. You can't shake hands, exchange business cards, *and* nosh on those pigs in a blanket all at once. Always eat before attending an event so you can focus all your energy on meeting people. You can eat all the dogs you want once you get your first paycheck!

HOW TO ASK FOR AN INFORMATIONAL INTERVIEW

Now's the time to put into practice what you learned in our chapters on sales pitches and cold-calling. Plan what you're going to say, practice, and go for it. The trick is to make it impossible for the person to say no! Don't forget these important points:

* Name drop as soon as possible when contacting someone who's been recommended to you. Your goal is to keep the person on the phone and hearing a name they recognize is sure to buy you a few moments.

* Ask if it is a good time to talk. People are busy and may not be ready for a long chat at the moment you first make contact.

* Be brief, to the point. Introduce yourself and use that thirty-second sales pitch.

* Be clear that you're not asking for a job, but for information.

* Ask for a meeting (coffee, lunch, brief chat) if possible.

* Don't forget to say thank you!

Here are some How-Could-Anyone-Say-No, I-Really-Did-My-Research ways to ask for an informational interview (or any networking meeting):

"Hello, Jane. I read the recent article about you in the *Baltimore Sun* and I really admire what you do. I'm very interested in pursuing a career in retail management and I was hoping you might be willing to provide some advice based on your experience. Would you be willing to meet me for coffee for about fifteen minutes to help me with my career? I know there's a Starbucks on the corner near your office—perhaps we could meet there at a convenient time for you?"

"Hello, Ms. Abrams. Barbara Pliskin from the Minneapolis Women's Network recommended that I call you. I'm looking to advance my career in journalism and Barbara thought you might be willing to offer some advice and perhaps some good magazine industry contacts.

I'm planning to attend the next Minneapolis Women's Network luncheon where you're speaking—would it be possible to set aside a few
minutes after the luncheon to chat?"

If your request is genuine, respectful, and well thought-out, how
could anyone turn you down?

TIPS ON INFORMATIONAL INTERVIEWING

You've convinced somebody to give you a slice of his or her valuable
time. Don't squander it. Be prepared, professional, polite, and to the
point. Be grateful, and let them know it. Decide one thing you wish
to accomplish in your meeting and stay focused. Remember that a
networking meeting is just that. It's a catapult to help you gain
insight into a particular field or to get the support of someone you
admire or respect. Your meeting will determine the next steps, but
be respectful of the opportunity and time you spend.

- Explain clearly to the person how you received his or her name
  and that you are interested in meeting for advice on your job
  search.

- Find out as much as you can about the person before the
  meeting so you can be sure to ask relevant questions, which you
  should prepare before the meeting. Never wing it. It's always
  impressive to be prepared. A simple Internet search will reveal
  lots of helpful information. Try to find something in common
  with your interviewer so you can form a connection when you
  meet.

- Without browbeating, be prepared to ask for specific advice
  on how they'd suggest you go about landing a job.

175

One-Minute Mess-Up

Don't Bring the Kids

Juggling kids and a career is certainly a challenge; yet don't use that as an excuse when looking for a job. As cute as your tot may be, kids just aren't welcome at professional functions, including career fairs and networking events. Arriving to an interview late and blaming it on your baby-sitter's tardy train will annoy even the most family-friendly employers.

Make alternative arrangements for child care, even if cash is tight while you're unemployed. Offer to return the favor to a friend who offers to baby-sit for an hour or two while you attend important meetings. Since you're looking for a job, not barhopping or shopping, you're likely to find a sympathetic pal to pitch in.

• Be friendly and enthusiastic at the meeting—people are generally happy to help when they see how pleasant and hardworking a colleague you're likely to be.

• Briefly tell about yourself: your background, experience, and what you're looking for.

• Ask for advice about finding the kind of work you want, about making yourself the best candidate for that kind of job.

• Ask if there is anyone the contact can refer you to for further discussions. Request permission to use his or her name or if they would call ahead for a personal introduction.

• Take notes.

• Don't ask for a job. That's not the purpose of this meeting. You are asking for information, advice, and the opportunity to contact this person for more help in the future.

• Don't stay too long. You promised a brief meeting, stick to it.

• Close the deal—near the end of the meeting don't be afraid to ask for the specific help you need—a contact at a certain company, information about how to get started in a particular career, a referral to the person's HR department. Be sure you leave with some information that made the meeting worthwhile.

- Follow up on any tips or suggestions they make, and keep your contact updated on the progress of your job search—particularly as you pursue their suggestions.

GOOD QUESTIONS TO ASK IN AN INFORMATIONAL INTERVIEW

Always come to an informational interview with prepared questions to prove that you've done your homework and you are serious about this meeting.

- How did you get started in this industry?

- Why did you choose to join your current company?

- What organizations or publications would you recommend that I access to become more involved in this industry?

- What's the best career advice you ever received?

- Would you share any pitfalls I should be sure to avoid?

- What skills or experience most impresses you when you are interviewing a candidate to work for you?

- When would be a good time to follow up with you to stay in touch and update you on my situation?

Remember, even if you're not wildly satisfied with the outcome of the meeting—meaning you weren't offered a huge job on the spot—always send a note of thanks. Graciousness will serve you well. Write a note neatly by hand or send an e-mail message—it doesn't have to be long, but make sure it's genuine and not generic. Reference some piece of advice that really stuck out so that your note is personalized and memorable. Include your business card or complete contact details so that it is easy to contact you in the future should they have an idea or lead for you.

PURSUING POTENTIALLY UNAPPEALING LEADS

Throughout your job search, it is inevitable that you will come across jobs that you do not necessarily think are right for you. Friends or colleagues may refer you to their only contacts, even though you might be overqualified, the industry is not exactly what you were aiming for, or the commute is out of your reach. "Should I even bother applying for this position?" will cross your mind more than once. However, there are issues to consider and tips to take into account before officially ruling out the potential opportunities.

Turn your informational interview into a networking opportunity and consider every contact a potential opportunity. Instead of just bowing out gracefully, make them want to hire you for another job or keep you in mind. Make an impression by saying you would have valued this opportunity two years ago when first starting out in public relations, but unless there is immediate room for growth, you are incredible at media bookings and know hundreds of producers across the country, which you are eager to put to use immediately. Use this time to wow them with your abilities. A successful marketing professional was called about an opening as a junior publicist at Lifetime Television. Even though she knew her experience far exceeded the requirements of this position and she was committed to pursuing business-to-business marketing, not consumer PR, she told the vice president at the popular women's cable channel that she'd welcome the chance to interview for the job. She made it clear upfront that she didn't think it was a right fit, but since the executive was willing to meet perhaps other projects or opportunities would emerge. Both women made new contacts through that meeting, which continue to be mutually beneficial.

You can also make contact with the hiring manager and ask if you can contact them in the future and state where your passion lies. "I'm best at sales and working directly with people. I would find a desk job too confining, but would be honored to represent your company should a sales opportunity open up in the field. I'm a real go-getter. Can I contact you again to discuss a future opening?"

Ask for a referral. Thank the person for her time, but let her know that you feel your talents would best be served in a more hands-on position. Ask if there is anyone else in the company who might be a good contact for you. Perhaps another department is hiring and the individual would give you a referral and allow you to use her name. This type of personal "door opener" would make even a dead-end interview worth your while.

Not interested at all in the job or the company? Consider the interview an opportunity to learn more about a particular business. Perhaps you will even learn a tip or two on how to pursue your job search in that field. What magazines are in the waiting room? What organizations does this contact belong to? What trade publications does he read? Don't leave the interview without learning something.

If you have gotten all dolled up for a meeting that didn't lead where you hoped it would, don't let that good hair day or pair of new hose go to waste. Remember that a job opening could be right around the corner. Take a shot and knock on a few doors and introduce yourself. Say you were interviewing right next door and the job wasn't the right match; perhaps their company is seeking the world's most efficient marketing expert. Keep in mind that around every corner is a potential contact and an opportunity that just might lead to a job. Remember there are no dead ends, only yield signs on your way to finding a job!

Writing a Notable Thank-You Note

A thank-you note is one of the surefire ways to make yourself memorable and let someone know their time was valued after a networking meeting, function, or informational interview. It's also the perfect way to let someone know that they made a difference by helping you. There are many reasons to write a thank-you note. Use the following tips to help you pen the perfect note:

- Always write (e-mail is fine) within twenty-four hours of your phone call or interview.

- Consider following up an immediate e-mail with an actual handwritten thank-you note sent by regular mail. If you have messy handwriting, avoid this step.

- Get the names right and be sure to spell everything correctly! Use your name, their name, and the name of anyone who helped make the connection.

- Identify yourself right away when writing.

- Remind them why you're contacting them—mention whatever they did to help you even if you don't land a job.

- Thank them in specific terms for their help, their consideration, their time.

- Briefly restate your qualifications if it's a thank-you for an informational interview.

- If appropriate, make a request for a follow-up interview, call, or contact.

- Keep your note short and focused.

- Attach a business card or copy of your resume, if appropriate.

Sample Networking Thank-You Notes
Thank You for the Informational Interview

Dear Mr. Austin:

Thank you for taking time from your busy schedule to meet with me this morning to answer my questions about retailing as a career choice. Your explanations about the many facets of retailing were a tremendous education for me.

As I told you, Deborah Bingham, a dear family friend, has been a buyer with Lawrence's for many years, and it was her descriptions of her job that inspired me to consider retailing. After meeting with you, I have a far clearer idea of the field, and also a sharper desire to make retailing my career.

Again, thank you for taking the time to share with me your knowledge and wisdom about such a fast-paced, dynamic industry. Your insights will be an inspiration as I pursue my graduate degree with an eye on retailing as my ultimate goal.

Sincerely,

Joan Alexander

Phone Call Thank You

Ms. Stone, this is Josephine Perrillo. Thank you for taking the time to chat with me on the phone yesterday. It was kind of you to provide me with contacts in the power industry to help my job search, and very helpful of you to offer to introduce me to members of the Professional Women's Association. I will be calling on Ms. Andrews and Mr. Jackson in the next few days. I appreciate your permission to use your name as a contact.

I look forward to hearing from you before the next Professional Women's Association meeting and attending with you. I will certainly keep you abreast of my job search results.

Again, thank you for your time and your generous offer of help. If I can ever be of assistance to you, I would welcome the opportunity to assist you in any way.

Thank You to a Friend or Neighbor

Dear Mike:

Thanks so much for your help in getting me contact names at the Williamsburg Fund. I've been looking all over for help, and found it right under my nose! It was great of you to call and set up a meeting for me.

If the occasion ever rises where I might reciprocate the kind favor in any way, please know that it would be my greatest pleasure. It's nice to know that such a generous individual lives right next door.

With warmest thanks,

Lynn

• • •

CHAPTER NINE

Networking, Networking, and More Networking

Already consider yourself a Networking Queen? There are many nontraditional places to network and off-the-beaten-path trails to blaze. Here's a list to jump-start your efforts in the event you have exhausted other traditional contacts. Warning: Gutsy girls only need apply for these tricks and tactics! But if you're motivated, go for it!

- **Get in for free.** Call the chamber of commerce and other major business organizations in your city to get a calendar of local events where you might make good contacts. Volunteer to help prepare, set up, clean up, or perform any other service that will get you into the event at no charge. Our favorite trick is to volunteer to work at the check-in desk where the name tags are displayed. This way you'll be able to meet and greet every attendee, then schmooze them later when you're off duty.

- **Use the power of technology.** Design a website about yourself and promote it to everyone in your address book. One woman we know got a job by writing a very clever e-mail about herself

Inside Scoop

Holidays

A holiday is much more than a classic Madonna single. It's a chance to sneak in a hello to anyone you want to reconnect with or want to meet. We're not just talking about Thanksgiving and Christmas, though sending a holiday greeting at these peak times is a great way to keep your job search moving forward when the rest of the world takes a break from normal business. Think Valentine's Day. Memorial Day. St. Patrick's Day. Australia Day. Halloween. Breast Cancer Awareness Month (October). There are special occasions every single day, week, and month.

Be creative and offer greetings that make you stand out from the crowd. You don't have to spend a lot of money on cards and stamps—e-mail is perfectly acceptable. Make sure the subject line is clever ("Can You Believe It's Already Arbor Day?!"), give a brief holiday greeting, then provide your contacts with an update on your career and the fact that you're job searching. Provide a concise, focused explanation of what you're looking for and how they might be able to help. And don't forget to provide all of your contact details at the bottom of the message so they can call to thank you and hopefully offer to help.

and sending it to everyone on her address list. She requested her e-mail buddies to forward her information to five friends. She received two job offers within three weeks!

- **Get published.** Promote yourself as an expert to association newsletters, local newspapers, community websites, and other publications. Most smaller pubs are eager for good content and happy to consider a well-written article or even a short tidbit. Getting published means getting your name out in public (in front of eyes who may be hiring) and a published article is always a good resume item or notable achievement to mention in an interview. If you've designed your own website, be sure to link to your articles.

- **Reach out and touch someone important.** Next time you see a newspaper or magazine article about a successful woman in your industry, drop her a note of congratulations and ask if she has any advice to offer a young woman in her field. Most women will be flattered that you read about them and happy to share some nuggets of wisdom. Why not ask to interview the most admired woman in your field—tell her it's for an article you're writing for an association newsletter. If the article is published, the featured woman will not only read the article, she'll share it with her friends and colleagues.

- **Learn your rights.** If your spouse was relocated, check with your partner's company to see if spousal support is offered for job placement. Many human resource offices of companies offer career assistance helping a spouse find a job. Just ask!

Associations and Networking Groups: Where the People Are

Professional associations and networking groups are the untapped goldmine of the job-search universe. These organizations exist to help people meet and do business with other professionals and students in their industry—the perfect venue for finding a job opportunity. Associations run the gamut from intimate dinner clubs to massive international membership organizations. Every industry has at least one association, and most industries have several, many of which include chapters designed specifically for women. Some associations, particularly in popular fields like accounting and marketing, even have collegiate chapters.

Large, multi-industry women's professional and networking organizations include the National Association for Female Executives

Inside Scoop

WITI Works

Carolyn Leighton, chairwoman and founder of WITI (Women in Technology International) says she started the organization "because there was no association for women in all aspects of technology." She "wanted to help women build serious networks with top professional women. You are most likely to land the best opportunities through your network of relationships. Always build your own brand inside and outside of your company by writing articles, developing a column, working toward being an industry leader."

185

(NAFE), Business and Professional Women (BPW), and the American Association of University Women (AAUW). Female-focused industry groups include fields ranging from Professional Women in Construction to Women in Film and Television. For the largest directory of women's organizations around the world, contact the Business Women's Network, a Washington, D.C.–based organization, at (202) 466-8209 or www.bwni.com.

SHHHH . . .

The secret about most associations—particularly those focused on women—is that they need members as much as you need a job. Most associations rely on membership dues and mailing lists to survive, so they are thrilled to talk to potential new members like you. So don't be shy about cold-calling your industry association or a professional women's networking group—membership directors will be more than happy to discuss the benefits of joining and answer your specific questions. Why not ask for the names of a few members to speak with about the association? This is a great way to meet active, involved professionals in your field. By mentioning that you received their name from their association they're sure to take your call.

Finding the Right Association

There are several ways to find associations serving your industry. For a general search, visit the website of the American Society of Association Executives (see, even associations have their own association!) at www.asaenet.org, or perform an Internet search by typing in a key word from your industry (e.g., "accounting") and the word "association." Then contact the national or local chapter of your industry's main association to find out when they hold meetings or events. Many cities list associations and networking groups on their chamber of commerce websites, and of course there's always the phone book. Visit the Resources section at the back of this book for a great list of industry associations, women's networking groups, and online organizations.

Associations vary greatly, but here are some general guidelines on how associations can best support your job search:

- **Events galore.** Association leaders understand that people join to meet others in their industry so one of their prime responsibilities is to host events where lots of schmoozing can take place. Call the associations that interest you and ask for their upcoming calendar of events—often they are thrilled when a prospective member (that's you!) wants to attend a function. Be on the lookout for professional development seminars, cocktail hours, "leads" meetings (when each member stands up and directly asks for the kind of job/client/partner/service he or she is seeking), picnics, fund-raisers, public policy or union briefings, and annual meetings. These are all great venues to network around, ask some questions, and make contact with active members of your industry.

- **Volunteer opportunities.** This is a great tip for recent college grads or career switchers looking to break into a new field. Call the local chapter of the industry's association and offer yourself as a volunteer. Many associations are nonprofit and run by people with full-time jobs, so they are thrilled for any assistance, particularly from a motivated job seeker. Consider volunteering for a task that will help build your experience (writing an article for their newsletter, balancing the books, organizing the catering for an event, designing a new feature of their website), then put this on your resume as experience in your field. Or, as mentioned earlier, if you can't score a professional task, volunteer for a position in which you'll meet the most association members—manage the database, work the registration table at an event, or make fund-raising phone calls. Remember, it's perfectly acceptable (encouraged, in fact) to list volunteer work on your resume, and nonprofit managers can serve as great professional and personal references.

• **Insider information.** Associations offer educational seminars, newsletters, and websites focused on keeping their members fully informed about their particular industry. This includes government regulations, new products or services, company news, and management changes. Small businesses often advertise job openings in their trusted association's newsletter before approaching the big Internet job sites or newspapers. Keep your eye out as well for companies doing particularly well (they may be hiring!) or new senior managers who may be increasing their staffs. Keeping up with industry news also helps in a job interview—you'll impress your interviewer with your savviness about their industry.

Wait a Minute!

Pamper yourself. You're worth it! Keep your spirits up with whatever turns you on. Think long baths, mini-massages, pedicures, chocolate (especially now that you're exercising more!). If shopping lifts your spirits, hit the thrifts and flea markets to hunt for the best bargain of the day. Consider a day at the beach or lake or a picnic in the park.

Scott Jordan, director of Corporate Development for Golden Key International Honour Society, gives us even more reason to stay active with professional associations. "Companies with hiring needs look to professional organizations as a resource for talent outside of their normal recruiting channels," says Jordan, who is also the former manager of College Relations for computer maker Gateway. Being a member of a prestigious association puts job seekers "in an elite group of people that is very attractive" to recruiters, yet it's up to the job seeker to utilize the "opportunities provided to distinguish yourself from the general candidate pool.

"The value is in direct relationship to the effort you put into using the mechanisms put in place by the organization," Jordan warns. "For instance, Golden Key offers members a resume exchange that employers can search for potential candidates. We also provide special recruiting messages from employers. Many interviews and jobs are secured through the informal networking provided at regional and national events."

Jordan's advice for leveraging the value of your membership in professional associations:

Inside Scoop

Gutsy Networking Technique

Ann King, founder and CEO of BloomingCookies.com, a highly creative company specializing in customized edible gifts in hand-painted containers, remembers a particularly innovative client. "A smart cookie who really wanted a job as a flight attendant had tried all the traditional avenues to no avail. She wanted something truly unique that would grab a recruiter's attention." She asked Blooming Cookies to include her resume in a customized flower pot filled with cookies, which featured the airline's logo hand-painted on the front. Of course, the finishing touch was that the words "Hire Me" were painted squarely on the front rim. "No less than two days after the cookies arrived, she received a plane ticket and an appointment for an interview with the airline," King proudly reports. And yes, the lucky lady landed the job.

- Ask directly if career assistance is a priority for the organization and determine the available resources.

- Research information about corporate sponsors that consistently support the organization, and use the relationship as a stepping-stone for making contact with that employer.

- Use every opportunity to put your name, resume, and credentials in an active organization's database.

- Attend regional and national conferences, conventions, and job fairs.

Adult/Continuing Education

We know what you're thinking: "I already went to college! What more do I need?" But adult education offers so much more than information. Even a one-day seminar or a series of night courses can provide the extra skills or certification you desire. Most continuing education classes are designed to accommodate the schedules of busy professionals so they are flexible in their offerings.

Adult and continuing education classes offer many benefits to the savvy job seeker:

- **Resume boost.** Particularly for career changers or rising executives, education demonstrates to an employer that you are motivated, eager to stay on the cutting edge of your industry, and willing to put in the work to achieve your highest potential. Whether you are in the midst of a course or have already completed one, additional education is always impressive and particular certifications may boost your chances (and your eventual salary range).

• **Industry contacts.** Adult education courses are taught by industry experts and attended by industry insiders. Make a point to learn about new industry trends, networking opportunities, and job leads by chatting with the other people in your classroom.

• **Leadership opportunities.** Instead of taking a course, why not teach one? One of our favorite PR pros got a job at NBC after volunteering to teach a class at her local university—when she was only twenty-one! For adult education classes, you don't need a Ph.D. or dozens of years of industry experience—just some solid work experience, a great syllabus, and lots of enthusiasm. Colleges and universities are always looking to expand their roster of professional teachers and lecturers—start by calling your local schools and asking about the process of becoming an instructor. Courses are usually held at night or on the weekends so teaching shouldn't interfere with your job search. Contact your local college, technical school, or even high school to find out about opportunities to teach a course in your field. It looks great on your resume, and, again, you never know who you might meet on the job!

TAILOR YOUR NETWORKING TO YOUR INTENDED CAREER

Networking works for every job and every career. But just like a dynamite cover letter or a knockout resume, tailoring your efforts to your desired results will get you more responses more efficiently. You don't want to turn down any help or contacts, but you'll do better looking for information on investment banking jobs in the *Wall Street Journal* than you will in a fashion magazine. Every career has a circle of influence in some way, and smart networkers think like their field of interest.

To illustrate just how pervasive networking is we even went to a registered dental hygienist for her advice. "When in school, try to develop relationships with the instructors in your field so that when you graduate, they will serve as excellent referral sources. I met many of the professionals in the School of Dentistry who then made contacts for me upon graduation. Read magazines to see who is often quoted, or go to the library to see if there are books written by individuals in your city," says Gail G. Heyman. "Surrounding yourself with the leaders in the field elevates your services as you can expand your interests. If you work for leaders in a specific field, you will automatically get connected with many other successful people who are attracted to the best service and product available."

Given her profession, Heyman has an even more apropos tip: "One of the best suggestions I can give anyone for getting your foot in the door is to have a great smile!"

Finding People and Networking Online

One place to tailor your networking is online. Think about those long-lost friends you once hung out with. Perhaps the kid voted the most likely to succeed is now a media mogul or running a huge software company and needs your services. You'll never know until you reach out and find out where they are now. Here are some quick places to find people online:

www.whitepages.com: A national online phone book.
www.classmates.com: A huge directory of high school alumni from over 30,000 schools in the U.S. and Canada.

www.highschoolalumni.com: Another source for old friends and classmates.

www.pueblo.gsa.gov: Federal agencies, military locator services, and private organizations that can help you locate possible contacts.

www.planetalumni.com: Includes schools, fraternities and sororities as well.

Also try browsing through alumni lists on the website of your college or university. There's often an "Alumni Notes" section where grads write in to share their news—read closely for tidbits about alumni in your city or industry who may be good contacts in your job search.

> ## Inside Scoop
>
> ### *Forwarding Her Success*
>
> The Internet helped one innovative woman find a job. While searching for a personal assistant's job, Merilee devised an Internet strategy offering helpful tips for getting organized. She built a database of her own contacts and asked all of her friends to forward her e-mail every week to their contacts. She called it Merilee's Tip of the Week and in every e-mail she offered suggestions for clearing a desk, organizing files, and even great restaurants that delivered lunch for busy professionals. She illustrated her writing skills and built a quick following showcasing her tips for helping others save time. Of course, each week her e-mail reminded recipients of her interest in securing a position as an executive assistant where she'd be an asset by organizing her boss's life. After just four weeks of her clever e-mails, she landed an interview with a relative of one of her close friends who ran a large business and was starved for time. Her clever campaign paid off: Merilee got the job!

CHATTING

Don't forget e-mail groups, chat rooms, and online bulletin boards as sources of information. With a little research, you can find rooms devoted to people in your industry, with your interests, in your area. Look to association websites, industry publication websites, and chamber of commerce websites. Be sure to sign up for Listservs as well—these are e-mail distribution lists in which the list members can send messages to their community, rather than a single source sending e-mails to a group list. You can even post your own message to your Listserv group, outlining your credentials and asking for help with your job search.

OVERCOMING SHYNESS

It's all well and good for us to pound networking into your head, but for someone who is shy or easily intimidated, cold-calling a stranger is a tall order. Walking into a room full of people is nearly impossible. With this in mind, we offer tips for overcoming shyness, which is a big barrier in everyday life and certainly in any job search.

- You are not alone. There's always someone else in your shoes. Be the first to say hello or to wish someone a good day and you'll be surprised at how welcomed your greetings are. No one wants to be alone and if you step up to the plate you are actually coming to another person's rescue.

- Remember the buddy system. Instead of attending events alone, find a pal to bring along to help you mingle with potential contacts.

- Read those name tags. At most networking events, attendees are required to wear name tags for the purpose of identifying associates and helping to initiate conversation. If you see a company name that's of interest to you, approach the person with a conversation starter about their employer: "Oh, hi. I see you work for Thompson Express . . . tell me what you do there."

- Give a compliment. Tell someone you're wild about his or her shoes, and then ask if they have any suggestions for where to shop

in the area. Spark up a conversation through common interests.

• Carry a best-selling book.
Books often attract a conversation—as evidenced by the
popularity of book clubs. Just
be sure you have read it and are prepared to discuss the subject
matter.

• Wear your best conversation piece. This could be a fabulous
pin or a fun purse. Everyone loves a handbag with flair and many
people will ask where you bought it. It doesn't have to be expensive to grab attention and get people talking.

• Stand in the food line. Lines are great places to meet someone
since you have a captive audience. Initiate a conversation by saying how hungry you are and how great the food looks.

• Ask for directions. The quickest way to get someone talking
to you is to ask for directions. Either they don't know or they will
be extremely talkative and help you get to your destination. This
is a quick way to drum up a conversation and has some natural
follows: Are you from this area? Where are you from? Do I detect
a southern accent?

• Spot a common interest. Try to identify someone who's admir-
ing something—whether it's the food or a piece of art. Initiate a
conversation based on that most basic interest.

• Talk to the wait staff. Anyone who is there to serve the event
or room is always thrilled to meet someone friendly. Never
underestimate anyone who you may view as beneath you because

you never know who they know. Plus, more importantly, being friendly is infectious. When you're nice it comes back to you.

- Whip out your card. Offer your card to someone and say, "I'd like to introduce myself. I'm looking for a job and you look like someone who everyone knows. What is your secret to success?"

Inside Scoop

It's All in the Detail

Our literary agent Meredith Bernstein is one of the most well-connected networkers we know, so we asked her to share her favorite secret with us.

"Key in on some personal aspect of a person you meet. What distinguishing characteristic strikes you? Let's face it: some people are just downright bland. I confess that as a visual person, this is a problem for me because I remember details because they are details and they can be crucial. Sometimes, after many years in the business, I will say to an editor I'm lunching with, 'I remember that fabulous chunky aquamarine necklace you wore with that lemon-yellow shift.' They are stunned that I have recalled that. It makes them feel special.

"Making people feel special because you have noticed and remembered something is one of the best things you can do. It binds you in some way and this can be important to the relationship." If you're meeting someone for the very first time, pay attention to a particular item or characteristic that you feel comfortable complimenting. Don't risk being insincere."

OUR FINAL NETWORKING TIP

Wear red underwear. That's right. Our final networking tip is to wear red underwear. It will make you feel powerful on the inside, where it counts. Of course it doesn't have to be red (though that's our favorite). Wear yellow if it makes you feel cheerful or energized. If our undercover tactics do not work for you, wear a polka-dot scarf if it makes you feel outgoing. Do the little things that give you the confidence—the extra oomph—to make a cold call, walk up and introduce yourself to a stranger, ask for a lead, or do any of the gutsy things you'll need to do to get that great job you know you deserve.

CHAPTER TEN

More Traditional Job-Search Methods

While you're out there pounding the pavement with gutsy networking and serious schmoozing, you can also pursue other, more traditional, job-search methods. Remember, you never know which path will lead to the illustrious pot of employment gold.

Career Fairs

Career fairs are popular and beneficial for entry-level and mid-career professionals. It is important to plan ahead and learn how to make the best use of your time at such events. Keep in mind that career fairs are not just for arranging interviews for specific positions, but also for exploring career options with participating employers, and perfecting your interviewing and networking skills.

FINDING CAREER FAIRS

Most career fairs are advertised in local newspapers and radio advertisements starting a few weeks before they are held. You can also register for any event-listing e-mail newsletters and regularly check event-listing websites in your area. Most major metropolitan areas have sites like www.citysearch.com or www.craigslist.org that announce the big community and business events. You can also perform an Internet search on "career fairs" and go directly to career fair companies' websites—like ours, www.womenforhire.com—to find out the dates they'll be in your town.

BEFORE YOU ARRIVE

Remember all the tips from your toolkit: Arm yourself with copies of your focused resume, a memorized sales pitch, a roster of available references, lots of business cards, a professional outfit, and a positive attitude.

Then get ready to flex that muscle you've worked so hard to build. Arrive with a clear idea of what you're looking for and why you deserve it. Know which companies are participating and what they're recruiting for. This is usually available on the website of the fair's sponsoring organization. Knowing the companies and positions makes it a lot easier to figure out if you'd be a strong match. Once you know there's some mutual connection, you can approach a recruiter with confidence. Many recruiters are simply there to select the best candidates to introduce to the actual hiring managers at their companies. They're looking to eliminate undesirables whose resumes probably won't make it to the next level. Your goal must be to get on their hot list—in other words, to make the cut, to convince someone that you've got the right stuff, that you possess the necessary skills and educational background, and that you'd be an all-around good candidate for their corporate culture. Proper planning on your part is key to making this happen. Without proper prep work you're bound to miss a multitude of opportunities.

CAREER FAIR TIPS

- **Be prepared and do your homework.** If the career fair has a website or placed an ad that lists the companies in attendance, visit their websites and print out a few key pages about the ones you are interested in. Get in the know and read up on them. Pull up company profiles at www.hoovers. com to learn about their strengths, weaknesses, and com-

petitors. And remember to show off your knowledge! Mention something about the company that illustrates you know what they do—a new CEO, a recent newspaper article, a new company initiative or advertisement. Make sure you are prepared to tell a recruiter what you'd contribute to their company and why you're excited about potential opportunities.

- **Target your resumes.** Bring at least fifty copies of your resume printed on plain paper, of course. Cover letters are not necessary at the fair, but don't risk running out of resumes. By researching participating companies before you attend the fair, you'll be able to bring resumes customized to each company you're targeting. Put each company's targeted resume in a different colored folder in your tote bag or briefcase so you don't hand over the wrong resume to an unsuspecting recruiter.

- **Bring a bag, a notebook, and a pen.** The bag is to carry literature and giveaways. The notebook should be professional with space for safekeeping of those resumes (no crumpled copies, please!) and a pad for notes. Bring two pens—just in case.

• **Look the part.** Dress as you would for an interview at the company's headquarters. This is no time to be casual. Wear your most comfy shoes since you'll be doing a lot of walking and standing.

• **Get some shut-eye.** Get a good night's sleep so you're rested and energized for the fair. Eat a good meal before you go to prevent tummy grumbles while you chat.

• **Arrive early.** Career fairs attract hundreds, sometimes thousands of people. Get there early, grab the directory or floor plan, and plan your attack. Recruiters are more alert and fresh early in the day so you'll get a better reception in the morning hours. Don't fall victim to their late-afternoon exhaustion because they've met with hundreds of candidates all day.

• **Map your territory.** Once you've checked your coat if the weather warrants, check out the place. Take a walk throughout the entire fair and get the lay of the land. Try to pick up as much literature as possible from the companies that are appealing to you. Don't just ignore companies you've never heard of—they may have positions of interest as well. If the fair is crowded, start in the back. Many people get stuck in the stampede at the front. Make your way to the back where there are representatives waiting for someone to appear.

• **Stay off the cell.** Nothing is more unprofessional than chatting on your cell phone while waiting in line to speak to a recruiter. At a career fair you have one purpose: to network to get a job. That should be important enough to turn off your phone for a few hours. Spend your time in line talking to the job seekers around you—you never know what contacts they might have. If you have to make or take an urgent call, do it outside.

SHOWTIME

You've finally inched your way to the front of the line. It's you and the recruiter face-to-face. Don't panic.

- **Make mental notes.**

Although recruiter styles vary, you can usually get a good feel for what you're about to encounter by slyly observing from a distance. Is the recruiter standing in front of the booth or sitting behind the table? Those out in front tend to be much friendlier and more approachable. They're eager to hear about your background and interests, and they're glad to tell you about their companies and available positions. The ones sitting seriously behind their tables may likely be systematic in their technique, with specific checklists or questionnaires that will determine their level of interest in you. These conversations tend to have a more formal tone. Look at body language. If a recruiter is upbeat and smiling this may mean you're in for a more relaxed, conversational style of interviewing. Once you've scoped out the kind of person you're about to face, mentally prepare for the kind of interview or conversation that you're about to have. Watching the person in line ahead of you will give you some idea of what to expect. Some recruiters conduct short, simple interviews designed solely to screen candidates. It's a couple minutes—just enough to allow them to size you up before deciding whether or not to call you for the next step. Kind of brutal, but true.

- **Briefly and succinctly explain how you meet their needs.** Time to whip out that thirty-second sales pitch. If you only have a few quick minutes of a recruiter's attention it's critical to point out the key factors in your background that make you qualified for the position. If you pay attention and listen to the gals in front of you and if you've reviewed some of that literature that you collected earlier, there's a good chance you'll overhear what those needs are.

- **More time?** The other possibility is a longer conversation— up to ten minutes—where you're asked to give a full accounting of your background and interests while explaining why you'd be an ideal candidate for that company. Be prepared to answer questions that relate to your field of interest, not just your particular background and experience. Put that three-minute sales pitch to work.

- **Next steps?** Don't forget one critical question before you leave each booth: What's the next step? Take the recruiter's card and make sure you know their procedures for follow-ups. Will they call you? Send you a letter? Should you call them? When?

- **Be a detective.** Sometimes a recruiter isn't willing to give out her card. After all, if she meets 900 candidates at an event and gives her card to each one, her e-mail inbox will self-destruct. In such a case, be sure to write down her name and figure out how to get to her on your own. Call her company and ask for her e-mail address, or look at the contact information on the company's website and figure out their e-mail system. Most companies follow standard e-mail formats such as Brad.Pitt@HunkCompany.com, Taye_Diggs@Model.com, or Jlopez@jlorocks.com. Play around and try them all—the worst that can happen is the message bounces back!

- **Don't leave empty-handed.** All is not lost if a recruiter tells you the positions she has open don't match your interests. If IBM is looking for account executives but you want to join their IT team, politely ask the recruiter who you might be able to contact. If she is unwilling to provide a name, quickly jot down the career fair recruiter's name and follow the above advice for following up.

- **Keep your expectations in check.** It can be awfully disheartening to be passed along after you were given a mere three minutes with the representative from the company of your dreams. That's a normal feeling—and it's the reality of the career fair process. Don't give up—you can appeal to other people within the company.

- **Final moves.** Before exiting the event, head back to the booths where you have some interest. Remind the recruiter of your interest (this shows definite enthusiasm), thank her for her time (this indicates class and professionalism), and be clear that you'll be in touch soon (this lets them know you're thorough and

One-Minute Mess-Up

Leave Your Partner at Home

At every Women For Hire event we see at least a dozen women arrive with a boyfriend, parent, or partner in tow. This is an automatic turnoff to potential employers, who immediately question the gal's ability to handle a job on her own. One recruiter remembers a time when a candidate brought her husband to the interview and said, "He's just here in case I need help. After all, this is the first real interview I've been on and I feel better having him at my side." Needless to say, she didn't get the job—and you won't either if you're not able to stand on your own. Leave your other half at home.

efficient). There's a good chance that this final gesture will leave a bit of a lasting impression that may serve you well.

BACK HOME

Two words, baby: Follow up! Too many job hunters make the dismal mistake of assuming that once their resume is in the right hands, or any hands for that matter, nature will take its course and the good ol' career fairy will call any minute with that fabulous offer. Wrong. Unless you were specifically instructed not to call, leave a short, well-rehearsed message for the recruiter the following morning so it's the first call they receive by voice mail the next day in the office:

> "This is **YOUR NAME** calling to thank you again for taking the time to talk to me yesterday at the career fair. I remain very interested in working for **COMPANY** and I'm confident that my **DEGREE/EXPERIENCE** will serve you well. I would appreciate the opportunity to take this to the next level and I look forward to hearing from you. I can be reached at **NUMBER**. Again, thanks for your time. Good-bye."

ONE LAST THING

Keep in mind, you won't leave the event with a solution to paying your rent or reducing credit card debt. Formal offers are rarely made on the spot. But if you're confident and you pay attention to the details of the follow-up, you'll be well on your way to securing a position.

Registering with Agencies

Placement agencies and headhunters are an often easy aspect of any job search. If the relationships are developed properly, these recruiters will actively arrange interviews for you with the goal of filling their clients' positions by getting you hired.

The catch? Placement agencies usually operate on a contingency basis. They get paid when they fill the job. This means that the majority of firms will present their clients with as many candidates as possible, which means stiff competition for you. Placement agencies are popular for entry-level positions in all fields, as well as administrative slots at all levels. Executive search firms handle middle-level slots and up and tend to be much more selective when determining which candidates to work with.

Search firms are usually retained by their clients. This means they receive a monthly or annual fee based on an expected number and level of positions they are likely to fill. They are used by companies looking for highly qualified candidates and they tend to focus on a specialty—from corporate marketing and public relations to hard-to-fill positions, such as a bilingual research scientist with experience in Asian epidemiology.

Placement agencies and headhunters are also keen on identifying candidates who not only possess the right skill sets but whose style and behavior will also complement the existing corporate culture. This is especially true when searching for candidates to fill more senior positions.

FINDING A REPUTABLE FIRM

Most major placement agencies advertise their services to job seekers in the Sunday Help Wanted sections. They can also be found under "employment agencies" in the Yellow Pages. The more selective firms are harder to reach, but can be found by doing a search online.

Before submitting your resume or signing on with a particular company, call to request a conversation with an account representative. Aside from selling your skills to get them interested in working with you, consider these questions that you should ask:

- What types of clients do you have?

- What type of repeat business do you have from those clients?

- What is your placement rate?

- What is your industry or specialty?

- Please describe the agency's history and philosophy.

- Do you provide any type of career coaching?

- Please describe the process for working with candidates.

- How do you determine which candidates are sent on interviews?

THE FINE PRINT

Remember, it's up to you to find the right firm to help aid your search. You have the right to quality service and personal attention.

- Be suspect of anyone who expects you to pay any kind of fee.

- Make sure the agency listens to your background and interests and doesn't simply send you out on any old interviews. This is especially a problem with agencies that work on contingency; many of them will send your resume anywhere and everywhere in hopes of it clicking somewhere.

* Some agencies will send resumes out without the candidate's permission. To avoid this be sure to clarify that you want to be notified before interviews are arranged on your behalf. This allows you to decide if you want your hat thrown into the ring.

* Truly reputable firms will give you all of the essential information up front, including the name of the employer they're recruiting for. If they hold back too much, your antennae should rise.

Inside Scoop

Don't Forget to Impress

In nearly twenty years as an executive recruiter and management consultant Arnie Huberman (www.huberman.com) has seen countless job seekers routinely make the mistake of assuming they don't have to impress associates at his search firm. The major misconception is that the candidate is the client. "Clients are the ones who pay the bills! Candidates are just that—candidates." This means it's essential to treat the headhunter just as you would a potential employer. "You have thirty seconds at best to get my attention. We look at the best-qualified people for the job," says Huberman. Do whatever it takes to impress the firm with your credentials. Make them believe that you are worthy of their time and that you will represent them well if they send you out for consideration by their clients. "I am very concerned and careful about you as a candidate, but my primary concern is meeting the needs of my client. So if you are not right, you will be told that we are not interested. We are not dying to find you a job," warns Huberman, whose top-tier clients include L'Oréal, General Mills, and Condé Nast, for whom he has successfully identified public relations professionals at all levels. The bottom line is that his focus, like most reputable search firms, is all about "working hard to get the client what they need."

* When they do set up an interview for you, insist on knowing as much about the position and the person as possible. It is in the agency's best interest to know that you're well prepared.

- Sign up with multiple agencies if you haven't agreed to exclusivity. They usually have different clients in various industries, which betters your chances for success.

- Maintain regular contact with the agencies you choose to work with. Since you aren't their only candidate, it's up to you to check in every day by phone or e-mail for a status on potential interviews or offers.

CHAPTER ELEVEN

Acing the Interview

You did it! You've resumed, you've cover lettered, you've networked. And now it's paid off: You've been invited to interview for a great job. First, pat yourself on the back—you've made it to the moment of truth. When you've advanced to the interview stage you know the employer is interested, so now it's time to close the deal and prepare the best way possible!

Let's begin by turning the tables and looking at the interview from the recruiter's perspective. There are three main areas all employers must evaluate when considering a potential candidate for a job. This is true in just about every industry and at every level. The more you understand what an interviewer is looking for, the more impressive you'll be. The three main areas are Knowledge, Skills, and Abilities. Be prepared to discuss all of your interview answers around these key areas. A careful review of job descriptions will enable you to identify the KSAs for any position you pursue.

KNOWLEDGE

An employer needs to know that, through your education and experience, you've learned the information, techniques, and industry vocabulary appropriate to the level and responsibility of the job you're seeking.

SKILLS

Can you perform the actual tasks required by this job function in this industry? This is particularly key for technical positions, management roles, and client service positions.

ABILITIES

An employer must determine if you're able to do the job. You'll have to demonstrate that you have successfully done this job elsewhere or that you have the necessary skills to succeed in this position. Your best chance of success is a combination of both. For recent graduates or career changers, it's important to emphasize your excellent general knowledge and ability to learn quickly.

Beyond KSAs, interviewers want candidates who are a good fit for the organization—personally and economically.

PERSONALITY TRAITS

The employer is looking for a genuine desire and passion in you for the type of work required in this position. Your personality also must be aligned with the culture and values of this environment. This includes how you'd interact with coworkers on all levels—below, equal to, and above you.

COMPENSATION

The employer will want to be convinced that you are worth what they'd be paying you.

PREPARATION, PREPARATION, PREPARATION

The number one rule for preparing for a formal job interview is to *over-prepare.* You want to walk into that meeting knowing everything you can about the job, the company, the interviewer, the industry, and the day's news. We're not talking about confidential trade secrets or totally insider information; but keep in mind employers want smart, motivated, and enthusiastic employees. Recruiters often cite a lack of research as a major pet peeve, so show what you know and you'll grab attention and offers. Here's what you need to know and where to find it.

Online Company Research

COMPANY SITES

For starters, zoom to the company's website and get right to the source. Many corporate sites have an "employment" or "careers" link especially for job seekers. Not only will you find current openings and application information, they all feature extensive information on the corporate culture and philosophies, plus plenty of details on their operations. Read everything from company philosophy to media releases to executive bios. So much to see—all in just a few clicks. It's inexcusable not to know this information inside out.

To research the company, check out www.hoovers.com, www.vault. com, and www.wetfeet.com. These sites have extensive information about companies and industries. For an executive look at the business

Every time we interview candidates for openings at Women For Hire, the first question is have you had a chance to look at our website? A full 50 percent of the time, a woman looks away and says no, she just didn't have time or her Internet connection was down. She tells us she figured we'd discuss that stuff in the interview anyway.

At that very moment, we let her know the interview is over. If she didn't have time for the most basic prep work, she doesn't deserve the job or our time. After all, we weren't asking for a thorough analysis of our competition—just a simple sign of respect for the interview process. While an interview is an appropriate forum for asking questions and learning more about an employer, it's essential for you to walk in having done your homework.

world, and for a comprehensive view, visit www.ceoexpress.com. This handy site is short on visual appeal but rocks on content. You can always count on Yahoo! Simply type in a company name and Yahoo! can provide a profile, stock prices, and recent news about the company.

GREAT BOOKS

Fabulous books like *The National Jobbank* are loaded with key info. Look for titles by Adams or Hoover's publishing companies. Resources published by these biggies provide great information on your favorite companies.

MAGAZINES

Several consumer magazines publish special issues rating companies on their hiring practices and employee satisfaction. Check out *Working Mother* for guides to companies with the most family-friendly policies. *Fortune* publishes an annual list of the Best Companies to Work For, as do most industry publications. Most magazines' websites will also feature archives from past years' rankings.

THE DAILY PAPER

Since most smart people keep up with current events, interviewers often ask interviewees where they get their news. It's absolutely crucial to read your city's most respected newspaper each day while you're job searching. You can never go wrong by reading the *New York Times* or the *Wall Street Journal* as well. Remember Tess McGill in *Working Girl?* The Melanie Griffith character earned a big promotion by clipping *New York Post* articles. Keep your eye out for companies in the news to see who's doing well even in a downturn. Don't forget to check out the Help Wanteds; it's even smart to watch the *Today* show or your favorite morning news program the day of the big interview to make sure you're fully prepared to discuss current events.

CONTACT THE COMPANY ITSELF

Why not? Most people don't think to contact the company directly. Many have recruiting offices that would be delighted to send you information. Try calling the company's own library with specific questions if the answers can't be found on the web. While contacting the company directly can be scary, it's a surefire way to get a leg up on the competition. With just a few pieces of "insider" information, you'll impress your interviewer and show your determination to get the job. Ask about new company initiatives, new management, company news, morale—anything that you can discuss in your interview to show that you've done your homework and you have made an effort to learn about the culture you might be joining.

WHAT TO KNOW ABOUT THE COMPANY

Once you've located several research sources, you need to know what to know. Basic facts you'll have easy access to—and that employers will expect you to know—include the following:

• Size of the company (Do they have 50 employees or 5,000?)

• Nature of the products and/or services offered (Do they consult technology companies or manufacture glassware?)

• Target market (Are their clients other businesses or consumers? What characteristics do their customers have?)

• General company history (Have they been around fifty years or five months? Have they merged or been acquired by other companies?)

• Company competitors (Who are the leaders in their industry?)

• Specific information about various departments (Marketing, IT, Accounting. Which departments are most profitable?)

• Company environment and culture (Cubicles and Casual Fridays or buttoned-up blue suits?)

• Recent news about the company (Mergers? Layoffs? New products? Expansion to other countries?)

• Information from the company prospectus or annual report (Public, private, profitable?)

If you're lucky, in addition to these essentials you might even run across information that outlines the organization's upcoming challenges and then be able to sell yourself on a problem-to-solution basis.

RESEARCH YOUR INTERVIEWER

To really stand out from the crowd, Paul Falcone, author of *The Hiring and Firing Question and Answer Book* and director of Employment and Development for Paramount Pictures in Hollywood, rec-

ommends conducting an Internet search on your prospective interviewer. Google, the mother of all Internet search engines, will retrieve information about individuals' publications, their "honorable mentions" in business societies or community groups, speaking engagements, and other activities. If the situation lends itself, ask the interviewer to confirm that she's the same Jane Smith who was quoted in the recent *Los Angeles Times* article about new recruiting efforts in corporate America. If you're right, you'll have won the heart of the interviewer. If you're wrong, she'll at least find it interesting that you took the time to find out more about her. In addition to performing an Internet search you can also ask the company's HR department for a bio or summary of the person you're meeting.

One-Minute Mess-Up

Easy on the Compliments

Shari Fitzpatrick began her career by wrapping Christmas presents at an Oregon department store and is now founder and chairman of Shari's Berries, makers of delicious mail-order chocolate-dipped strawberries. She recalls a time when she did not hire a woman because the candidate really overdid it on the compliments. While it's definitely appropriate—and even encouraged—to offer compliments when you feel that they're genuine, be careful not to go overboard because such behavior may appear insincere, especially to a stranger.

MAKING SMALL TALK

Those casual first few moments of an interview—the "Hi, nice to meet you" stage—are just as important as the more formal questions to come. The interviewer knows you'll be a bit nervous, but it's important to show grace under pressure. Now's the time to mention the article you saw in the newspaper that morning, or to mention a recent study on your industry. You don't want to suck up, but you do want to show that you're prepared and comfortable engaging in conversation with new acquaintances. Most likely the interviewer will initiate conversation, but arrive prepared with a few ideas in mind so you're not racking your brains for something to say.

Laurie P. Selzer, national director of marketing, Metro Networks and Shadow Broadcasting, shares this advice on chitchat: "During interviews I try to respond to something personal, like interesting items on the interviewer's desk or wall—something that will get them to talk about themselves and their lives outside their professional life. I always ask how they got started in what they are doing."

Pay attention to the smallest signs of what you might be able to do to "ingratiate you to them," says Hillary Rivman, senior vice president, Planned Television Arts. "I remember one potential client mentioned that she had a passion for cooking gourmet food but didn't have all that much time between work and home. I forwarded her a website [that offered tips on this very predicament], which she greatly appreciated and remembered."

Preparing Answers to Likely Questions

Although each job interview is different, there are several common questions that arise in the majority of interview situations. It is essential for you to be well prepared to answer the questions for which you can be prepared. Most interviews will contain a few unexpected zingers, but there's no reason not to be prepared for the questions you can anticipate.

Remember:

- Highlight your knowledge, skills, and abilities.

- Quantify your success whenever possible.

- Never point out flaws in your resume or experience. Let the interviewer bring them up.

- Make sure you are presenting yourself in the best possible way. Mark Victor Hansen, coauthor of the bestselling series *Chicken Soup for the Soul,* suggests videotaping yourself being interviewed and watching the playback.

It's a good idea to wait at least three seconds before answering any interview question so you have a quick moment to get over your nerves and mentally prepare your response. Here are some common interview questions and sample answers to help you get ready for the big day:

Q: Tell me about yourself.

A: This is about as wide open as it gets. The best rule of thumb is to reveal a tiny personal tidbit along with some interesting professional stuff as they relate to the company you're interviewing with or the position you're interviewing for. Sometimes it'd be fun to just tell them what you really feel, especially since it's so easy to go off on a tangent or get too personal. But, unless you're applying for a job at Weight Watchers, there's no use mentioning that you'd like to lose ten pounds. If you're not looking to work in a retail shop, don't mention your favorite clothing brands.

Q: What is your greatest strength?

A: The best way to approach this question is to imagine that you're really being asked something much more straightforward: Do you really have what it takes to effectively do this job? This is your golden opportunity to toot your horn and make the case for why you know that you're up for the task. If the most important requirement of the position is dealing with customer complaints, then you will want to discuss in detail your past experience with customer service, why you enjoy the challenge of turning an unhappy client into a happy one, and specific, quantifiable examples of how you successfully managed customer complaints in a past position. Have a list of character traits in mind that you feel comfortable attributing to yourself, along with supporting details to back them up.

12. Forgetting to bring writing samples.

13. Using lowercase letters in all of your e-mail correspondence.

14. Misspelling words on press release samples.

15. Ignoring a request to discuss creative ways to promote a beauty salon, or any pre-interview assignment.

16. Acknowledging that your use of Microsoft Word is "so-so."

17. Requesting your second week off to travel with your boyfriend.

18. Demanding to know in the first ten minutes how soon you would get a raise.

19. Admitting that you don't read a newspaper.

20. Drawing a blank when asked to come up with an on-the-spot idea to promote a jewelry store.

Q: What is your greatest weakness?

A: Now they're really digging for dirt. This is the interviewer's safety net. Here's the perfect opportunity for you to tell them something they were not able to get out of you any other way. Too many honest applicants make the mistake of being brutally candid. We're not suggesting that you lie, but for goodness' sake be careful! For example, even if it's true, you should never admit that you're a horrible procrastinator or that you're terribly disorganized. If you're interviewing for a position that requires a team player, this is not the time to admit you're somewhat of a loner.

Some failsafe possibilities that shouldn't land you in trouble:

• At times I can be impatient with those whose standards aren't as high as mine.

- At times I can be too sensitive and caring about other people's opinions.

- At times I can find it difficult to make time to relax.

- Sometimes I am a bit aggressive in my desire to close a deal.

With each of these responses you're basically saying that you do not approve of sloppiness, you have a heart, you are a workaholic, and you are a hard-nosed salesperson. Not exactly bad attributes in an employee!

Q: How would you evaluate your last boss?
A: There's only one right answer here: a positive one. No matter how tempting it may be to blab on and on about someone you just couldn't stand, do not do it. Never ever trash a former employer. It'll kill your chances for the job. By no means should you go overboard with compliments for a real jerk or a total incompetent. Find something neutral to say if you are not able to offer anything nice.

Q: What would your last boss say about you?
A: The best answer here is to focus on the best aspects of your relationship with your last employer. You might say that your last boss would praise your ability to follow directions, work as part of a team, and achieve measurable results while also taking initiative on specific projects. This is a great chance to show how you improved in your last position if you received regular performance reviews. Again, focus on the positive side of your relationship with your last employer—no bitterness even if the relationship was acrimonious.

Q: Why wasn't your summer work experience in your field of choice?

A: This is a genuine concern among recruiters who are looking to fill entry-level positions where little if any training is provided. As stereotypical as it may seem, plenty of women right out of college have loads of experience waitressing throughout school. Some recruiters interpret that as a lack of professional ambition. It's fairly easy to bat this one out of the park: "My experience as a waitress was valuable training in customer service, which will serve me well in a variety of professional environments. Not only did I have to think on my feet, I interacted with all types of personalities with one main goal: to ensure the satisfaction of the patrons. I also had the opportunity to train numerous new staffers, which has helped prepare me for future leadership roles."

Q: What do you think you'll be doing in five years?

A: Most of us can't plan next week, let alone years down the road. Yet this is among the best-loved questions, so you'd best be ready for it. Use this as an opportunity to demonstrate your commitment to growing in a particular industry or company. Combining your professional growth with loyalty to the employer will serve you best:

"I don't think it's really possible for any of us to truly know where we'll be five years from now, but I can tell you my hopes. For the immediate future I want to immerse myself in this business to learn from the ground up. Beyond that my goal is to contribute to the success of the company, which will hopefully enable me to grow within the company."

Q: What do you know about our company?

A: Your goal is to show off a depth of the knowledge you learned from your research. And of course it's essential always to remain positive. "I know you love putting anorexic supermodels on your covers" would not be an impressive response when interviewing at *Vogue* magazine. Instead, you'd want to address the quality of editorial content and what differentiates it from the competition. You would also want to address how *Vogue* fits in to the Condé Nast empire of magazines. It's inexcusable not to know basic information on the company size, products, reputation/image, history, philosophy, management, and competitors because just about all of this is available on their website. Your answers should project an enthusiasm for the company and the industry—and you should feel free to pose one or two questions on this subject.

Q: What makes you the ideal candidate for this position?

A: "I've always wanted to work here" is a bad answer. "I really need a job" is the worst answer. An employer wants to hear what you'll bring to them, not how they will help you pay your bills. If appropriate, talk about how you'd solve a problem, lower costs, increase sales. You can apply your previous successes/knowledge/ skills in this area.

Q: What's the most appealing part of this position?

A: Be able to provide one or two strong examples, although salary and location should not be among them.

Q: What's the most unappealing part of the position?

A: Focus on something minor and try to associate some type of positive comment with the unpleasant task. For example, a clerk at a law firm might hate transcribing long depositions, yet by doing so she would learn the ins and outs of effective questioning.

Q: What do you think are the most important qualifications of a BLANK *{position you're applying for . . . sales exec, operations manager, executive assistant}?*

A: Be able to provide two or three action- and results-oriented responses.

Q: What is your management style?

A: Open door is ideal, but don't lie if it's not true. Be sure to work in that you communicate well with your entire staff, you solicit their opinions, you keep them informed, you get the job done, and you interact well with upper management equally well.

Q: How do you handle difficult situations at work?

A: Never say you get along with everyone so there are never ever problems and never say you avoid people who aren't cooperative. Big bells go off when candidates are overly defensive when answering this question. Instead, talk about your ability to negotiate and compromise while understanding that different people have different perspectives, and that new ideas often develop from controversy.

MORE QUESTIONS TO THINK ABOUT

Management/Performance

- What skills do you look for when hiring new employees?

- How many people have you had to manage?

- What's the most difficult part of being a manager?

- What do you think your direct reports think of you?

- Have you ever been in a situation when you had to say something although you knew it wasn't popular?

- How have you specifically helped to increase sales, profits, success?

- How have you reduced costs?

- What were the best/worst parts of your previous job?

- What were your greatest accomplishments in that position?

- Have you ever lost a customer?

- What is the most difficult decision you've ever had to make?

Work Style

- Do you prefer staff or line work? Do you prefer working with figures or words?

- How do you handle conflict on a team project?

- Have you ever had to fire anyone, and if so, how did you handle the situation?

- How do you enlist the help of others in your work?

- What do you do to put coworkers at ease?

- How do you solicit feedback from others on your work?

- How do you stay cutting edge?

- How do you learn from failure?

- Describe your listening skills.

- How do you handle working under pressure?

Personal

While interviewers cannot ask about your age, sexual preference, religion, marital status (see Questionable Questions in chapter twelve), they're certainly able to get a sense of your personal side with other pointed questions.

- Which business leaders or role models do you respect?

- If you could have dinner with someone famous, living or dead, who would it be and why?

- What kind of books do you read?

- What type of recreational activities do you enjoy?

- What are your favorite Internet sites?

- How do you avoid excess stress? How do you relax?

- How do you get along with and embrace people who are different from you?

- Where do your ideas come from? Describe your creative process.

- What's the most out-of-the-box idea you've ever had?

Sometimes an interviewer asks a "trick" opinion question to catch you off guard. For example, you may be asked if you object to drug testing. The only correct answer is no. If you do not wish to consent to testing, you should consider looking at other employers that do not engage in such practices.

NEGATIVELY PHRASED QUESTIONS

More times than not you will be asked a negatively phrased question that the interviewer hopes will reveal a weakness *and* a strength.

- Describe a time when you missed a deadline on an important project.

- Describe the type of bad decisions you have made as a manager.

Your answer not only reveals a mistake you made, but it also says a lot about your ability to handle stressful or negative situations. This is your opportunity to turn a negative into a positive because the ability to acknowledge a mistake is often seen as a sign of maturity and leadership.

Assuming that you can wing it is a bad approach to negative questions. More times than not that leads to disappointment—not to mention you probably won't get the job. When responding to negative questions, keep in mind these three points, which will help ensure thoughtful and winning answers.

- Briefly state the incident in which the problem or mistake occurred.

- Explain how you overcame the problem as it related to that particular situation.

- Describe the steps you took to ensure that such a problem would not happen again.

The end result is to convince the interviewer that you learned from this experience and have overcome this particular weakness.

THE DREADED SALARY QUESTION

More than any other topic, "the salary question," "What are your salary requirements?" dominates the fear of women who attend Women For Hire Job-Seeking Strategies Seminars. So many women are uncomfortable even talking about money, let alone asking for it.

We consulted Paul Falcone, author, for his tips on handling a discussion of salary in a job interview:

"First of all, be open and honest about your salary history. Too many candidates seem to think that sharing salary history information up front gives them some disadvantage in the hiring process. Truth be told, most recruiters can tell your salary (plus or minus $5,000 to $10,000) just by looking at your resume for a few minutes. Still, they want a candidate who's up front about salary expectations because, more often than not, that tends to be the ultimate deal breaker."

SO, WHAT ARE YOU WORTH?

Remember, a recruiter will offer you a salary the company thinks you're worth, not always what you think you're worth. But of course you need a response in mind when the salary question comes up. If possible, hold off on discussing your salary expectations until you really know if you want the job or not. Once you're sure, ask yourself these key questions:

- At what point salary-wise would I accept this job, and at what point would I walk away from it?

- What's my ideal salary versus my minimum salary for this position?

- What benefits are crucial to me and would make up for a lower salary? Consider such commodities as tuition reimbursement and 401(k) matches when thinking about your monetary needs.

Don't make the mistake of telling a recruiter what kind of salary you need to survive. In any major company, that doesn't have a great effect on the negotiation. Your best bet is to arm yourself with knowledge about the industry range for such a position. But remember, you have to be comfortable with the bottom of the range you provide, because that's what you'll likely be offered.

Preparing Questions for Your Interviewer

Show your interviewer how interested you are by preparing great questions to ask in the interview. We can guarantee that the interviewer will say, "So, do you have any questions for me?" and you must be prepared. They say that you can tell more about a person by the nature of the questions they ask than by the statements they make. That's because well-focused questions demonstrate a quick insight that's both instinctual and intellectual. Falcone recommends these questions:

- I understand the primary responsibilities of the position at this point. What would be some of the secondary duties—things that may only occur once a quarter or twice a year?

- What would you add or subtract to the background of the individual who held this position before?

- What are some of the immediate challenges facing the department in the next ninety days? What role will this position play in tackling those challenges?

• What would be the ideal personality of the individual you hire that would match your department's culture? Are there any strengths or weaknesses that stand out in particular?

Since it's impossible to predict what might come up during your conversation, it's important to be prepared with a range of questions to pose. Some other options include:

• Would you be able to tell me why this position is currently available?

• What are the qualifications of individuals who have excelled in this position or a similar position?

• What type of training is typically provided?

• What are the company's (or this division's) growth plans?

• What is your background and how did you get your job with this company? (Remember, people often like talking about themselves, or at least being asked!)

• What are the next steps in the hiring process?

Inside Scoop

Questions

Women For Hire asked Suzanne Welch, vice president, Corporate Marketing for fiber optic maker Corning Incorporated, when and if it's okay for a candidate to probe her interviewer with questions about a company's values.

"Timing is everything. First, do your homework about the kind of company you want to work for and seek jobs at those companies. Then, you don't need to worry about your values matching theirs. Interview for the jobs and sell yourself. A potential employer is seeking to learn how you would perform in their environment. Candidates often make the mistake of thinking 'selling' themselves means 'bragging' about themselves. What's worked for me is helping my potential employer know how my background links to what they want to have done. When you get the offer, the balance of power shifts a bit, and there's an opportunity for you to ask more questions about the environment. If you feel it is necessary up front as part of your evaluation of the opportunity, you want to do so in a way that does not dampen the enthusiasm your potential employer has for you."

PHONE SCREENINGS

Oftentimes a smart recruiter opts to talk with a potential candidate by phone before deciding if they'd like to invite someone in for a more formal session. Not-too-smart candidates typically mistake such conversations for idle chitchat. Bad move. This is not a casual event. Now's not the time to wash the dishes or paint your nails. Instead, treat it as seriously as an in-person interview. Be sure to bring the phone to a quiet space with a pad and pen handy.

Work It, Girl!

Asking Questions Develop twenty questions that a recruiter might ask a potential candidate who is interviewing for the position you are going for. More important, plan your knock-'em-dead responses to each one.

_____

_____

_____

_____

_____

_____

_____

_____

• • •

Interview Day

Interview Dos and Don'ts

Preparation is crucial, but the day of the interview will ultimately arrive. Make sure that your knowledge and talent are allowed to show through. An interviewer will make an initial judgment about you within the first few moments of your meeting, so follow these tips to make sure you shine from minute one:

- **Map it.** Make sure you have directions to the office. If it seems confusing, consider a trial run the day before.

- **Arrive early.** There is *absolutely* no excuse for lateness in an interview. Plus, by arriving a few minutes early you'll be able to check out the company and perhaps glean some last-minute information from the atmosphere and staff. Instead of whipping out the current issue of *Cosmopolitan,* try chatting up the receptionist instead. If you're sitting alone, be sure to have a copy of the newspaper or an industry journal to read while you're waiting. No novels—show your professionalism.

- **Be hungry for the job, not for a sandwich.** Eat something light before you arrive. Nothing too heavy to make you sick, just something to leave you satisfied. Bring some extra breath mints, but never chew gum or candy during an interview.

- **Dress appropriately.** Appearance does matter in an interview situation. Err on the side of formality—wear a suit, minimal jewelry, and a neat, professional hairstyle.

- **Treat support staff politely and professionally.** Interviewers often ask their assistants how candidates presented themselves on the phone and in waiting areas. Consider every contact with the company as part of the interview process. In fact, getting an administrative person on your side may be the best thing you ever do—they are the gatekeepers who answer the phone, do the scheduling, and open the mail!

- **Bring collateral materials.** Remember, this is a sales pitch and you want to be prepared with support materials for the product, you. Bring extra copies of your business cards, resume, and any additional information about yourself. Come prepared with examples (writing samples, websites you've designed, grant proposals you've written, articles published about you—anything to demonstrate your past success). You may never remove these items from your briefcase, but it's better to have them with you for a little show and tell.

- **Have references ready.** You may be asked to fill out a job application, including a list of references, so be sure to have their contact details with you at the interview.

- **Never bad-mouth former employers.** Even though it might feel like loads of fun, it's essential to resist the urge to spill the beans on what you really think of your old boss. The momentary pleasure you'd have knowing the recipient got your tongue wagging just isn't worth the long-term headache it's likely to create. Remember, you never know who they might know. Rest assured that it's natural to feel anger toward an unfair boss. What's not okay is to burn bridges—with a long career awaiting you—based on those feelings. Recruiters see huge red flags when talking to candidates who harbor ill will toward former employers. Leave the baggage behind.

• **Aspire to sparkle.** Emily Viner, a recruiter at Guardian Life Insurance Company, looks for spark when evaluating potential candidates. "Regardless of what someone has done before, they must have a *passion* for something—anything. Whatever it is they're talking about—jobs, family, or an event in the news—I want to see excitement. You can see it in their eyes and hear it in their voice. It tells me they're in the game. This shows me that I'm looking at a person of action and vision with the potential for great things."

Wait a Minute!

If you must get the evil thoughts about a layoff or evil ex-boss out of your system, whip out a pad and scribe the letter of your dreams. Include every bad wish and all the nasty things you're itching to say. Once your note is perfected and you have crossed the T's and dotted the I's, tuck it away for safekeeping or tear it to shreds. Never mail it!

One-Minute Mess-Up

Follow Directions!

One recruiter makes a point of telling interviewees to meet on the twenty-third floor of her office building, even though her office is on sixteen. She says that more than half of the people show up on sixteen because that is where she is listed in the company directory, even though security does not prevent them from going straight to twenty-three. Before the interview even begins, they have one strike against them.

MORE INTERVIEW DOS AND DON'TS

● **Don't** become too familiar with the interviewer. Remain professional at all times.

● **Do** establish commonality—remember to use the research you gained and find a commonality with your interviewer.

● **Don't** respond in basic "yes" or "no" answers—always elaborate.

● **Don't** be shy about asking the interviewer to repeat the question or clarify what they're asking if you're unsure of something.

● **Don't** rush into an answer you're unsure of. If you need a moment to compose your thoughts, it is okay to have a silent pause. This may be seen as a sign of thoughtfulness.

● **Do** speak specifically about your role in any previous successes. Let the interviewer know what you did, said, and thought.

● **Don't** argue with your interviewer, no matter what. If you don't agree with something the interviewer says, you can acknowledge their point by saying, "I understand how you feel about that," and move on to another subject.

RESTAURANT INTERVIEW ETIQUETTE

Some recruiters make a point to interview candidates over a meal. While the free lunch or dinner at a nice place might come as a welcome treat to the unemployed, remember that you are there to get a job, not to eat. This means you must focus on your answers, not on your plate!

During mealtime interviews you are always being watched. Recruiters are paying close attention to how you might represent their company when dining with clients. They are looking at the way you balance conversation and consumption.

- **Make a dry run.** Particularly if you are a picky eater, visit the restaurant a day in advance to review the menu and make a mental note of what to order.

- **Talk while the interviewer eats.** While your guest responds, it is appropriate to take a bite or two. This keeps the conversation flowing without awkward pauses.

- **Do not order expensive items.** While you should not ask for a skimpy side dish instead of the entrée, be careful not to order the forty-eight-dollar fillet.

- **Avoid ordering messy food.** Spaghetti is definitely not the best choice.

- **Stay away from finger foods.** Unless everyone's having pizza, steer clear of clumsy stuff that may require you to use your fingers—oversized sandwiches, ribs, French onion soup with tons of melted cheese, crab claws, and fried chicken.

- **Never drink alcohol.** Even if the interviewer orders an innocent glass of wine, do not be tempted.

- **Don't play with your food.** Some women tend to push food around on the plate. Now is not the time to worry about your diet. Eat the food you ordered.

- **Cut one piece at a time.** Sounds like nursery school advice, but when adults tend to get nervous, many of us may cut up all of our food at once assuming that it will appear less clumsy. Eat each piece before cutting another.

- **Follow proper etiquette.** To signal that you are finished, place the knife and fork across the plate parallel to each other.

BONUS TIP: STEER CLEAR OF THE SALT

There is an old trick among recruiters, even though it is nearly impossible to get many of them to admit to it. They are watching your salt intake and it is not because they're concerned about your blood pressure. A person who douses her food in salt or pepper before tasting it is believed to be someone who routinely rushes to judgment before knowing the facts. She may also be considered someone with firm habits that are not adaptable to different situations. Since you will never know if your interviewer buys into this theory, it is best to never automatically dash the salt or pepper until you have tasted your meal. Once you have tried it and determined that your food could use the extra flavor, by all means sprinkle away.

HOW BADLY DO YOU WANT THE JOB?

Every woman who goes after a job isn't always the best candidate. However, on many occasions the person with the best attitude, the most enthusiasm lands the job and the interviewer's vote of confidence. The key is to deliver what the interviewer is looking for, but you also must look good in the interviewer's eyes. Your best attributes and skills are the key to landing it. And then there's that one special ingredient that matters after all is said and done. How much do you want this job? If you want it because you're in desperate need of income, that will show. However, if you want it because you are the ideal candidate it's critical to make that point loud and clear and go for it.

Close the Deal

Close the interview by asking for the job! Don't be shy if you're really interested. A respectful close might sound like this:

> "Mr. Werner, I appreciate your taking the time to see me. I just want to let you know that I'm very interested in joining your company. I came to know your firm by the research I did before coming in, but now that I've met some of the people I'd be working with and have a better understanding of the job, I'm that much more excited about it. I would love the opportunity to contribute to the success of XYZ Company."

At the very end of the interview, it's appropriate to ask what the next steps in the hiring process will

---

Inside Scoop

Smile and Shine

Resume expert and Harvard graduate Anne McKinney tells us, "lack of experience in the field is frequently the last reason why candidates are not offered jobs. Job hunters should realize that the interview is an opportunity to show their curiosity and personal warmth as well as their enthusiasm for and curiosity about the job. Don't be passive in the interview, waiting for the interviewer to do all the work. Show initiative and ask questions that reveal your intellect and curiosity; ask pertinent questions that show you care about what the interviewer is really looking for. Don't forget to show your personal warmth; in a way, the interview is a personality contest among other things. The interviewer is trying to identify the person who would be the best to work with. Interview research shows that 'those who smile at interviews are perceived as more intelligent than those who do not smile.'

"Interviewers know that an interview *is* stressful, so if the job hunter is a relaxed and smiling individual, the inference is that she must be comfortable with the job requirements while seeming pleasant and agreeable. Go into an interview with the goal of really trying to find out what the organization is looking for, and also go into the interview intent on showing off the most congenial aspects of your personality so that you will appear to be someone whom customers and coworkers would want to work with."

be and to ask for a business card from your interviewer so you can follow up. Listen carefully to the answer and jot it down when you're in the elevator or out of the building. If the interviewer tells you to follow up in a week, mark the date on your calendar and follow up to show your listening skills (in addition to your standard thank-you note follow-up). If she mentions she's going on vacation to Hawaii for two weeks, write it down and remember to welcome her back with an "Aloha!" Not only will you win points for your personal touch, you'll know not to panic when you don't hear from the recruiter for fourteen days.

Inside Scoop

It's Not All About You

Catherine Hughes, chairman and co-founder of Radio One, Inc., offers this advice: "When you are going on a job interview, remember to express your loyalty and commitment to that job, and also how you are going to bust your butt for that company. I'm impressed when a job applicant tells me something they know about my company. For example, are they familiar with Radio One? Do they know who the president of the company is? Who founded it? Instead of sitting there impressed with yourself, express how impressed you are with their company and why. Find out what community service projects the company is involved in and commend them for their efforts. Keep in mind, you are not entitled to a job. You have to impress the person and stand out. It's what you are bringing to the table besides an appetite. Women stand out by being knowledgeable. Remember that you're not just looking for a job, you're looking for an opportunity to make something great."

PSYCHOLOGICAL PROFILING

During the interview process, some companies will utilize employee selection assessments or tools and have you tested by an additional individual who is either a psychologist or a professional with the appropriate training retained by the company to screen applicants. A psychological assessment might make the final decision and the goal is to make sure you are completely screened to match the job that you are applying for. This might include testing and verbal interviews, and all are designed to determine your work habits and appropriateness for this job. Don't be scared—this is common practice and shouldn't intimidate you if you think you're qualified for the position.

According to Dean Stamoulis, Ph.D., executive director at Russell Reynolds Associates, which is an executive recruiting and assessment firm, "Sometimes the information gathered will be used to help the hiring manager make his overall decision, and in other situations the assessment will be used as pass/fail in nature and will require a certain score to obtain that job. A good idea is to ask how the assessment you will be given will be used so that you can prepare. You will likely not be shown the results or allowed the right to see them. If you do get the job, there is the possibility that this information might be shared with you in a helpful manner to assist you in your work."

BEHAVIORAL INTERVIEWING

We know life isn't always fair. Sometimes the job doesn't go to the person with the best credentials, but rather to the candidate

Inside Scoop

Responsibility 101

Gone are the times when Mom yelled, "Who smushed chocolate ice cream all over the sofa?" and you could get away with replying, "Not me!"

Big girls have to fess up.

These days employers want to know—and will ask—about your failures as well as successes. Nobody, not your parents, boss, or best friend, thinks you're perfect, so put aside the excuses and take responsibility for your actions.

You didn't get that D in economics because your professor didn't like you. You got it because you didn't turn in your best work.

You weren't late for an important meeting because of bad traffic. You were tardy because you didn't leave early enough.

Nobody told you to bring resumes and wear business attire to a career fair? What were you thinking?

Don't play the victim. "It wasn't my fault" statements give the worst impression possible. We know life's unfair sometimes. Deal with it, girlfriend. Regardless of your age, a potential employer is looking for someone mature enough to handle responsibility and someone who can demonstrate that she's able to learn from her mistakes.

Among the worst lines to avoid:

"My boss didn't like me so I didn't get the promotion."
"I didn't make dean's list because my professors were unfair."
"It's not my fault I'm late. I had to wait for a long train to cross the tracks."

continued

Stay away from the woe-is-me stuff. Those kinds of downers bring attention to your flaws and they certainly hurt your chances of impressing someone. Instead, show some honesty. "The project wasn't as successful as I thought it would be. And from that disappointing experience I've learned that I have to communicate my ideas better to my team."

who's able to navigate the process most effectively. As we've discussed, basic interviews tend to focus on resume-based questions. They revolve around your education, previous work experience, and future interests. Savvy employers do not stop there. They have adapted their own versions of behavioral interviews, which require candidates to elaborate on prior experiences often using very specific criteria, as opposed to the open-ended and more general questioning in the basic interview.

- Describe a time when you were part of a team where there was conflict between the members.

- Describe a time when you had to put in extra hours to complete a project or assignment.

- Describe a time when you had to satisfy an unhappy customer.

Even with solid work experience, many people just aren't comfortable answering these questions. This is usually because they're not prepared. We'll help you anticipate the likely questions so you're not thrown off guard.

Difficult Topics

EXPLAINING GAPS IN WORK HISTORY

The longer you've been working, the more likely there are to be some gaps in your employment history. Short gaps or transition periods of

Work It, Girl!

Assessing Your Behavior Consider twenty of the most popular behavior-based questions as they relate to your previous experience. Even recent grads can relate educational or part-time work experiences. Make notes about the anecdotes you would share during an interview.

Describe a time when you:

Solved a difficult problem

Worked effectively under pressure

Adapted to a difficult situation

Prepared a presentation that was well received

Failed to complete a project on time

Were disappointed in your behavior

Anticipated potential problems and identified preventive measures

Prioritized the elements of a complicated project

Got bogged down in the details of a project

Made a big decision with limited facts

Surmounted a major obstacle

Persuaded coworkers to do things your way

Defended an unpopular decision

Tolerated an opinion that was different from yours

Delegated a project effectively

Dealt with an angry client

Made a bad decision

Hired the wrong person

Fired someone

Set your sights too low or too high

up to a few months need no explanation. For example, if you graduated in May and became employed full-time in September, there's no need to account for the three months in between. Likewise, if the hiatus occurred several years ago, followed by some solid experience, it's not necessary to include it. Longer periods need details, but it's best to be short and direct. Common explanations include time off for education, travel, parenting, or caring for a sick relative. If a period of unemployment has stretched beyond a few months, it's important to put a positive spin on any accomplishments you've made during this time. We know you haven't just been lying around with a tub of ice cream watching Oprah, right? If you've been training for a marathon, doing volunteer work, gaining proficiency in a computer program, or coordinating your high school reunion, by all means, say so. Be confident of the fact that you were fortunate to have the ability to make those life choices:

"I'm proud to have had the opportunity to take a year off to [travel, care for my aging mother]. It was a rewarding time for me personally, and now I'm of course eager to jump back into the corporate world full-time."

If you've worked interim jobs while trying to establish a career,

Inside Scoop

Sharing Personal Choices

Revealing your association with controversial causes and organizations is a delicate matter that requires serious thought. There's a lot of debate on this issue. Some people believe that candidates should be open and honest about their affiliations. After all, if an employer is unwilling to hire you because of personal choices, then perhaps it's not the right fit. Others are more conservative and believe it's better to research a particular company to determine the tolerance level. Such hot buttons might include alliances with Planned Parenthood or GLAAD. A company like Microsoft, which has a solid reputation as supportive of all minority groups, isn't likely to be offended with such mentions. However, not all employers fall into this category, which is why it's essential to know your audience. Remember, if in doubt—and you're determined to work at a particular company—leave it out. This is especially true if the omission does not compromise your skill set or credibility.

that's okay too. It's nothing to hide; in fact, it shows drive and a great work ethic. While it's important not to lie, it's not necessary to go out of your way to be completely truthful if the reason for your time off may nix your chances at the job. For example, time away to overcome an addiction to drugs or alcohol may be disguised as "travel" or "caring for an ill family member," even if that relative is you. If pressed, you may be forced to open up in confidence to someone in personnel, which is okay as long as it's near the end of the hiring process and you're close to being offered the position.

Avoid sounding skeptical about your time off as it raises unnecessary red flags among potential employers. Do not apologize for those worthwhile responsibilities that required your time and devotion. If you sound positive and proud, recruiters will likely respect your choices.

EXPLAINING BEING FIRED OR LAID OFF

Many job seekers find themselves out of work because of corporate downsizing or the demise of failed start-ups, particularly dot coms. You can almost always count on an interviewer asking about the circumstances surrounding your unemployment. If you have been downsized, you will want to attribute your layoff to changes in the economy and the elimination of your position. If your entire division was eliminated, you will definitely want to include that detail. Do not be ashamed or embarrassed to explain that through no fault of your own, the company made a bottom-line decision that affected you and many other employees. HR managers understand that these things happen all the time, so it will not come as a shock to them.

If you have been fired for other reasons, especially something performance related, you want to avoid addressing that directly. Generally the interviewer will not know those circumstances and you can talk around it. "I left the company because I wanted to seek a more challenging opportunity," "I left my position because I wanted to explore opportunities in other industries," and "I left that job to redirect my career and learn another line of business" are some possible options.

No matter what the circumstances of your situation, the goal is to craft a response that focuses on something positive. Even if you are a victim of downsizing, do not take the opportunity to trash your former employer as unable to compete effectively in their industry. Do not blame incompetency on their part for the shutdown of your division. Explain what you learned from the process and how much you are looking forward to moving on.

Questionable Questions

Occasionally an interviewer ventures into territory you'd rather leave unexplored. Questions that probe for personal details of your life may not be merely awkward, they may, in fact, be illegal. No matter how badly you want a job, you don't have to answer illegal or inappropriate questions. Proper questions focus solely on the job and your ability to do it. What are your rights?

THE LAW IS ON YOUR SIDE

While exact standards vary from state to state, questions may not be asked for the purpose of discriminating on the basis of age, marital status, religion, race and national origin, sex, physical appearance, or disabilities. Don't make a citizen's arrest quite yet, however. "What an unusual name! Where's it from?" may be a devious—and illegal—attempt to extract your ethnic origin, but more likely it's an innocuous conversation starter. An interviewer, after all, wants to get to know you; but an inexperienced one may not know the fine lines of the legal limits. According to author Paul Falcone, larger companies tend to train their managers about the dos and don'ts of interview questions. Smaller companies tend to be more lax about preemployment questions. After all, it's not uncommon to find an entrepreneur who reasons, "This is my company, so I'll select who comes aboard and who doesn't."

While most skilled recruiters know to stand clear of the forbidden topics for fear of potential lawsuits, others manage to find ways to get the answers they're looking for without appearing to cross the line. This holds true particularly with recruiters who prefer a less formal, less structured interview style. Casual or chatty conversation may very well include topics traditionally considered taboo. What to do? Answering outright may reveal something the employer takes as a negative: The friendly question "Is that an *engagement* ring?" may lead to the discovery that your wedding is planned just as their high season kicks into gear.

On the other hand, refusing to answer may make you come across as a potential troublemaker—someone who is uncooperative and confrontational. An appropriate answer is evasive but friendly. In answer to the engagement ring question you might respond, "It is a very special ring, thank you for noticing. It is lovely, isn't it?"

Prohibited topics are not always obvious. The key is to be tactful and prepared. If you're eight months pregnant, it's natural that someone will likely comment on the impending birth, which may in fact be a completely innocent gesture. Being prepared for the potential questions or topics will make you feel more at ease. The first step is to try to recognize the interviewer's intent. One or two seemingly innocent personal questions are probably a blunder; a series of them may signal blatant discrimination, or at the very least, a disrespect for the employment law.

The easiest route is to simply answer the occasional, inoffensive inquiry and move on. An alternative is to ignore the question altogether and continue to another topic. A more offensive question merits: "I'm not really comfortable discussing that." Period. The most graceful maneuver is to figure out what they're really after and address that concern. Make your point without making the interviewer feel embarrassed. Questions regarding marriage, family, and pregnancy plans are often a ploy to see how committed to the job you'll be in terms of extra hours, travel, or child care "emergencies." Assure the interviewer, "I have no problem devoting the necessary time to making sure my job is done."

Take the opportunity to emphasize a positive trait about yourself. Questions about religion may disguise concern over prohibited workdays and holidays. Turn it around to: "I'm hardworking and have never had a conflict between my job and religious beliefs. I get along great with people of all backgrounds."

MORE STICKY ISSUES

Whether a question is permissible often depends on the wording. An employer can't ask if you were born in the United States, but they can ask if you're authorized to work in this country. Interviewers can list the required job duties and ask whether you would be able to perform those functions even though your answer could reveal a disability. If your disability does not prevent you from performing the tasks related to the job, the employer is prohibited from using information about the disability to deny you the job.

Some other red flags:

- How old are you? What's your date of birth? When did you graduate? What they should be asking is whether you meet the minimum age requirements to work.

- Would you like to be addressed as Miss, Mrs., or Ms.? Is that your maiden name? My husband hates when I travel. Does yours?

The interviewer may ask, "How would you like to be addressed?" Questions such as "Would you be willing to relocate/travel/work weekends?" must be asked of all candidates and be part of the job description.

- Where'd you learn to speak Spanish? Do you consider yourself part of a minority group?

If it is pertinent to the job, employers are allowed to ask what languages you speak, read, or write, as well as question your mastery of those languages.

- How tall are you? Have you been tested for HIV? Are you taking any prescription drugs?

Certain positions like flight attendants or firefighters have height or other physical requirements, in which case knowing your stats is key. As a general rule, employers may ask if you are physically capable of performing all of the functions required by the job.

- Have you ever been arrested?

Most states require the question to specify whether an applicant has a felony conviction, not simply an arrest.

In all cases, you should always feel free to ask the interviewer to explain to you the pertinence of the question. For example, "I'm not really sure how that question relates to the position I'm applying for. Would you mind helping me understand so I can give you the most direct and thorough response possible?" If the interviewer is know-ingly treading on thin ice, this gentle reminder will help get things back on track. If the question is truly innocent, your question will force the interviewer to clarify that for you.

If you do sense a pattern of discrimination, don't burn your bridges just yet. One lousy interviewer doesn't make a law-breaking company. When you leave the interview, jot notes on questions you found inappropriate. If you feel any of them relate to not getting a job offer, remedies can include talking to the interviewer's supervisor, the HR manager, or filing a complaint. Check out the EEOC website (www.eeoc.gov) for more information.

Second and Third Interviews

At many organizations the next step after a successful interview is more interviews. You will know if this is a possibility when you ask about next steps at the end of your first interview, so you should always be prepared to go back to the company for an encore. As we mentioned, some companies start with a phone screening and then move to face-to-face interaction. Other companies start with an HR behavioral interview, and then move on to an interview with the manager you'd be reporting to, then invite you in for testing. Still others require several interviews with several members of the team you'll be working with. It's perfectly all right to ask during your first interview what to expect, but often the process will change depend-ing on the level of job you're looking for and the number of candi-dates the company is considering.

Second interviews (and any interviews beyond that) should be treated with as much professionalism as the first meeting. At this point you know they're interested, but you have a few more runs around the bend before reaching that finish line. A huge mistake job seekers make is thinking the second interview is just a formality. You don't have the job yet. Follow these tips to make sure you're in top form until the very, very end:

- Dress formally for every interview, even if the company is casual.

- Get business cards from everyone you meet with at every interview, and send personalized thank-you notes or e-mails to each person, even if you've met with them before. This will really set you apart from the crowd.

- Before each additional interview, review your notes from your first meeting. Make reference to issues you discussed to show your great listening and follow-through skills.

- Review the interview questions you prepared before the first interview. Just because you weren't asked about something in the first meeting, doesn't mean it won't come up later on.

- Never show fatigue at the process or criticize an interviewer for asking the same question in multiple meetings. "I already told you that!" is not an acceptable response.

- Keep up the positive energy at every meeting. Don't let your guard down—be as fresh at interview 27 as you were the first time you walked through the door. An enduring positive attitude will really set you apart from other candidates.

DON'T LET YOUR HAIR DOWN YET, RAPUNZEL

We've heard too many stories that go like this: After her second or third round of interviews, a young woman is feeling pretty good about her chances. The HR manager responsible for filling this

251

position has guided her through the process and the candidate has come to trust this person and feels they've developed some type of bond.

"You're doing so well here with all of these interviews. We're almost ready to wrap it up, which must make you feel great. I know it'll be a load off your shoulders to find out either way," says the manager. The conversation continues and the manager finally asks, "So, I know what your professional interests are, but what about you personally? Are you planning on starting a family soon?"

In a moment of weakness, the woman lets down her hair. "Well, actually, yes. Once I start a job and have a steady income and benefits, I'm definitely hoping to get pregnant."

She feels like she's confiding in a friend. After all, these two women have known each other for several weeks and the HR manager has taken what appears to be a genuine interest in this job seeker.

Don't let yourself fall into this trap! Most women are quick to make friends and share confidences and usually this is a wonderful characteristic. But not in an interview situation. The interviewer is not your friend. Interviewers may be extremely nice, genuine people, but their job is to probe in any way they can to find out whether you are the right candidate for the job they need to fill. They may even create a false sense of security to catch you off guard. Certainly do not treat the interviewer as an adversary, but remember to remain professional and "on" at all times. All times. We mean it—we have seen this ruin the chances of many a qualified, hardworking job seeker who revealed too much to a friendly recruiter. Be friendly, but also be smart. And be careful.

Effective Follow-Up

The most fabulous interview in the world can be ruined by ineffective follow-up. Polite persistence is the key to moving forward and crossing the finish line. Composing a thank-you note following a job interview is slightly different than writing a note after a more casual networking meeting or even an informational interview. Your goals are very specific—reiterate your interest in the position and the key reasons you feel you are a good match for the position.

ANATOMY OF A POST-INTERVIEW THANK-YOU NOTE

- Send or e-mail a thank-you note no more than twenty-four hours after your interview.

- Thank the interviewer for their time and any information they provided.

- Refer (very briefly) to something specific in the interview— a commonality with the interviewer, a specific aspect of the position you feel is perfectly suited to your skills, a mutual contact.

- Reiterate your interest in the position.

- Sign off by saying you look forward to following up according to the instructions provided at the end of your interview (Aren't you glad you jotted them down?).

DOS AND DON'TS OF THANK-YOU NOTES

- **Do** write a thank-you note even if you think you didn't get the job. You'll be remembered as a total professional and potentially dedicated person. Plus, you never know who was next in line should a job ever open!

- **Do** thank everyone you met with during the interview process, but . . .

- **Don't** send the exact same note to several people. Colleagues compare notes and you'll look lazy if you send the same note to five people. A small personalization (one or two unique sentences are fine) for each note makes a big difference.

- **Do** provide your full contact details along with your thank-you note. Make it easy for the recruiter to follow up and offer you another interview or make the offer.

Sample Thank-You Notes

Dear Ms. Simon:

Thank you for taking the time to discuss the assistant investment broker position at Los Angeles Investment Bankers with me. After meeting with you, I am convinced that the financial world is exactly the career I was looking for as I completed my college years. I was particularly impressed by your enthusiastic description of the work environment at LAIB and the cultural climate in Los Angeles. I already knew that LAIB has the best reputation for performance as well as integrity; I was impressed to see how professionally and soundly your people make it function.

I appreciate all the time you took to introduce me to the company and the industry. I feel certain that my qualifications would help me to fit smoothly into the team at LAIB, especially since I've interned with your partner firm, Mississippi Investments Bankers, for the past three summers. As promised, my mentor at MIB, Lyons Heyman, will be sending you a letter of recommendation this week.

If I can provide any further information to help you reach your decision, please contact me at any time. Again, thank you for your time and consideration.

Sincerely,

Sue Castle

. . . .

ARE YOU SURE IT'S OKAY TO E-MAIL A THANK-YOU?

Until recently, an e-mailed thank-you didn't illustrate the same warmth and sincerity as a handwritten or typed thank-you on your letterhead or personal stationery. However, the world is changing and e-mail has become an acceptable and efficient way to communicate. The job market is a fast-moving one, so it can be best to get back to people instantly. If the employer gave you his or her personal e-mail address, then under some circumstances this could be appropriate. However, some individuals keep their e-mail private and you will do best by sending it care of their assistant or secretary to be forwarded.

E-MAIL THANK-YOU ETIQUETTE

- Make the subject line specific so they'll open the mail. It might read: A Special Thank You From Karen Emery.

- Write the same letter you'd have written for "snail mail."

• Don't type in all caps. It's difficult to read and is considered rude.

• Do not e-mail the person a follow-up to see if they read your thank-you note. If you are concerned about that, then also send a hard copy in the mail. It's perfectly fine to send both an e-mail thank-you and a written note.

SOMETIMES WORK DOES MEAN HAVING TO SAY YOU'RE SORRY

If you've made a mistake, or forgotten an interview, or neglected to send a thank-you note, don't shrug it off. A heartfelt apology will almost always be accepted and can more than erase the negative of the original "sin." Always admit a wrongdoing and exhibit your character. Apologize professionally, briefly, and ask for the opportunity to start over. Here's an example:

Dear Ms. Bartholomew:

Please forgive my horrible breach of etiquette in missing our appointment last Friday. I hadn't realized that the Labor Day weekend traffic would be so incredibly bad. I left Ann Arbor at 10:00 A.M. for our 2:30 P.M. appointment, for what is normally barely an hour's drive. I sat in unmoving traffic until 4:00 P.M. because of that fatal bus accident on the highway.

By the time I reached an exit and called, you had closed for the long weekend. I am so sorry to have missed you. I do hope you will allow me to call and reschedule our appointment. As we had discussed on the phone, I am certain you will be as impressed by my credentials (my judgment of driving time in traffic excepted) as I am by the opportunities available at Barth Media.

Again, please forgive me. I will call on Wednesday morning to request an interview and hope you will welcome my call.

Sincerely,

Carla Lovell

CHAPTER THIRTEEN

Evaluating Offers and Sealing the Deal

Hurrah! Whoopee! After all of your hard work, you finally hear the magic words: "We'd like to make you an offer." You did it. Congratulations. You rock. But keep your head on straight 'cause it ain't over yet. First, be sure to thank the recruiter or person offering you the job graciously for offering you a position. Generally the job initially will be offered to you by phone, so you'll have the opportunity to ask a few questions and find out the exact details of the offer. Always keep a pen and paper near your phone (or in your handbag in case the call comes on your cell phone) so you can take notes.

When you are offered a position, there are some essentials you need to know in order to evaluate the situation. At this point, you're in a great spot—they want you!—so don't be afraid to find out all the information you need to evaluate the offer:

- What is the proposed start date for the job?

- What is the compensation package, including all possible benefits: sign-on bonus, relocation allowance, vacation days, bonus structure, 401(k) match, overtime policy, tuition reimbursement, stock options, profit sharing, gym membership, mileage allowance, commission bonuses, performance/salary review after the first ninety days, company-sponsored discounts on popular goods and services, parking and/or commuting allowance, and of course, various health and dental benefits? Be sure to ask when benefits (particularly health coverage) will begin.

- What are the travel requirements of the position?

- What is the title?

- Is the offer subject to any conditions, such as a background check, past employment verification, drug test, or security clearance? Some companies are required to do this before making an offer, but others will wait for your acceptance before wasting their time and money on tests or checks. It's important to establish what the company's policy is and what the consequences will be.

When you have the answers to the above questions, you'll need some time to think. Remember, many of the elements of your offer are negotiable (we'll get to that in a minute), so you need to think about what's most important to you. Tell the person offering the job: "Thank you very much for offering me a position with your company. I'd like a little time to consider your offer. May I get back to you in twenty-four or forty-eight hours?"

QUESTIONS TO ASK YOURSELF

Although it's hard to turn down an offer for any job, especially if you've been unemployed for a long period of time, you must feel confident that you'll be happy in your new position. Sit down with your pen and paper and ask yourself the following questions. Remember to refer back to the self-assessment activities you completed at the beginning of this book.

- What is the potential for career advancement in this position and this company? Ultimately, the potential in a position is worth more than the starting salary.

- Is this the industry you want to be in right now? Consider this question particularly carefully if you are a recent grad. Is this the field where you want to pay your dues and start working your way up the ladder?

- Will I be happy with the lifestyle and work schedule associated with this position?

- Am I happy with the size of my team and the size of the company in general?

Avoid making the mistake of accepting a position that won't make you happy. If you accept an offer that doesn't meet at least your minimum requirements, chances are you'll be job hunting again in no time.

Salary Negotiation

When you do choose to accept an offer, the final step of the process is negotiating your compensation package. The average woman still earns about seventy-three cents for every dollar a man earns. Frankly, we're sick of it. Inequality is old-fashioned. And smart women are worth a lot. Don't just take it from us. We called on the experts at www.salary.com for advice on negotiating the big bucks that we know we deserve.

Women For Hire: What are the top three rules for job seekers to follow to successfully negotiate the best possible compensation package?

Salary.com: Successful negotiation is based on preparation and patience. Always anticipate what you may need to know when you next speak with any potential employer.

- **Research your value.** Research the value of your talent in the employment marketplace. Find sources that tell you what companies pay for the job you're considering. The sources should take into account the size of the company you work for and its industry and region. It is even more helpful if you can use a source that helps you calculate the potential value of your personal skills and background such as education, length of experience, certifications, and management responsibility. In addition to www.salary.com, check out these websites to compare salaries: www.jobstar.org and www.wageweb.com.

- **Don't be the first to disclose a number.** If possible, try to get the employer to disclose the pay for the job before you tell your requirements. If you find this too difficult or awkward, consider providing a broad range (based on the research you did above) and say you expect "a fair total pay package for the job and my unique set of skills, including . . ."

- **Prepare a counteroffer.** About half of all job seekers accept the first offer that's put on the table, but some employers make offers expecting candidates to counteroffer—so go ahead, ask for what you want. Remember that your counteroffer can include more than just base pay; it can include bonuses, stock options, vacation time, and a flexible working schedule. Every time you speak with a potential employer, you should be prepared with a complete, prioritized summary of your ideal offer and you should know in your mind how negotiable you are on each item.

Women For Hire: What mistakes are often made by job seekers when negotiating compensation?
Salary.com:

● **Not being prepared with relevant information.** Spending a little time learning how the relevant labor market values a particular job and how your unique skills may further increase those values can have a dramatic impact on your ability to maximize your total compensation. Knowing the facts and being able to speak intelligently about them can support and justify your desired pay.

● **Neglecting to negotiate things beyond base pay.** Base salary is just one of the negotiation points. There are many more items to consider when negotiating your initial employment package, such as performance expectations, benefits, and schedule for salary increase. Once the salary negotiation is complete, moving on to the other components of total pay can be rewarding.

Relocating

Career moves often require geographic moves. If you are negotiating a job offer that involves moving, you'll need to figure out how much it will cost to ship your worldly possessions to a particular place and the cost of living in that location.

The web is the best place to look for cost of living comparisons, from salary calculators to housing costs. HomeFair.com (www.homefair.com) has a variety of tools that calculate the cost of moving, the cost of living, and the quality of life in various places. 1stmovingdirectory.com (www.1stmovingdirectory.com) also covers aspects of moving your stuff and your family.

Don't forget the psychological costs of moving. Will your spouse like the new climate? Will your kids be happy changing schools? Does your new location offer social activities and organizations that are important to your personal life? If you're single, will your new location be a hard place to date or meet other singles?

Women For Hire: If a job seeker has been earning $30,000 and the position they're applying for typically pays $48,000, what can the candidate do to avoid being lowballed by the employer?

Salary.com: Again, do your homework!

- **Be sure you're qualified for the new position.** A dramatic difference in pay like this (60 percent increase) may actually indicate a promotion or perhaps a position that is significantly more demanding than your current role. Be prepared to answer the questions on these issues.

- **Determine the differences, if any, between the content of the current job and the new job.** Knowing the differences between the jobs will help to explain why the pay packages are different. It will also help to demonstrate that you have the skills to meet the challenges of the new position. For instance, if you are moving from a nonprofit or government organization to a large corporation, you will most likely be able to increase your pay significantly.

- **Determine all the differences in the total rewards packages including pay, schedule, benefits, and intangibles.**

There may be differences other than just the base pay—this is particularly likely if there's a vast difference in the base pay but not a major difference in the job responsibilities. You may find differences in bonus opportunity, profit sharing, stock options, benefit plans, and vacation time.

- **Reconcile the real differences between the jobs.** Create a side-by-side summary of the individual job responsibilities, qualifications, compensation, benefits, intangibles, etc. Add an extra column to summarize the magnitude of the differences. Note the key differences in each category for use in negotiations.

- **Focus salary discussions on the market data for the new job (rather than your current pay at your current job).** Your current pay is not really relevant if the market data for the job establishes a reasonable pay of $48,000 and your skills and experience demonstrate you're a fit for the job. Of course you shouldn't tell a potential employer that the information is not relevant, but you can lead them to that conclusion by focusing on the much more relevant market data and value of the job in question and your value as an employee with a set of skills that qualifies you for that job.

- **Avoid disclosing your current salary if possible.** If the potential employer does not know your current salary is $30,000, there is no problem. If asked what your current salary is, you can try to deflect the question by responding with something like, "I'd expect to be paid reasonably for someone with my skills [name a few] working in this job. Based on what I've seen, it seems that would be between $46,000 and 53,000."

- **Keep discussions focused on the new job, the salary for that job, and you in that job. (Leave the past in the past.)**

Being underpaid at your current job doesn't give your new employer license to underpay you as well. It does, however, give you a justifiable reason to look for a new job.

• **If your current salary is known, use the three to five most compelling differences to justify why you deserve at least the $48,000.** Don't try to overwhelm a potential employer with an impressive litany of differences between the two jobs that justifies the pay differential. Selectively choose three to five of the major reasons. Including a lot of the minor differences will simply dilute the impact of the major ones.

• **If possible, use other current salary offers to justify what you are worth and to mitigate the effect of your current pay.** If the employer thinks your current salary is relevant, you can bring in salaries from other current job offers. These have the added effect of implying a value for you in the job as well as the fact that you are a desirable employee for this type of job. (Of course, this cannot work with the first new offer.)

• **If you're gutsy, try to justify why you deserve $50,000 to $55,000.** The job *typically* pays $48,000—perhaps you're better than typical. If the employer sees that, then you should be worth more than $48,000. Go for it!

GET IT IN WRITING

Remember, you don't have the job until you have the offer letter in hand. Be sure to take careful notes during any negotiation with a company so you have your own record of the discussion. Ask for any special compensation or flextime arrangements to be included in the offer letter. If the letter doesn't outline everything you discussed, you can, politely of course, negotiate further. Now is the time to ensure you have the arrangement you want. You'll lose much of your negotiating leverage once you start the job. Remember, it is your right to a clearly outlined offer letter. Don't start a job without one.

How to Say No Gracefully

It's a problem we all want to have, but a problem nonetheless. Sometimes a position, salary, or company culture just isn't a good match. How do you turn down an offer? It's important never to burn bridges—especially with those who offer you a job. Tact is key.

When a company offers you a job you choose not to accept, give yourself some time to think about your response. Thank them for the offer, then ask if you can get back to them in twenty-four or forty-eight hours. It's okay to turn down an offer by phone and formally in writing. Tell the recruiter the job is not for you, but thank him for his time and tell him you'd definitely like to stay in touch. Be honest and show respect for his time. Also let the recruiter know that if you come across anyone who might be a good match, you'll let him know.

As with any contact, keep in touch with recruiters you've turned down. Tell them where you end up and send them periodic hellos if you think you may be interested in working for their company in the future. Also remember that recruiters are mobile too—they may leave and work for another company where you may encounter them again.

Handling Rejection

GET OVER IT AND GET ON WITH IT!

Like so many other things we're involved in, a job search brings its fair share of stress and failure. A call we place to a recruiter seeking an interview that goes unanswered for days or weeks may be seen as a failure. Our inability to land an interview after sending out dozens of resumes may feel like a failure. It's all around us and we can't escape, but we can control our reaction to it.

- Ask for feedback. If you don't get the job, call and ask the person what you could have done differently to have been hired. Ask for specific recommendations and honest guidance. Be sure to send a thank-you note expressing how much you appreciated the feedback.

- Reassess the situation. If you keep getting big fat *no*s, consider what might be the problem. Are you overqualified or underqualified for the positions you're pursuing? Do your skills match those required? Are your tools for communication effective?

- Always ask for referrals. Even if the person you are talking to cannot help you directly, ask if they might refer you to someone else. The more you build your network the faster you'll find success.

* Propose part-time work. If you're turned down for a full-time slot, you might consider offering to work on a part-time or trial basis to prove yourself and save the employer money. While they might not be able to extend an offer for an $80,000-a-year position, they may have $3,000 to spend on a project consultant. Flexibility could land that money in your bank account.

* Suck it up. While we want you to maintain your pride most of the time, some of the time it's essential to keep checking back with contacts who've been less than helpful. Don't shy away from continuing to touch base. Jobs open regularly and you may stumble upon some lucky timing.

* Change courses. If one person rejects you, it doesn't mean another person within the same company can't assist you. *Fortune* 500 employers especially are mighty big. Even if one division says no, don't give up hope on the whole company. Try other departments and find new contacts.

* Rejection rhymes with perfection. As corny as it sounds, being rejected should force you to rethink your strategy and perfect any flaws. Consider your resume, presentation style, even your phone manner.

* Don't underestimate the power of your personality. Women are hired often because of their determination and willingness to do what it takes to learn the necessary skills to succeed, even if they do not already possess all of the requirements. This is directly attributed to the power of persuasion from a convincing communicator.

* Refuse to give up. You have the opportunity to land a job through the oddest places—from contacts at your hair salon and

neighbors in line in the grocery store to alumni contacts and former colleagues. Commit to keep plugging away every day no matter how difficult the task appears.

- Fight back. For every rejection you receive, make it a rule to send resumes to five new contacts. By increasing the number of jobs you pursue, you will most definitely increase your chances of landing one.

CHAPTER FOURTEEN

Day One and Beyond

First of all, *congratulations!* You've made it through the ups and downs of job searching and you've negotiated a great salary and benefits. Now it's time to shine. While your first few weeks will likely be dominated by HR paperwork and getting up to speed on company processes and individual job tasks, there are many actions you can take to pave your way to employee stardom. Happy employees are productive employees.

Meet and Greet. From the CEO to the mailroom clerk, now is the time to say hello and introduce yourself around the company. You never know which colleagues you'll need help from in the future, so be sure to greet everyone with the same enthusiasm and friend-

Inside Scoop

Prediction from Faith Popcorn

The famous futurist predicts that a growing trend among women is that many of us will start our own companies at some point. In preparation for that, Popcorn says that throughout your career "start to look around for potential partners, educate yourself on how to run a company. Learn from HR people and the financial people. Learn from everyone, not just in your department. Get a total picture of how that company is run."

Recession-Proofing
Your Career

Resume expert Anne McKinney says the best way to recession-proof your career is to gain as many skills and as much knowledge in as many different areas as possible. "Welcome opportunities to cross train in new areas of operation within the company that currently employs you. Use initiative to go get new knowledge or skills; for example, enroll in community college courses that will advance your knowledge. If you are a young person, aggressively seek to diversify your base of competencies so that you will have two or three areas of strength that would be fertile job-hunting avenues. Finally, do the kind of work in your current job that you will be able to show off on a resume—if you find yourself in a job hunt. Increase market share, boost sales, cut costs, improve customer satisfaction, and make a difference in the bottom line of your employer."

liness. Making a good first impression will help you for years down the road.

Ask Questions. Take advantage of your New Girl status and ask lots of questions (without becoming annoying of course!). Now is the time to find out how to send FedEx packages, where the coffee filters are kept, how to order office supplies—don't wait until it's 4:59 P.M. on a Friday and you're desperate!

Set Goals. Writing down your goals is one of the best ways to ensure achieving them. Think about the projects you can complete in your first three months and make a list of colleagues or clients you'd like to meet with over lunch. We recommend sharing your goals with your boss to let her know you're ambitious and anxious to demonstrate your skills quickly.

Keep Networking. Be sure to send a message announcing your new position to everyone who helped in your job search. Keeping these contacts is crucial to the long-term success of your career—particularly the networking contacts you made in your industry.

Mentoring

We know how hard you've worked to land a great job. We know you've worked just as hard to start off on the right foot with your colleagues and clients. Now it's time to start planning your rise up that infamous ladder of success: It's time to turn your job into a career. Finding a mentor is a crucial step because it's easier to advance with confidence when someone is cheering you on. A mentor serves as an adviser, coach, role model, cheerleader, and all-around helping hand for your career. According to Sheila Wellington, president of Catalyst, the preeminent nonprofit organization that monitors the progress of executive women in the workplace, and author of *Be Your Own Mentor,* the single most important reason why men tend to rise higher in their careers than equally talented women is that most of them have found mentors along the way. Sounds like a challenge to us! Every smart woman needs a mentor so we can break that glass ceiling once and for all.

BEEN THERE, DONE THAT

Mothers, grandmothers, big sisters, teachers, counselors, friends. Every step of our lives we've looked to more experienced people to help us along—to offer encouragement and evaluate our choices and decisions. We value their advice because they've traveled along a similar path—the "Been There, Done That" school of expertise.

A mentor is someone in our lives who has "Been There, Done That" professionally: A more experienced person who is willing to share wisdom to help someone else grow. A mentor may just be more important to your career advancement than degrees, experience, hard work, and lucky breaks. So don't be shy—asking for a helping hand may be the best career move you ever make.

Wait a Minute! ....

"Everything a woman does is a job," says former CNN anchor Lynne Russell. "We find it so easy to make commitments and so difficult to walk away—whether we're running a marathon or an office." To balance the endless pressure of always being on the go, Russell, who wrote *How to Win Friends, Kick Ass & Influence People,* advises women to "make a point of asking ourselves if we're having a good time. If we aren't, then we should feel free to make adjustments. We tend to ask too much of ourselves, trying to be all things to all people, answering everyone's needs, often at our own expense. So, as you start your exciting new position, remember to take care of yourself. You're worth it."

....

FIVE STEPS TO FINDING AND KEEPING A MENTOR

The key is to choose a mentor who has valuable professional expertise in your field and the time and willingness to help guide you through your career.

- **Start with a clear focus.** Take some time to think about your long-term career goals, time frame, and commitment level, just as you did at the beginning of your job search. What are your biggest issues right now? What are your biggest obstacles? Where do you feel you need the most guidance (networking, education, company politics, work/life balance)? Write down your answers.

- **Look under your nose and far beyond it.** Make a list of all the people you admire professionally. Look both to your personal network and to leaders in your field. Consider former colleagues and clients, professional association members, family friends, and alumni of your college or university. Also consider formal mentoring programs offered through your company or professional association. Start off by considering anyone as a potential mentor—you have nothing to lose!

- **Interview prospective mentors.** Once you've decided on your top choices for mentor, ask each of them out for coffee or lunch. Tell each prospect that you are looking for a mentor to guide you in your career, and explain what goals you are hoping to achieve. Show them your plans and share your issues. Be honest about what you hope to get out of the relationship, and be honest about why you think each person might be a good choice. Most people will be flattered that their guidance is of interest to you, and most people will be honest about their ability to commit to helping you.

- **Be clear about time commitments and expectations.** While many people may want to help you, not everyone has the time to take on the commitment of mentorship. Be clear about how much time both mentor and mentee can commit to the relationship. Try starting with monthly chats or meetings to get to know each other and set clear goals with time frames attached. With modern technology, mentoring can take place by phone, e-mail, or even instant messaging, but it's important to be clear about expectations on both sides so that no one feels overburdened or neglected.

- **Remember that mentoring is a two-way street.** For mentoring to be effective, both the mentor and the mentee must benefit. Mentors can learn from the freshness of the mentee while working through her career issues together. The best professionals learn from all experiences, including teaching and coaching others. So choose your mentor wisely and constantly reassess the helpfulness of the relationship to your career. Relationships may change over time.

QUESTIONS ABOUT MENTORING

Can my mentor be a man?

The choice of a mentor is very personal so it's up to you whether you feel more comfortable with a man or a woman. In some male-dominated industries, it may be necessary to choose a senior man who is well connected and encouraging of a woman rising up the ranks. Comfort level is more important than gender when forging a successful mentor-mentee relationship.

Can my boss be my mentor?

We recommend against a mentoring relationship with your direct report. Try strategizing your salary negotiation with the person who's making the decision! It's crucial to have a good relationship with your boss, but it's wise to have an outside adviser as well. In fact, former bosses often make great mentors.

Can I have more than one mentor?

While it's best to start with one committed mentor relationship, there's no need to limit yourself to one mentor throughout your career. Issues will come up and your path will certainly change, so be open to different mentors at different stages of your career. Some professionals assemble an informal board of directors—a group of people—friends, colleagues, professionals—they call upon with different issues and questions.

MENTOR MISTAKES

Sheila Wellington of Catalyst shares three mentoring mistakes that can ruin a relationship:

- Don't expect miracles—that big promotion, an instant network. Your mentor may open some doors for you, but don't assume that she will open all of them.

- Don't be defensive—in order to gain the most from a mentoring relationship, you must be open to advice and feedback.

- Mentoring is not a one-way street—you must give back, be loyal, return favors.

Inside Scoop

Professional Coaches

While most mentor-mentee relationships are voluntary, more and more professional women are seeking the guidance of professional career coaches. Coaching is a relatively new profession: A career coach is paid to help you develop career goals and achieve them in an agreed-upon time frame. Kind of a career therapist! As with all professional service providers, it's important to evaluate a coach's credentials and his or her style. Coaches can be very expensive, so choose wisely if you decide on this path.

MENTOR MOMENTS

Once you have a committed, enthusiastic mentor, be sure to use his or her time wisely. Set clear goals from the start and write down new issues as they arise. Mentors cannot solve every problem or strategize about every daily decision, so be choosy about the issues you bring to your mentoring relationship.

Issues that merit mentoring include:

- Evaluating new job offers and compensation packages.

- Acclimating to a new position, company, boss, or project.

- Negotiating work/life balance issues.

- Dealing with difficult colleagues or clients.

- Decisions regarding adult education or returning to school for an advanced degree.

- References to other professionals or organizations that might help to advance your career.

DON'T JUST HAVE ONE, BE ONE!

Once you've secured a mentor for yourself, give some thought to mentoring someone junior to you. Even in your first job you can mentor an intern or college student. You'll feel good about helping someone else succeed and we guarantee you'll be surprised at the amount you can learn from a beginner in your field. Consider a mentee to be a source of information about the future of your company or industry—you'll be sure to garner some crucial tidbits for your own advancement to higher and higher levels. The best mentoring creates a web of professional relationships that grows as each mentor and mentee weaves her own path of success. Human resource consultant Dr. Ava S. Wilensky adds, "If someone mentors you or helps you and the situation or job opportunity does not work out for whatever reason, before you make the decision to quit or turn a job down, it's important to check with the person who initially connected you and invested a great deal of time in helping you get there. It's a courtesy to acknowledge their efforts and keep them in the loop. Let them know because it could impact them and their perception of how they choose to help you in the future."

A Final Note

DON'T FORGET HOW YOU GOT THERE

There are endless occasions in life to express your appreciation to another person who has guided, mentored, or assisted you in some small or big way. Express your genuine thanks in writing and with a phone call. It's a lifelong talent and art to remember those people to whom you owe gratitude. Give credit to anyone who has helped you along the way. A note to someone's boss can also work wonders offering positive feedback about a person who was kind enough to assist you. The bottom line is not to forget who helped you climb the ladder to success. The key to being grateful, however, is not just to thank someone, but to celebrate that person's contribution to your life. Down the road, send an update to say how you are doing and let them know you haven't forgotten their generosity. Another way to honor someone's deed to you is to pass one along to another job-hunting candidate in the future.

Remember how you got where you are today and know that you'll need ongoing support to achieve your dreams. Anything is possible with solid skills, a strong network, and all the smarts and gutsiness you have inside. Dream big and go for it! We believe in you.

JOB SEEKER'S CHECKLIST

O Focused job search goal

O Notebook to keep track of networking and job contacts

O Exploration of volunteer, internship, and freelance
   opportunities

O Impressive, clear, error-free resume

O Cover letter template, to be customized for each position

O Resume posted on general and industry-specific job-search
   websites

O Business cards

O List of stellar references

O Professional interview outfit

○ Sales pitch and cold-calling script

○ Attendance at networking events, associations, career fairs

○ Coordination of informational interviews and networking meetings

○ Registration with job placement and temp agencies

○ Extensive research before interviews and preparation of questions for interviewer

○ Practice answers to likely interview questions

○ Thank-you notes after every interview or networking interaction

○ Research of salary ranges in your industry

○ Assessment of most important benefits

○ Request for job offers in writing

○ Announcement of new position to all networking contacts and references

○ Mentor at new company

○ Celebration of success!

RESOURCE GUIDE

INTERNET JOB-SEEKING RESOURCES

General Job Listings
www.careerbuilder.com
www.monster.com
www.hotjobs.com
www.wetfeet.com
www.flipdog.com
www.worktree.com
www.nytimes.com/jobs
www.careers.wsj.com

Especially for First Timers
www.collegerecruiter.com
www.jobweb.com
www.jobtrak.com

Executive Job Listings
(note that some of these sites may require a fee)
www.6figurejobs.com
www.execunet.com
www.futurestep.com

Media Industry Job Listings
www.mediabistro.com
www.journalismjobs.com
www.mandy.com
www.nynma.org/careers

Finance Job Listings
www.careers-in-finance.com
www.jobsinthemoney.com
www.financialjobs.com
www.fjn.com
www.nbn-jobs.com

Marketing/Advertising/PR/Sales Job Listings
www.marketingjobs.com
www.tigerjobs.com
www.jobs4sales.com
www.odwyerpr.com

Technology Job Listings
www.tech-engine.com
www.dice.com
www.computerjobs.com
www.techies.com

Government and Nonprofit
Job Listings
www.govtjobs.com
www.usajobs.opm.gov
www.nonprofitjobs.org
www.idealist.org
www.opportunityNOCS.org
www.fedworld.gov/jobs/
jobsearch.html

Out-of-the-Ordinary/Nontraditional/
Adventure Job Listings
www.jobmonkey.com
www.funjobs.com
www.backdoorjobs.com

Diversity Job Listings
www.imdiversity.com
www.hirediversity.com
www.latpro.com

ONLINE SELF-ASSESSMENT RESOURCES

Michigan Occupational Information System Self-Assessment:
www.expage.com/SelfAssessment
This site offers a number of surveys to evaluate an individual's personality and strengths and weaknesses. The goal is ultimately to inform them which work environments are best for them.

The Princeton Review Career Quiz:
www.review.com

Campbell Interest and Skill Survey:
www.usnews.com/usnews/nycu/work/
wocciss.htm

Career Explorer: Career Explorer's Assessment Test
www.careerexplorer.net/features/
career_assessment.asp

The Career Key:
www.ncmentor.org/InterestSurvey/

The Keirsey Temperament Sorter:
www.keirsey.com/

Self-Directed Search:
www.self-directed-search.com/
www.test.com
Secure preemployment testing.

www.assessment.com
Free career analysis lets you figure out your strengths, temperament, and job type preferences.

www.acareertest.com
This site helps you identify the top careers that match your interests and career aptitude, your personality and work style patterns.

ONLINE SALARY RESOURCES
www.salary.com
www.theshadownegotiation.com
www.wageweb.com

COMPANY RESEARCH TOOLS
www.hoovers.com
www.wetfeet.com
www.vault.com

NETWORKING ORGANIZATIONS AND ASSOCIATIONS

You're not alone. There are organizations waiting to help you network and learn the ins and outs of your profession. Once you've chosen a field, you'll find many specific groups aimed at helping you.

Associations and Resource Organizations

American Academy of Actuaries
www.actuary.org

American Association of Medical Assistants
www.aama-ntl.org

American Association of Dental Assistants
www.dentalassistant.org

American Association of University Women
www.aauw.org

American Bar Association
www.abanet.org

American Business Women's Association
www.abwahq.org

American Chemical Society
www.chemistry.org

American Dental Association
www.ada.org

American Health Care Association
www.ahca.org

American Health Information Management Association
www.ahima.org

American Hospital Association
www.aha.org

American Institute of Architects
www.aia.org

American Institute of Certified Public Accountants
www.aicpa.org

American Medical Technologists
www.amt1.com

American Nurses Association
www.nursingworld.org

American Society for Information Science
www.asis.org

American Society of Journalists and Authors
www.asja.org

American Society of Mechanical Engineers
www.asme.org

American Society of Women Accountants
www.aswa.org

American Women in Radio & Television
www.awrt.org

American Zoo and Aquarium
Association
www.aza.org

Association for Women in
Communications
www.womcom.org

Association for Women in Computing
www.awc-hq.org

Association for Women in Science
www.awis.org

Association of Women in the Metal
Industries
www.awmi.com

Association of Women Professionals
www.awoman.org

Business and Professional Women
USA
www.bpwusa.org

Business Women's Network
www.bwni.com

Catalyst
www.catalystwomen.org

Cosmetic Executive Women
www.cew.org

DigitalEve
www.digitaleve.com

DigitalSistas
www.digitalsistas.net

Editorial Freelancers Association
www.the-efa.org

Executive Women International
www.executivewomen.org

Federally Employed Women
www.few.org

Financial Women International
www.fwi.org

Financial Women's Association
www.fwa.org

Institute of Industrial Engineers
www.iienet.org

International Association of
Administrative Professionals
www.iaap-hq.org

MilitaryWoman.org
www.militarywoman.org

National Association of Career
Women
www.nacwonline.org

National Association of Insurance
Women
www.naiw.org

National Association for Female
Executives (NAFE)
www.nafe.com

National Association for Law
Placement
www.nalp.org

National Association of Securities
Dealers
www.nasd.com

National Association of Women
Business Owners (NAWBO)
www.nawbo.org

National Association of Women in
Construction
www.nawic.org

National Black MBA Association
www.nbmbaa.org

National Society of Hispanic MBAs
www.nshmba.org

National Network of Commercial
Real Estate Women
www.crewnetwork.org

National Society of Black Engineers
www.nsbe.org

9to5: National Association of
Working Women
www.9to5.org

Promotion Marketing Association of
America
www.pmalink.org

Public Relations Society of America
www.prsa.org

Securities Industry Association
www.sia.com

Society for Human Resource
Management
www.shrm.org

Society of Manufacturing Engineers
www.sme.org

Society of Women Engineers
www.swe.org

U.S. Hispanic Chamber of Commerce
www.ushcc.com

Women Executives in State
Government
www.wesg.org

Women in Cable &
Telecommunications
www.wict.org

Women in Government Relations
www.wgr.org

Women in Packaging
www.womeninpackaging.org

Women in Technology International
(WITI)
www.witi.org

Women Unlimited
www.women-unlimited.com

Women's Council of Realtors
www.wcr.org

WorldWIT (Women in Technology)
www.worldwit.org

EVENT LISTINGS
*These sites cover major markets. Check
your local area for similar resources filled
with a variety of events relating to all
interests.*

Major Cities
Craig's List
www.craigslist.org

Citysearch
www.citysearch.com

Digital City
www.digitalcity.com

Atlanta (www.accessatlanta.com);
Austin (www.austin360.com);
Boston (www.boston.com);
Chicago (www.chiweb.com);
Dallas (www.guidelive.com);
Denver (www.denver.com, www.
dodenever.com);
Houston (www.houston.com)
Los Angeles (www.la.com);
Miami (www.miami.com, www.
miamiandbeaches.com);
New York (www.newyorkmetro.com,
www.alleyevent.com, www.
bernardoslist.com);
Portland (www.portland-oregon.com);
Sacramento (www.sacramento.com);
San Diego (www.sandiego.com);
San Francisco (www.sanfran.com);
Seattle (www.seattleinsider.com);
Washington, D.C. (www.dcregistry.
com)

BOOKS
There are probably as many books written about jobs as there are jobs. You'll find volumes on every facet of job hunting, job keeping, quitting, and switching. How to dress, how to act, talk, think—it's all written down somewhere. Here are some top titles to support your career advancement efforts.

Be Your Own Mentor. Sheila Wellington. New York: Random House, 2001.

Do What You Are: Discover the Perfect Career for You Through the Secrets of Personality Type. Paul D. Tieger and Barbara Barron-Tieger. New York: Little, Brown, 2001.

I Could Do Anything If I Only Knew What It Was: How to Discover What You Really Want and How to Get It. Barbara Sher and Barbara Smith. New York: Dell, 1994. This book focuses on helping you decide your dreams, determine your goals, and helps you reach them.

The Hiring and Firing Question and Answer Book. Paul Falcone. New York: AMACOM Books, 2001.

What Color Is Your Parachute: A Practical Manual for Job-Hunters & Career-Changers. Richard Nelson Bolles. Berkeley, CA: Ten Speed Press, 2001. The best-selling job-hunting book in history, crammed with career advice and thought-provoking exercises to help find the career and job that are right for you. And if you enjoy the book, you'll want to visit Bolles's website, www. jobhuntersbible.com, for more tips and tools.

The Shadow Negotiation: How Women Can Master the Hidden Agendas That Determine Bargaining Success. Deborah M. Kolb and Judith

Williams. New York: Simon and Schuster, 2000.

Resumes and Cover Letters That Have Worked. Anne McKinney. Fayetteville, NC: PREP Publishing, 1997. McKinney is also the author of several industry-specific guides to cover letters and resumes.

Who Moved My Cheese? An Amazing Way to Deal with Change in Your Work and in Your Life. Spencer Johnson and Kenneth Blanchard. New York: Putnam, 1998. Your career is a journey, and this book makes the trip, with all its ups and downs, an adventure rather than a chore.

CONTACT WOMEN FOR HIRE
AND THE AUTHORS

We would like to hear from you.

Please share your success stories and job search experiences with us by e-mailing them to book@womenforhire.com.

Visit www.womenforhire.com to register for our free e-mail newsletter filled with even more of the best job-seeking tips and strategies. You can review information on who's hiring and for what positions, get the dates and locations for our upcoming Women For Hire events throughout the country, which are free for job seekers and provide excellent networking opportunities, and learn about one-on-one career coaching sessions and job-seeking seminars held year round.

INDEX

Page numbers in *italic* indicate figures; those in **bold** indicate tables.

ABOUT THE AUTHORS

Tory Johnson is the founder and CEO of Women For Hire (www.womenforhire.com), a business that produces career fairs connecting America's leading employers with smart, diverse women in all fields. Each year Women For Hire events enable more than 500 top employers to meet directly with more than 30,000 high-caliber job seekers at a time when workplace diversity is essential and recruiting is competitive.

Johnson conducts job-strategy seminars, lectures on networking, and coaches job seekers on career development throughout the country. She is a frequent media guest on career issues and has appeared on CBS, CNN, CNNfn, CNBC, and numerous ABC, CBS, FOX, and NBC stations throughout the country. She has been featured in the *Wall Street Journal, Miami Herald, Atlanta Journal, Chicago Tribune,* and *Dallas Morning News,* among other coverage, providing extensive career advice.

Johnson is highly involved with all aspects of her business—managing staff, planning events, and personally inspiring the women she serves. Through her work at Women For Hire, Johnson has helped hundreds of women find jobs that will start them on—or advance them in—successful professional career paths. She lives in New York City with her husband and three children.

Robyn Freedman Spizman (www.robynspizman.com) is an award-winning author and has written over sixty parenting, inspirational, and how-to books. She has authored *When Words Matter Most, The Thank-You Book* and is the coauthor of *Getting Through to Your Kids, 300 Incredible Things for Women on the Internet,* and *Good Behavior.* She has reported for the past twenty years as a consumer advocate on many how-to topics from saving time and getting organized to gift giving and the hottest products for NBC WXIA-TV in her popular *Been There, Bought That* weekly segment. Spizman has also been featured as a guest on over 5,000 leading national and local television talk and radio shows including NBC's *Today,* CNN, CNNfn, the Discovery Channel, and the Oxygen Network, and her advice and books have appeared in many national publications including the *New York Times, Cosmopolitan, Woman's Day, Family Circle, Redbook, Parents, Child,* and *USA Today.* A well-known speaker, Spizman has spoken to thousands of women across the country and was named one of Atlanta's top Divas in Business. She lives in Atlanta with her husband and two children.

Lindsey Pollak is a writer, speaker, and consultant on women's career issues and marketing to women. Her experience reaches across the government, nonprofit, corporate, and new media sectors. She is a contributor to several websites, a frequent conference and seminar presenter, and an active member of several national women's organizations. Pollak is a former director of Business Development for WorkingWoman.com, where her responsibilities included creating strategic marketing relationships with over fifty professional associations. Previously she served as program coordinator for the American Woman's Economic Development Corporation.

A native of Connecticut and graduate of Yale University, Pollak received a Rotary Ambassadorial Scholarship to Monash University in Melbourne, Australia, where she completed a master's degree in Women's Studies. She lives in New York City.